HISTORICALLY
INACCURATE

HISTORICALLY INACCURATE

SHAY BRAVO

PENGUIN BOOKS

PENGUIN BOOKS

UK | USA | Canada | Ireland | Australia
India | New Zealand | South Africa

Penguin Books is part of the Penguin Random House group of companies
whose addresses can be found at global.penguinrandomhouse.com.

www.penguin.co.uk   www.puffin.co.uk   www.ladybird.co.uk

Published in Great Britain by Penguin Books in association
with Wattpad Books, a division of Wattpad Corp., 2020

001

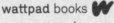

www.wattpad.com

Printed and bound in Great Britain by Clays Ltd, Elcograf S.p.A.

A CIP catalogue record for this book is available from the British Library

ISBN: 978-0-241-46079-5

All correspondence to:
Penguin Books, Penguin Random House Children's
One Embassy Gardens, 8 Viaduct Gardens
London SW11 7BW

MIX
Paper from
responsible sources
FSC® C018179

Penguin Random House is committed to a
sustainable future for our business, our readers
and our planet. This book is made from Forest
Stewardship Council® certified paper.

Para mis padres y mis hermanas.

Por siempre creer en mí.

CHAPTER ONE

There is a fifty-fifty chance that I will go to jail because of what I'm doing right now. Is it a good idea? No. Which shows what a fool I am. But don't just blame me, also blame the stupid system of societies and their initiations—at least the one at Westray's community college.

The door handle clicks and turns, confirming the key they gave me was, in fact, the key for this house. This raises two slightly worrisome questions: Why does Anna have a key to the Winstons' house? And why do the people at the history club want a fork?

Granted, they might want an old fork. You'd expect an old house to have antique forks, but Anna wasn't that specific. The letter Carlos handed me after my meeting with her just told me to get a fork from the kitchen, take a selfie, and get out of the house—with the fork, of course. All of that to get into the club. It's not even a nationally recognized club, but it fills space on my resumé.

The Winstons' house is not the fanciest in our town. It's two stories, made out of sturdy wood and with a sloped roof reminiscent of early twentieth-century architecture. They bought the house in the '70s for a ridiculously low price since the building was nearly falling apart. They got a plaque for remodeling the place, and with time the neighborhood grew around them, including my parents' old house—they moved to Westray after they eloped.

Mrs. Winston has a pretty big garden planted in front of her house, which extends to the back. As a little girl, I would ride my bike down the street and see her working in that garden in front of that beautiful house that I'd never step a foot into. She should be well into her eighties now, but even back then her energy for gardening surprised me. My family lived in this neighborhood for a while, before what happened a year ago, when we had to move from a house to one of the few apartment buildings in town. It's a nice area of Westray, where the trees grow tall and the grass always seems greener. I only have fond memories of this neighborhood.

I shake my head, trying to concentrate on the task at hand. If I wasn't being lied to by Anna, the club president, the Winstons go to bed pretty early. The darkness of their corridor should mean they are asleep; I hope it doesn't mean they're lying dead somewhere.

My phone buzzes inside the pocket of my jeans and I nearly jump out of my skin.

Anna: Sol, you've been standing in the same spot for

like an hour. Are you doing this or not?

I glare at my phone and drop it back in my pocket. She can think whatever she wants—I'm taking my sweet time doing this if it means I won't leave the property handcuffed.

College kids do stupid stuff like this, right? Besides, white guys get away with much worse stuff. Forget the fact I'm not a guy—or white, for that matter.

Straightening up, I turn on the small flashlight I brought with me so I wouldn't get distracted by whatever might pop up on my cell phone. The hallway comes to life with portraits of people I don't know and decorations of cats in various styles. The narrow hall leads to a small living room where more pictures and a couple of plants adorn nearly every surface. A fat calico cat is sleeping on one of the couches; it perks up when I slowly step around it then goes back to dozing like nothing happened.

The house smells like old people. Visit your grandparents or (in case they're no longer with you) a local retirement home, and you'll understand. And they'll appreciate the company.

The living room connects to a dining room via a small foyer that also faces the stairs; the hallway I just walked through seems to serve as a way to connect the living room to the backyard and a small bathroom. In the dining room is a table with six chairs and a small bowl holding fake bananas, apples, and shiny grapes. An archway leads to a buttercup-yellow kitchen with white cabinets and clean, dark countertops, where a vase of sunflowers rests on a smaller table. Not even when Dad and I both clean our home together does it end up as spotless as this place, old-people smell aside.

Next to the refrigerator, and right beside a door (possibly

leading to the garage) is a decorative spoon and fork set that is large and sturdy enough to knock out a man. While it would make a nice gag to take a picture with *those* and skedaddle outta here, I'm pretty sure the people at the club would bitch at me for it.

I toe my way to the drawers and open the one closest to me slowly, but there are only spatulas and other large utensils. Closing this one as silently as possible, I move to the next one, closer to the sink, and slide it out. Forks. Other cutlery is also stashed inside the small drawer, making me feel like I'm in an Indiana Jones movie and I've just uncovered a treasure chest.

Grabbing one of the bottom forks, I take out my phone, open up my camera app, and quickly take a selfie before slipping both in the back pocket of my jeans. Looking over my shoulder to ensure there isn't a startled eighty-year-old ready with a pickaxe, I extract a dollar-store fork from my right boot. It doesn't feel or weigh the same as the fork I'm stealing, but I place it inside the drawer, close it, and walk back the way I came.

Someone turns on the light in the dining room.

Fork still in hand, I freeze, gaping at the guy standing under the arch between the foyer and the dining room.

He screams.

Shrieking, and then ducking in time to avoid what he's chucked at me (I'm pretty sure it was his phone), I push a chair in his way as he rushes forward. The instant he falls down I book it out of there.

My breath rushes out of my body when my stomach slams against the railing of the staircase.

"Hey!" the guy shouts, scrambling up.

Instead of running to the door where I originally entered,

like any person with common sense would, I panic and make a split-second decision to climb up the stairs.

Sprinting to the first door along the hall, I cross myself—praying there's no eighty-year-olds sleeping inside—and enter, quickly closing the door behind me and bolting it.

Turning on my flashlight, I sigh in relief.

There is a messy bed in the middle of the room, a desk on one side, and a chest of drawers on the other. The walls have a few posters and decorations, but what is most important is on the left side of the bed.

A window.

A loud knock on the door makes me jump in the spot.

"Hey, open the door!" the guy screams.

"Look I'm not here to steal anything!" Slowly, I back away from the door, getting closer to the window.

"Like hell you're not!"

"I swear, I just needed a fork." The latch of the window is tight, and my fingers protest in pain as it opens.

There is a pause in the loud hammering on the other side of the door. "What?"

With a grunt, I push the window open. A tree is nearby, and I can survive a jump to one of the branches, I think. "What what?"

"What did you just say?"

"I only came for the fork."

"A fork?"

"Yeah, that thing you use to eat with—"

"I know what a fork is!"

"Then why the hell do you ask?"

A small flower box sits below the window and then the

slanted roof follows. I *could* slide down, but that would be more likely to end with a broken leg.

There is a sudden click, and I turn around to see the guy standing by the door, a multitool in hand, the doorknob on the floor.

I take the fork out of my pocket and hold it out for the guy to see.

"Look, I'm just taking the fork, I swear." Reaching for the window, I put a foot over the ledge and climb up.

"Whoa, what are you doing?" He comes closer and I take a step back and nearly fall out, grabbing the inside of the window.

"Stay back!" I swing the fork around like a weapon. "I am going to fall and die, and it'll be your fault."

"You broke into my grandparents' house!"

"For a fork!"

"What do you want it for?"

"I'm—that's none of your business."

"Is this some stupid high school prank?"

I gasp, nearly losing my grip on the window frame. The cool January air chills the back of my neck. If it wasn't for the fact that my body could plummet to the ground at any moment now, the breeze would feel nice. Carlos did mention it was a great night tonight on the way over, before Scott interrupted him with ". . . to commit a crime."

"High school? Do *I* look like a high schooler?"

"You sure act like one."

"You little—" I look at the tree. "This conversation is over."

I shove the fork into my boot this time and cross the window sill with a deep breath, letting myself fall partially on my side to protect my phone and my foot with the precious cargo. The dark shingles are wet with dew and excruciatingly cold. Wearing black jeans was a bad idea. As my body slides at a faster velocity than I expected, all that comes to mind so I can make the jump from the roof to the tree is to stick my heel out. Said heel gets jammed in the drainpipe and gives me enough of a break to leap and body slam a branch.

This, of course, sounds fancier than what actually happened, which was me screaming the whole way until I met the painful embrace of an oak tree.

Shouting comes from the window but the blood rushing in my ears is too loud for me to pay attention to it. Instead, I focus on the tree. Some of its branches have been pruned recently, and they stick out in strange places, like tiny ladder steps.

"Oh good, you're not dead."

The guy looks out of the window, his curly hair moving slightly in the breezy night. "I thought I'd have to call my grandparents to tell them there was a corpse in the garden—now I'll only have to tell them you broke into their house."

"Here's the deal." My arms are about to give out; the tree bark bites into my skin. "You never saw me, and this didn't happen."

"Are you taking the fork?"

"I'm taking the fork."

My foot slips and the shock of the fall rips a scream from my throat. Rolling and covering the back of my neck is all that I manage as the roots of the tree meet my body. White flashes behind my eyelids and pain blooms in my left leg, but when I open my eyes, I'm still in one piece and no limbs seem broken.

"Oh shit! Are you alive?" he shouts from above.

Carefully, I flex my fingers, assuring myself nothing's damaged, and get up. My leg protests mildly but it's nothing I can't look at later. Patting my butt, I confirm my phone is in place. All I can hope is that the screen didn't crack, because I can't afford a new one.

"I'm fine."

"Serves you right."

"Being fine?"

"Nah, falling down."

The amusement in his voice makes me scoff, and my retaliation is lifting a single finger at him. The guy raises both of his hands, flipping me off too.

"Like I said, this *never* happened." Behind the tree is the gate I used to enter the garden. Close to a small shed and a vegetable patch, the path is decorated with stones, and leads to the gravel alleyway behind the house.

"I heard you the first time." He leans against the window ledge, looking thoroughly entertained.

"I mean it this time."

"I'm calling the cops."

I limp my way to the gate, trying to ignore the laugh coming from the second floor when I halt.

"Can you close the back door? I think I left it unlocked."

"Wait, you have a key for the house?"

I run, ignoring the pain emanating from my leg.

"Hey!"

"This never happened!" I push the gate open and step into the alleyway.

Someone grabs my arm and yanks me away from the fence. If it wasn't for my handler's blue hair, I would have screamed. We race down the alleyway, steps quickly filling the street as more people join our small entourage.

Turning sharply to the left, we sprint down the sidewalk, feet splashing through puddles every so often, until we reach the maroon soccer mom–looking van that got us to this side of the city a mere half an hour ago.

Anna pushes me inside the back of the van while the other members of the club climb into different spots. The driver is Scott, who works at Pizza Hut—which explains the faint scent of marinara and mozzarella cheese.

"Why were you screaming?" Anna asks as soon as Scott gets the van going. "More Than a Woman" by the Bee Gees plays on the radio.

"You sent me on a suicide mission for *this*!" I shove the fork into her hands. "And didn't remind me the Winstons had a grandchild. Why do you want a fork? This doesn't even look like a hazing."

"Do you want to be hazed?" Carlos asks from the seat behind us.

"*Callate*, Carlos." He's my best friend—technically the reason I'm here to begin with. Said he couldn't miss seeing how I pulled this off.

"At least you didn't have to take a picture on top of the city founder's shoulders." That had happened last October, and he had done it only wearing underwear, which made the pictures he showed me later slightly more amusing. His comment doesn't calm my anger.

"You didn't have to break into a house."

"That's strange, no one was supposed to be—Did he call the cops?" Anna puts the fork inside her bag. She has a dark-orange jacket on that she really should not have worn if she was planning on breaking the law.

"No . . . at least I don't think so."

Scott takes a sharp left, the streetlights blurring past us as he bobs his head up and down to the music. The downside of being in the very back of his car is that there are no seat belts, and with his driving skills, the most I can do is hold on to the back of Carlos's gray seat for dear life.

"Then you should be fine. How old did he look?"

"Between eighteen and twenty-two, I guess."

"When you said grandchild I thought of a six-year-old or something," Scott says from the driver's seat.

"Dude, why would I be screaming for my life? If it had been a six-year-old I could have lied and told him I was the tooth fairy."

He lifts his index finger at me, maintaining his eyes on the road.

"It doesn't matter anymore. Send me the picture and you should be all set." Anna brings my attention back to her, a car honking at us as Scott goes through a yellow-turning-red light.

"Why do you guys even do this?"

"It's fun," Scott says.

"And you're here safe now," Carlos adds.

"And it's been done since the club started." Anna hits my leg with hers. "You'll be fine."

As long as the guy doesn't sue me. I bite the edge of my thumbnail, anxiety pooling in the pit of my stomach. All that there is to do now is wait for tomorrow and see what happens, but as the van reaches the entrance to Westray Community College, or WCC as we call it, I can't help but feel like this won't be the end of seeing the Winstons' grandson.

CHAPTER TWO

The kitchen is half of our living area, so Dad and I usually eat sitting on the couch. The window over our sink faces east, and in the morning rays of sunshine beam through the small rectangle. Whenever I can't sleep, I get up extra early, make a pot of coffee, and stare out of the window for long periods of time with a warm mug between my hands, like today.

We have a small balcony to the side of the apartment, but I remember being small and seeing my mother do the same at our old house, holding her cup of coffee and taking the morning light by the kitchen window. Two birds are perched on the high wires that pass above the duplex. Breathing out close to the glass, I carefully draw a third one over the fog.

"*Buenos días.*"

One of the birds flies away.

"Buenos días." Yawning, I turn to look at my father as he walks over and places a good morning kiss on my cheek.

"It's Monday. Why you look so tired?" He smiles and moves over to the counter where a green mug is already waiting for him next to the pot of coffee.

Trying not to think of all the shenanigans I got up to last night, I take a sip from my own cup. "Mondays are reason enough to look tired."

My father has an uncanny ability to crave work like an addict, working forty to fifty hours a week on construction projects and finding little things he can do on the weekends to make himself busy. Thankfully, he sleeps like a rock, so I didn't have any problems last night when I snuck into the apartment around two in the morning.

"Morning classes, huh?" He's already dressed in work attire even though it's six thirty in the morning.

"Mm-hmm." I have class around nine, but considering I bike to school, I need to leave home about eight thirty. Sometimes it feels as though the school only has a rack for twenty bikes or so. Students compete for them, especially during morning classes, and this is not ideal when you're running late. If I can find a pole close to my building and not get a ticket, that is a blessing.

I once saw a bike chained to a bush outside the nursing building. Nursing kids aren't messing around with their education, I'll tell you that.

"At what time do you get home?" he asks.

"I should be back by five."

"You work today?"

"If I want to eat out, I do." I work at the library as an aide, shelving books, helping people find that text that is obviously right in front of their faces, signing people up for library cards.

"There's plenty of food at home." Dad points to the fridge. "You won't go hungry for days."

"I haven't gone grocery shopping, actually."

"You won't go hungry for a day."

"For hours, probably. There was a little *carne seca*, so I made you some tacos for lunch." I walk to the microwave and extract the small bag I'd wrapped for him minutes before he entered the kitchen. (I did not microwave them, I left them there so they'd stay warm. I'm not that bad of a cook.) Mom used to wake up early every morning to make him lunch, so I do whenever I can so he won't have to eat fast food every day. "See? I'll make a good housewife."

Dad chuckles, taking the bag. "Thought you didn't want to be a housewife."

"I don't, I'll make my husband do half of the work like it's meant to be. But I know *abuelita* asks you about how I cook." My grandma has not seen me since I was a baby, and we seldom talk. But from what I know, she understands the world is different these days, though she still thinks I should cook and clean for my dad since Mom is gone.

Dad places a hand on my head and messes my hair up. I move away, playfully swatting his hand as he finishes his coffee.

"Gotta go or else the boss gets angry."

Dad's broken English is something he hasn't fixed throughout the years; in fact, it's something that bothers his boss because it keeps him from moving up in the company, but I doubt he ever gets angry at my father. He's a hard worker. Dad used to be very fair skinned when he was younger, but after years of working under the cruel California sun his skin darkened, nearly matching my own skin color, though I got mine from my mother's side of the family.

"Okay, be careful."

After Dad leaves I consider going back to sleep for thirty minutes or so, but I'd probably snooze my alarm five times before actually getting up again, and then be really late. Instead, I hop in the shower, cursing when the cold water hits my skin, and wash my body as fast as humanly possible. Once that's done, I brush my teeth, hop into some jeans, struggle to get the button to close, put on a sports bra—because a girl can't deal with underwire today—and find a random shirt from the pile I washed last week and haven't put away yet.

I am halfway on my way to the front door when a key aspect of my life makes me stop in my tracks.

"Michi? Michi?" I put my backpack down and wait for her to meow back at me.

As I check her water and food bowls to make sure they're full, she comes, purring, between my legs. Assuring myself she won't die without me here, I put on my backpack once more, grab the key for my bike lock, and head out the door.

Westray is a fairly small town; people say that it'd be even smaller if not for the opening of the community college in the '80s. The city is located an hour and twenty minutes northwest of Chico and really close to the mountains, which look blue in the distance. A lot of people who have lived here all their lives know each other, especially in smaller neighborhoods like the one I grew up in, but the college brings in more people from the areas around the town. The downside to Westray is that it is a hilly ho, and biking up and down those rises does become a chore.

The sound of screeching tires followed by a honk nearly throws me off my bike. My heart jumps to my throat as I look up at the shining pedestrian crossing sign and then back at the gray sedan that nearly ran me over seconds ago.

"I have the right of way, asshole." It's a mumble, not the shout I want to give the driver, but there's no time to throw it down a couple of blocks away from school.

I continue pedaling to the other side of the intersection before someone else tries to kill me, my mind reeling back to the last time a car did not miss.

Considering I'm earlier than usual, I find a decent spot for my bike. We got Starbucks vending machines last fall, so the students always hog those, but the Social and Behavioral Sciences Building—the SBS—also has a small coffee shop owned by the college. I get a cup before class, making it my second one of the day. My record is twelve in under twenty-four hours.

"Caffeine already? You're going to get the jitters." Diane hits my shoulder with hers as soon as I'm out of the coffee shop, the weight of her backpack nearly knocking me off my feet.

"Dude, this is my second cup of the morning."

"You're an addict." She recently changed her wig style from wavy hair to long braids that nearly reach her lower back, and they look gorgeous as she pushes them off her shoulder as we walk to class.

"I'm a normal student. You, on the other hand, are superhuman."

She pushes a braid behind her ear. "I already know that."

Diane and I met last semester, but we're already on cursing terms, which means we're pretty close friends in my book. We had three core courses together and spent more nights than we can remember going over materials and cramming study guides, including crying over exams that we completely failed.

"I feel so dead, I don't want to go to class," I say.

"Don't do it, skip."

"The semester just started, woman. I don't want to fail yet."

She laughs as we enter our American Heritage 102 class. "Oh please, I know you're only coming to class because of . . ."

There is no need for her to signal for me to know she's talking about the guy sitting in the last seat of the second row. I made a comment about him being good looking once and so she teases me about him every now and then. In reality, though, I like the class—the material is rich and the professor is funny, which usually keeps me from falling asleep.

"I'm not the one who stayed up messaging someone all night."

We sit in adjacent desks, waiting for the class to start, as the room slowly fills with more classmates.

"Excuse me? I go to sleep at a decent time. I don't know what you're talking about."

"Diane, you messaged me at two in the morning asking whether or not to send her a good night text."

Diane began talking to Natalie two weeks ago and it looked like they were really hitting it off. Diane, however, is the kind of person who falls really easily, if the dopey grin on her face is any sign of that.

"She's so fine, I can't help it."

"Then tell her."

With a huff, she smacks my hand with her pencil.

"Ow!"

"You didn't tell me how it went last night."

If she thinks I didn't catch the change of topic she's really underestimating my powers of intuition. She hits my hand again.

"Ow, calm down." Taking into consideration the bruises I discovered on my torso this morning, I can now start a grunge blog on Tumblr. My ankle was also possibly sprained and pedaling was a bit of a struggle, almost car accident aside. "I was very nearly murdered last night, if that serves as a summary."

"What?" Diane says.

"Don't look at me like that, it's freaking me out. Murdered might be a bit of a stretch, but I did fall out of a tree."

"I can't say I'm surprised. You broke into someone's house—"

"Who broke into someone's house?" asks the guy who sits in front of me, his eyes shining with interest.

"My uncle." It's a quick save, and Diane ignores my dirty look by pretending to be scrolling on her phone. "Someone broke into his house last night."

"Wow, that sucks, man."

"I know."

The professor enters the room, and my chest feels lighter as she places her bag on top of the desk at the front of the classroom.

"I keep telling him to move."

"Where does he live?"

Fuck.

"Minnesota."

It's clear in his eyes that he's ready to shoot another question.

"Good morning, class," says Dr. Olivarez.

My interrogator turns away from me and I turn my attention back to Diane, who gives me an apologetic look.

If I end up going to jail it will be her fault.

I clock in around eleven. The second floor of the library is bursting with so many people that the teeny space of the sweatshop we call the back room is like a little piece of heaven to me. Here we have all the damaged books and the ones that need to be shelved; in other words, my job. It's the wet dream of an English major, being surrounded by books all of the time.

Last November I joined the library staff more out of need than want. Dad was struggling with paying our bills, and I felt like I wasn't giving enough to my family, so I decided to try to do more. A lot of places turned me down for not having previous experience or a reliable source of transportation, so I looked for things within the school that would allow me to study and not have to worry about not making it to work on time. My English 101 professor, Dr. Mendoza, overheard me and Diane after class one day and mentioned one of her master's students worked at the library, and that they had some openings.

At twelve dollars an hour, twenty-five hours a week, it's about enough money to help out with groceries and a couple of utility bills. Furthermore, Dad was able to take whatever he was saving in money and send it to Mom.

Pushing the cart marked *Sol* out of its rack, I blow a kiss to Matilda, whose shift just ended, and who replies by cupping her hands on her face.

"Have fun!" she calls.

"You know I will."

Students flock to the library the first two weeks of school looking for books and materials they need that will surely break the bank. The campus bookstore is on the first floor, so the rest of the building being busy really cannot be avoided. The flux of people in and out of the building is stressful enough the first week, but the second one drags out even more. It'd be nice if it was only the bookstore that was busy, but a lot of people also go looking for books on the other floors, so the peaceful halls of the library become akin to a mosh pit.

Now that it's the beginning of the third week of the semester things should simmer down a bit more, but from the number of students still looking around and trying to find free cubicles, I have a bad feeling that this week will still be a bit hectic.

I place a large tome of the *DSM-IV* back on its shelf.

"Sol, can you help Karim at circulation?" Miranda asks as I'm returning the cart to the back room.

"Sure."

The circulation station is literally a desk in the shape of a circle in the middle of the library, where students can get information and library cards. Usually we don't have many students come to us, and I spend my time spinning around in my chair while Karim pretends to look busy.

Karim is talking with some students when I push open the small door that leads to the inner circle of the desk. I grab my chair and tell the next set of students that I can help them, settling into the calm drag the day has fallen into.

Fifteen minutes later I see *him*.

To be honest, I don't recognize him right off the bat. What I remember from last night is his dark-brown skin, short curly hair, and, more than anything, his voice.

Lifting one accusatory finger at me, he shouts, "You!"

That's when I scream. Karim jumps in his seat, turning fully to look at me, but I know my job well enough to know what

I've done is verboten, the golden code of the building we're all currently in broken.

Rule number one of the library: no screaming.

Rule number two of the library: no running.

Rule number three of the library: no losing your shit.

Okay, I made the last one up, but case in point: I'm so getting fired.

"Sol, are you all right?" Karim eyes me curiously when I stand up and push my chair to the side.

"I forgot something in my backpack, I must go." I sprint out of the circular desk, nearly falling over the door.

"Wait, come back!" says the guy from last night.

David, who was by the photocopier, hushes him and I pick up my pace, bookshelves and students becoming blurs until my destination is within hands' reach. My entrance is rewarded by Frank and Olga stopping their conversation, but I wave them off as the door closes behind me with a quiet click.

"I'm fine, ignore me." This is said while I find a good shelf on which to rest my back and raise my hands to cover my burning face—something that to anyone listening to me would not look fine, but I appreciate the fact they go back to what they were doing before.

The door opens and I stop myself from saying, "*Chingada madre*" out loud. It's not language you want to spew out in front of your supervisor, who is the person that walks in.

Miranda is a five foot, thirty-seven-year-old woman who has two cockatoos and five lizards. She told me the names of all of her pets when she was passing me books or hanging out with me on our lunch break, usually accompanied by laughter and photos of said pets. She's not laughing now.

"Sol, what happened?"

"I'm sorry, I shouldn't have screamed. I saw someone and he brought back bad memories."

"The young man outside?"

"We didn't exactly meet under the best circumstances. It won't happen again, I promise."

Nothing really happens with me in general. I'm good at keeping a low profile when it comes to work and classes, hell, even in high school I wasn't a popular or unpopular kid in school, I was just Soledad.

"Make sure it doesn't happen again," Miranda says. "You freaked some people out, myself included."

I can feel my face becoming hot and my stomach twisting. This is possibly the most publicly embarrassing thing that has happened ever since I fell during recess in middle school. Like straight-up face-planted the ground. You never get over something like that, not with the cute guy from fourth period watching.

"Don't worry, it won't."

"Okay, but that was pretty funny."

"You're laughing at me?"

"A little."

I try to laugh it off, too, but I can't get the image of him out of my head.

"Can you help Karim? You left in the middle of your shift." Miranda holds the door open for me. "By the way, if you have any trouble with the guy from before, tell me. We'll get security to boot him out."

It'd feel wrong to ask that of her, in every possible way. I should be the one getting in trouble and not him.

When I walk outside, a few students look my way, hushed laughter audible from behind their hands, but I ignore them as I make my way back to the inner circle of the circulation desk. Karim is finishing up with someone as I sit. The guy from before is nowhere to be seen.

"What happened?" Karim asks, rolling around to grab some papers from the printer.

"I didn't get fired," I say.

"I mean with the guy. That was some Cinderella moment right there." He gives a quick scan around the library, then takes out his phone and passes it to me. "Someone put you guys in the school's story."

My blood runs cold. I quickly open up his app and move past the camera option and into the stories he's following. Sure enough, I find the video. It starts right after the guy points his finger at me and says, "You" way too loudly. Then I'm screaming and running away. The girl taking the video laughs and mutters, "Oh my God, what?" as she follows me with her phone. The short video finishes before I enter the back room, though this doesn't matter because the following video is also of me and the guy, from a different angle. No wonder everyone was staring at me.

"What if you become a meme?" Karim takes his phone back.

Internet fame, the most sought out and yet most despised thing a young person these days really cares about. There is no way that little video will ever compete with the true overlords of the internet, cat videos, but it's an interesting thing to consider nonetheless.

"If I become a meme I'll get rich, and I won't be sharing any of my money with you."

"Salty."

I throw the nearest paper clip at him, and fake a smile as a student approaches the desk.

I'm stepping out of the elevator when I remember I have to go grocery shopping. It's not really a hassle, considering the nearest supermarket is two blocks away from the north side of the college. The problem is getting all I need into the basket on my bike.

I don't bike to be eco-friendly. Dad and I don't have enough money to get another car so I'm stuck with biking; at least it keeps my legs looking hot. I can't wait for summer so I can wear shorts and dresses.

Waving a quick good-bye to Linn at the main desk of the bookstore, I push past the glass doors of the library and welcome the cool January air as it hits my cheeks. The sun peeks through the trees planted outside the library, which offer enough shade for it to feel like it's colder than fifty degrees.

"Hey."

The guy from yesterday leans against one of the trees, one earphone in while the other one falls across his maroon jacket, both hands in the pockets of his jeans. Since the current set of classes doesn't end until 5:45 p.m., the sidewalks are empty. A few students hang out by the picnic tables, but they're out of earshot. It doesn't surprise me that he's here—in fact, I've got to give it to him for thinking out this plan—but it does bother me a little that he thought about waiting for me in the first place.

"Should I get a restraining order?"

"Shouldn't that be my line?" he responds.

"You're the one who came to my work."

"The library is open to *students*, which is what I am. You were the one who screamed like I was going to shoot you."

The bike rack for the library is set nicely underneath a tree about ten feet away from me, so there is no easy way to ditch him. When I walk toward my bike, he follows close behind.

"Look, it was lovely meeting you again—" I move my hand in his direction.

"Ethan."

"Well, *Ethan*, I have to go."

"Are we going to ignore the fact you broke into—"

Whirling around, I make an attempt to slap a hand over his mouth but he deflects easily with a step backward. Still, though, my heart pounds a hundred beats per second as I try to figure out if any of the students close by could have heard him say that.

"Be careful what you say in public."

"This could be considered assault."

"You're the one who's following me around. That's harassment."

Ethan doesn't look like he believes me at all, which is rude, and continues to follow me to the bike rack.

"Look, I didn't call the cops on you last night."

The tension in my shoulders eases. The lack of police officers within my area had given me a good idea that he hadn't said anything, but hearing confirmation coming from him is a relief.

"That is greatly appreciated. Would you like a pat on the back? Some Skittles? A coupon for Burger King?"

"The key for my grandparents' house would be more appropriate."

"I don't have it."

"Bull."

"I swear, I don't." My lock gives and the chain comes undone. Some people warned me about bike thieves at school, so Dad got me a good padlock and a thick chain to ensure my only form of moving around didn't get stolen one day. "If I did, and I *don't*, I'd give it to you. It wasn't my idea to enter your grandparents' house, but I can promise you it'll never happen again."

"But the thing is, shorty, that I don't want a copy of my house key somewhere—"

"Wait . . . did you call me *shorty*?"

"You *are* pretty short."

"I am five-five and a half."

"I'm six foot two. That means you're shorter than me."

The sun filtering through the branches above us creates patterns over his skin and clothes. He reminds me of someone, but I can't quite remember who. Possibly his grandparents, whom I have met before, or perhaps he and I met before and we forgot everything about each other; I'm not too sure. If he's a student here, there's a possibility I've seen him around somewhere and simply not noticed him until now.

"I know you don't trust me—"

"I don't."

"But I promise on my honor that no one will break into your house from today onward."

"Your *honor*?"

"Why is it that you make that word sound so sarcastic?"

A small breeze pushes through the campus, rustling some of the trees around us and making me wish I'd worn a hoodie. Our winters are mild enough that a light sweater or a long-sleeved shirt usually does the trick, but today has been a wild ride already, and I should have expected Mother Nature wasn't done with me.

"I find it hard to believe that a person who broke into my house for a fork has much *honor*. You haven't even told me why you needed the fork in the first place."

"Do you think I'm going back to your house to steal your cat?" There's no denying, that's a possibility.

"He's a twelve-year-old family relic. I have to keep him safe."

"What's his name?"

"I might tell you if you tell me your name."

"I don't fall for cheap tricks like that, Ethan."

"Pity, I wanted to file a police report."

Okay, he's good, but I have no time to keep stalling here. Stealing a glance at the sky, I can see that the sun from this morning has turned to a gray afternoon, and with the wind blowing colder by the minute, I'm beginning to think a storm might be rolling in tonight. Rain is always bad news when I have to bike home, although I can bother Carlos or Diane if it gets really ugly.

"Fine, I'll get you the key, but I won't be able to get it until I meet with my cl—people." Though getting the key from Anna seems impossible, considering all the club rules and traditions that she mentions.

"I don't trust you."

"You're going to have to or call the police, as you said, though I'd appreciate it if you didn't." I take off my backpack and rest it in the back basket of my bike. The front one is small and can only carry a few things, but Dad pulled through and found me a large metal one that he welded to the back, and which allows me to carry a lot of things to and from home.

Before I climb on, I extend my hand to Ethan.

"Your phone."

His brown eyes narrow but he removes his phone from his pocket, unlocks it, and hands it to me. I can tell by his body language that he half expects me to take off with his device. Can't say that I blame him, but it is a tad dramatic.

I input my phone number, using the sun emoji as my name as an inside joke, since my nickname means sun in Spanish, as well as a way to keep my anonymity.

"Here. Send me a message and I'll save your number. I'll text you when I have the key."

"When do you think that will be?"

"Whenever I text you."

"You don't reveal much, you know that?"

I can't tell if the way he says that is with interest or annoyance, but either way, he takes a step back, allowing me enough space to push my bike onto the sidewalk. With a kick, I check that none of my tires have lost any air since this morning. My bike has gone through a lot of things this past year, so I've become used to checking it's in top shape at all times.

I place one foot on a pedal. "A proper thief keeps her secrets well guarded."

"I'm home," I call when I push the door of the apartment open, plastic bags hanging off my arms. Michi runs toward me, meowing as if I'd left her alone for a decade instead of ten hours. "*Hola, mi amor.*"

Except for Michi, the house is empty. Dad usually gets home

around six thirty or so, which means I still have time to make something for dinner or order pizza, depending on how lazy I feel. Mom used to have food ready by the time he got home, *carne guisada, entomatadas,* flautas, or even mole if she felt like it—all while she was a teacher herself and didn't get home until about an hour before he did. While I know my concoctions are nothing compared to hers, I do the best I can.

My phone buzzes and I instinctively look at the clock.

Ah, she's probably on the bus by now, I think.

Dusting my hands against my jeans, I open up the text message.

Mami: Just got out of work. How was your day?

Me: Good, I'm home. How's the weather in Monterrey?

It happened too fast. People involved said that's the way it happens these days.

Mom was teaching me how to drive to the farthest grocery store from home; I was getting good at it actually. The day was sunny and dry, and the traffic was light for a Saturday afternoon. If the colleges I had applied to contacted me, my parents were going to help me get a small car.

We were on the freeway and a truck got off the highway at a faster speed than I thought it'd take and merged right into us. Our little Pontiac got so twisted that I wondered if the crash would have killed me if the truck had struck a bit before it did.

Everything kind of flew by after that, but I remember waking up and seeing Dad in the hospital, his hands over his eyes. They'd detained my mom—Immigration and Customs Enforcement, ICE—and she was being processed for deportation. She said that she was going to request a voluntary departure because the people who'd detained her scared her into thinking she'd never get a second chance if she didn't.

"That's illegal, isn't it, though? We can do something about it—can't we get a lawyer or something, call up Tio Ramon, or . . ."

"Nothing." He'd shrugged. "They've processed her information already, there's nothing we can do . . . nothing."

He said that we couldn't do anything about it.

I don't think Dad ever cried over what happened. For my part, I tried to keep up the appearance that everything was going to be fine around him. If he was going to handle it well, so would I. Except when I was around Mom or alone at night— then the walls came down and the tears poured.

Michi pushes her head against my thigh, reminding me that she's hungry and that I have not opened that can of tuna she's been meowing at since I took it out of the plastic bag. Once I've put her meal bowl on the floor, I look through the new onslaught of messages that have come through.

> Anna: *Remember about the meeting this week. We'll have a little costume party*
>
> Carlos: *Anna it's Monday*
>
> Anna: *Only wanted to remind you in case you guys forgot ;)*
>
> Scott: *Yo, can I dress up as Hamilton?*
>
> Alan: *Dude I was going to dress up as Hamilton*
>
> Scott: *I'll dress as Lafayette if you dress up as Hamilton, bro*

I mute the group chat while I get everything for dinner ready. They can all have my attention later. The door handle clicks and Dad walks in, toolbox in hand and his gray button-up shirt nearly black with sweat.

"*¡Ya llegue!*" I'm home.

"Welcome home," I respond, unlocking my phone to see the new message Mom sent me.

Mami: It rained today. I miss you guys

Outside, thunder makes the kitchen window shake a little. The first few droplets of rain fall on the sidewalk outside. At least the rain unites us today, even if now she lives thousands of miles away.

CHAPTER THREE

A nun walks into the Liberal Arts Building.

No, that is not a joke. There is a nun in the Liberal Arts Building.

It's me.

I'm the nun.

Here's the thing they don't tell you in Sunday school: nun habits are uncomfortable as hell. They're heavy, hot, and surely were not meant to be flattering. Before anyone starts throwing stones, I grew up Catholic. (It's rare not to be Catholic in a Mexican household.) I haven't stepped foot inside a church since I was about twelve, though, and I'm fairly sure I will burst into flames if I do.

Why is it, then, that I am dressed as a nun?

Sor Juana Inés de la Cruz.

She was a badass mofo, I'll tell you that. Born in the 1600s, she was hungry for knowledge, and joined a convent instead of marrying because, back in ye olde days, marriage would have gotten between her and her studies. Sor Juana was so smart forty (male) scholars were invited to test her knowledge. A philosopher, playwright, and poet, she wrote for the king of Spain and was renowned for her skill.

I *could* have bought a fancy old dress, like the kind she wore before she became a nun, but most of her work became known after she joined the convent. Besides, that would have cost more than this costume, which consists of white bedsheets and a butchered brown hoodie. Bless Diane's heart for her sewing skills.

I must be offending so many people right now. I turn into the hallway that'll lead me to the club room. It's simply a classroom the history club occupies each week for its meetings. There is no official room, but it always happens to be the same one that is available for reservation, so we have somewhat taken over it every Saturday. In fact, Scott mentioned once that he was going to write our names under the chairs, but Alan reminded him that was vandalism. Carlos instead suggested writing "Property of the History Club" on a white sticky note and pasting it to the ceiling.

"Oh shit, no you didn't." Scott jumps off of the professor's desk, on which he was sitting a second ago, and appraises a slice of pizza from the boxes he provided. He makes an exaggerated bow. He is wearing a white turtleneck and a blue coat—really, he's in the same crafting department as I am (at least we tried). His blond hair is pulled back in a founding-fathers-but-make-it-fashion way, and I've got to admit, it looks pretty good on him. "Sister, what brings you here?"

"To smite your ass." I move past him, making a beeline for the pizza.

"Oh, I would love for my ass to be smitten."

"Goddamn it, Scott." I give a small laugh. "Don't make Alan jealous."

Alan and Scott have a flirtatious friendship that I've quickly gotten to know in the past two meetings I've been a part of. When I finish my comment, Alan gives me a pointed look over the top of his cup.

"Don't steal my man, Sol."

"I could never," I assure him, taking a slice of pizza from the box close to Scott.

The new members aren't supposed to bring food, since it's supposed to be a sort of party for us. While we don't have that many members, I'm still surprised at the amount of food they were able to gather. Four boxes of pizza, four large bottles of Coca-Cola, orange soda, Sprite, and Dr Pepper, as well as a couple of bags of chips and a case of water.

Junk food is what college students are made of.

"Who are you supposed to be?" Alan leans on one of the chairs closest to the board. He's dressed more like the version of Hamilton from Lin-Manuel Miranda's play than the historical figure. He is part or fully Puerto Rican, from what I deduce from his Spanish, and his black hair nearly reaches his shoulders, so he, too, pulls off the look very well.

"Take a guess." I mean, this *is* a history club. If they don't know, I'll be slightly offended. Carlos, who is sitting against the wall, opens his mouth, but I hold my hand up. "You're not allowed to cheat, you're Mexican."

His mouth promptly shuts.

"That's not fair. Do you have any idea how many nuns are famous around the world?" Scott asks, crossing his legs.

Anna struts in, followed by the other two missing club members.

"Oh, I know—"

"Sor Juana." Anna answers before Alan can. Her chin-length blue hair is covered by a dark-brown wig that falls in waves over her shoulders. She's wearing a yellow and white striped dress that opens up to show dark jeans underneath. Not what I would consider fashionable, but she manages to pull it off.

"That's me," I say. "But who are you?"

"Sylvia Rivera." Anna pushes her hair with a flip. "A great figure for the trans movement and my queen."

"I dressed up as Nikola Tesla because I think he was chill, had some really cool electrical engineering ideas, and I had enough clothes to pull it off." Carlos shrugs, standing up.

"You're such a party pooper."

"I'm practical, unlike Sol."

I raise my eyebrows. "Are you? Remember what happened in sixth grade?"

In sixth grade Carlos jumped out of his second-floor room's window with an umbrella because he thought that Mary Poppins kind of had a cool trick and he needed to test it out for science.

"Hey, *no abras la boca o les digo que pasó en* eleventh grade—" *Don't even open your mouth or I'll tell them what happened in eleventh grade.*

Long story short: we both got detention at school for "disturbing the peace of the classroom." It was art class and when Carlos smudged blue paint on my white shirt, I had to take revenge—there was no other way around it, and the fact our teacher got between us was partially her fault.

"Boy, don't even think about it."

"Don't you love when people start talking in a language you don't understand?" Alan asks.

"Yeah, I live for it," Ophelia, one of the club members who entered the room with Anna, responds. She always reminds me of '20s art deco posters, except with long red hair, which is undone at the moment. She is wearing a gray dress that trails a bit behind her.

"Quick, Scott, say something in German." Alan hits Scott with hits elbow.

"I don't know German."

"Anything works."

"*Ich spreche kein Deutsch*," he says.

Carlos and I stop to look at Scott, dumbfounded. Alan seems mildly impressed.

"What the hell did you say?"

"I told you, I don't speak German, and I only know how to say that." Scott shrugs, the buttons of his coat glinting as he leans back against the desk. "I know how to say that in most languages, in case I'm ever lost in an unknown place."

"Oh really?" Ophelia has flowers in her hair, and now that I pay attention to her costume, it reminds me of the painting of *Hamlet*'s Ophelia by John William Waterhouse. "What about in Japanese?"

"私は日本語が話せません。"

Carlos grabs my elbow. "I somehow feel like he's insulting us in different languages."

"What about Spanish?" Alan takes a mouthful of chips as he speaks.

"*Yo no hablo Español.*"

"Well." Anna straightens up and walks to the middle of the classroom. "Before Scott starts speaking in Vulcan, we should get the meeting started."

"The boss has spoken." Scott gets up and dusts off his shirt.

"The *queen*," Ophelia says.

"The *empress*," Alan says.

"The *fairest of them all.*" Carlos takes a swig of his soda.

"I hate you all," Anna says, laughing, as she sits on the desk while the rest of the club members take seats in front of her.

As ridiculous as our club is, there are still some things we do the traditional way. We need community credit hours, so we help out at school events and promote ourselves as much as possible. There are volunteering opportunities at the local museum and the history department at the school, and we have fund-raisers and club parties every now and then. Really, the only weird thing about our club is our initiation process.

"So, our dear Soledad finally completed her challenge last week." Rummaging through her bag, Anna takes out a printed picture of the selfie I sent her last Saturday. My side still hurts from the fall from the tree outside Ethan's house.

My phone feels heavy inside my jean pocket. Ethan has sent me three messages in the past four days asking whether or not I've retrieved his house key, but I promised myself I wouldn't contact him until I had valid information about his key in order not to give him information about myself. The more anonymous I am, the better.

"Now she is an official history club member." Anna encourages everyone to give me a round of applause, which feels misplaced and puts me on the spot, but I try to own it and hope we never have to bring up again what I did for this organization.

After this we discuss hours and Carlos—who is the vice president of the club—and I sign up to help in the history department.

"Remember to ask your professors whether or not you can make an announcement about the club," Anna says, taking a piece of onion from her pizza slice. "We need three more members to meet the requirements."

"What requirements?" I ask.

"We need a certain number of members to be considered a school organization. If we don't have that, we don't get funding and we might not be able to participate in certain school events." Carlos shrugs. "Or something like that."

Alan, our unofficial graphic designer (because he's the only one of us who can draw anything aside from stick figures and because he has an Adobe account), hands us all a couple of posters before he leaves. They are designed to look like Victorian-era ads, and would grab *my* attention if I was to walk by them.

THE HISTORY CLUB

Afraid of never being satisfied?

Hungry to spend time with dead people at the local museum?

Trying to find a way to kill time because you're a lonely history nerd?

Fear no more! We've got the right answer for you!

Meet us each Saturday at 10 a.m. at LA 135.

The password is cornbread (don't question it).

Seems legit. There is a bit of guilt in my gut at the thought of luring unsuspecting students to a society that asks them to do daring tasks in order to join; nevertheless, I place the papers inside my folder and then fumble in my seat to get my backpack. As I do so, Anna finishes up her conversation with Ophelia, and I stand to ask her about Ethan's little problem.

"Is there a possibility of getting the Winstons' house key back?" I say.

Anna reaches to the back of her head to undo a clip in her wig. "Forgot something in there? Interested in elderly voyeurism?"

"What? No!"

"I'm kidding. Not everyone shares Carlos's tastes."

"I heard that!" Carlos shouts.

"Anyway, why?" She pulls her wig off to reveal a cap covering her bright-blue hair.

"Their grandson. You remember I told you about him."

"I happen to have a terrible memory." It could be sarcasm, but I still don't know her well enough to know for sure. When I first met Anna a couple of weeks ago she seemed a bit cold. Carlos assured me that's the way she is, holding herself high as the face and leader of the club. Older members seem to really like her, though, so maybe I simply haven't gotten to that point yet.

"He threatened to tell the police."

"Ah, right, him."

"He asked me to get the key to his house back."

"Have you told him to change the locks?" Her hair comes undone, blue strands falling above her shoulders. In a way, I like how it clashes with the colors of her outfit.

"I hadn't thought about that."

She taps the side of her head, gathering some documents from the desk.

"Look, it is possible to give him the key back, but it'd be breaking club policy. The system we run is information sensitive, and we wouldn't like word getting around to the wrong people about what we do." A smile creeps up her lips. "Although . . ."

"Why do I have a bad feeling about this?"

"If you recruit him into the club, all this would be fixed."

Words are flying out of my mouth before I can thoroughly think about her statement. "That's a terrible idea. Inviting him to join the club could not only put me in an awkward position, but he could also represent a threat to the whole club." Not only would he get to see what we do inside the club, but if he wanted to, he could bring the entire Westray Police Department. Just because he didn't call the cops on me once doesn't mean he won't be tempted to do it in the future. In the history of bad ideas that are very unlikely to actually work, this is up there with the Trojan Horse.

"If he wanted to, he would have already, don't you think? Who knows? Maybe he's more interested in us than we are in him. Besides, we need all the members we can gather."

She pulls out a weathered envelope made of thick, cotton-like paper and that has a golden wax seal with the history club's logo on it. It's a direct invitation that is only given to top priority candidates. I've only seen a letter like that once, when Carlos presented me with one.

During my first semester I felt lost. Yes, I had Carlos and Diane, and I had my job, but it felt like I was spinning my wheels. Without Mom around, I lost a pillar of my core family—it was strange not having her here, and now that a new chapter of my life had begun, not having her here was startling, even physically painful at times. For someone who had never really met her extended family, losing my mother was like losing a part of myself.

I couldn't leave Dad alone, not in that situation and not considering the amount of debt we were quickly looking to get into for legal fees in the future, so WCC was the only option aside from online classes. My future went from being an exciting adventure to look forward to, to me wandering aimlessly through a haze.

Carlos had made many attempts to get me to socialize more, but after the summer all I wanted to do was focus on school and not get into the kind of trouble that would worry my parents even more. So over winter break he showed up with an envelope, promising a place to hang out that wasn't home or work— somewhere I could relax and see more people. A club that I was already overqualified for by being a history major.

Anna hands the letter to me. "Doesn't hurt to try."

I reluctantly take the envelope from her.

"If he refuses to join, I'm sure we'll find the right arrangement," she says.

"How can you be so sure?"

She shrugs, shouldering her backpack. "You aren't the first member to get caught and you won't be the last, Sol. Don't worry, we'll find a way to put your worries to rest."

"That sounds kind of ominous."

"We have our methods." Anna winks. "The meeting is over, guys. Remember about your hours and that we'll meet a week from now. If you have any questions don't be afraid to message me or Carlos."

Then she is out, looking as grand as she did when she made her entrance.

Once I'm in the hall, I take out my phone to text Ethan. Nothing too complicated or something that'll alarm him.

> Me: I have an update on your key, can you meet at the café at Social and Behavioral Sciences tomorrow or Monday?

Carlos puts his arm over my shoulders.

"Where are we headed, Sor Soledad?" The corner of his Tesla moustache is slowly peeling away from his upper lip, and I have a deep urge to yank it off.

"Want to go to Starbucks and weird people out?"

"Hell yeah." He holds out the crook of his elbow for me to grab. I take it with evil happiness. "It's on me."

"What did I do to deserve you?" I rest my head against his shoulder.

"Possibly sacrificed a person or two in your past life."

"Nuns don't believe in past lives."

"That's what makes you special, you're a heathen nun."

"Pray during the day and do *brujería* at night?"

"Exactly."

I've known Carlos so long we should legally be siblings at this point. When I was younger, I'd ask my parents for a brother or sister, but it was only when I was older that I learned I had been a high-risk pregnancy, and that after three miscarriages the doctors had advised my mother to stop trying for her own health.

Then in sixth grade, Carlos and I became friends. I had other friends of course, but Carlos was like the brother I never had, as if my own wishes had taken form and stumbled into my second period science class, lost in school after moving to the United States from Sonora, Mexico. Carlos's dad is an American, so he already knew English when we met, and they didn't hold him back in the school system. We were both very far away from our extended families, and were only children, and for the last seven years we've always been there for each other during the lows and highs.

Even though I was dating Tyler when Mom was deported, it was Carlos who I called sobbing that night from the hospital. He stayed on the phone with me for five hours even though he was spending winter break in Mexico. In fact, Carlos was the only one who tried throughout all those months to help me through it all, since I didn't want to hassle my parents with my volatile emotions. I honestly don't know where I would be if he hadn't been there with me.

CHAPTER FOUR

Dad was the one who came up with the idea of morning calls with Mom. They happen twice a week on Tuesdays and Thursdays, and it was his way of giving us a girls-only call so we could catch up on, as he called them, "women things." He also said that as he walked out the front door waving me away when I asked him if he was going to get coffee on the way to work. There's a possibility he also said that because once a couple of months ago I dragged myself in the kitchen complaining about cramps and he wasn't sure about how to handle that.

We didn't necessarily need an extra hour of talking. In fact, Mom and I texted and called each other a lot on our own terms, but she ran with it, and it was nice to have an extra hour in the morning two days a week dedicated to getting up to speed with her.

"Because Thanksgiving is an American holiday, I think I should visit you on Christmas." I push the door of the fridge closed and carry the jug of milk to the kitchen counter where my bowl of cereal is waiting. "And I'd be paying for my plane ticket; you guys wouldn't have to worry about the money."

I had visited Mom only once since she "moved" to Mexico. That was the term she wanted to use and that was the term we settled on. Monterrey is a large city, and she lives in what's called the metropolitan area. It's the third largest city in Mexico, and about an hour and a half away from where she grew up before she was brought to the United States when she was six. When Mom returned, a distant aunt of hers helped her find an apartment and got it into someone good's ear that my mother was an excellent English teacher.

We helped her move into her little one bedroom apartment and made jokes about it being like a holiday home, but when it was time to say good-bye at the door, Dad pretty much had to pry me and her away from ugly crying in each other's arms. She promised we could come visit whenever we had time, especially for holidays—after all, I am a US-born citizen and Dad got his residency through the Immigration Reform and Control Act of 1986 after working in agriculture in his teens. We could still visit her, and it was something we were looking forward to, but after a couple of weeks living by herself, she got a call from an unknown man telling her they knew she had family in the States and that they had her under watch.

Her aunt assured her those calls happened every now and then, usually from people pretending to be part of a cartel or other criminal organization in order to get money out of unsuspecting people, but Mom didn't feel safe anymore, and she didn't want me or Dad visiting as often.

"Hmm." Mom's voice fills the air, her cup of coffee the only image on my phone screen while she prepares her breakfast. "But who would your dad spend Christmas with?"

"He can come if he wants to, he's a resident," I reply.

"He already said he has to work, remember?"

"Yes, but I want to see you."

My mother is beautiful, with thick black hair and skin that never seems to age. She's forty-two yet could be taken for someone in her early thirties; however, lately I've begun to notice the signs of stress in her—the circles under her eyes and lines across her forehead as she furrows her brow and thinks about the risks of bringing her young daughter to a city many say is dangerous. I'm not scared, though. Carlos visits his family in Sonora every two months or so and is completely fine. It always feels unfair my parents have sheltered me this way, even if it comes from a place of love.

"We'll see what happens. I don't want Dad to be alone," Mom says.

I shrug and eat a spoonful of my cereal. It's not like I want to leave Dad alone on Christmas, either, but I didn't visit her for the holidays last year, and it feels like forever since last February. Dad has visited her twice since everything happened, but I haven't gotten a chance to see her since that day in her apartment, and I'm the citizen in our household.

"Aren't you running late? Your students are going to get there before you," I say.

"*Ay sí*, they should use the time I'm not there to actually do their homework instead of asking for an extension." Mom teaches English classes at a private school in Monterrey, and while it does not have the best pay, it gives her enough money for rent. "How's school going?"

"Good." Responding through a mouthful of food is quite possibly not very ladylike, and she seems to share the same thought based on the look she gives me.

"Have you joined any clubs this semester?"

"The history club." She glances quickly above her camera, something that shows I was right about her running late, but these morning calls feel like my life before everything happened, sitting down at the kitchen table in the old house, sharing breakfast before school, thinking over spring break plans or weekend family trips.

"Do you like it?"

"Yep, it's fun and Carlos is in it." He used to make more appearances in my house when we were in high school, after many assurances to my parents that we weren't dating. Sometimes we'd even take him camping by the lake; after all, Dad appreciated having an extra pair of hands to look for wood and someone to go fishing with.

"That's great. *Corazón*, I've got to go, I'll message you later."

"Okay, *mami*, be careful." I send her a kiss and she returns it before hanging up, her image freezing and then going black.

Ethan and I had agreed to meet at a coffee shop at the school; that way I could work on my homework after he left. I have a bad feeling, and it's not the fact that I probably won't be doing my homework and instead will roam on social media for the majority of the afternoon. It's easier to see other people be happy in their own posts—it makes life look easier and more bearable than what it actually is.

The envelope Anna gave me glares at me from the table. I open up my messages and read over the last few.

Ethan: I'll meet you inside then?

Me: Yeah, I'll be there around ten

Ethan: Okay
Ethan: omw

Michi jumps on the chair next to mine, purring when I pet her head. I reach for the envelope.

"Well, here goes nothing."

I push my hair away from my shoulder, looking around as I open the door of the café. There are a few college students typing away at their laptops and one or two elderly people, possibly professors, talking among themselves while drinking from their cups of coffee. The lighting is dim to allow the hipsters to thrive, and soft jazz music plays in the background, providing a study-blog aesthetic.

Ethan is wearing a denim jacket over a yellow shirt, the golden color of which nearly matches the rim of his round glasses. He looks up when I approach.

"About time. I thought I'd be late for class," Ethan says as I take a seat in front of him and try to resist looking at his cup of coffee. Caffeine would be nice right now.

"What class do you have?" It's such a student-y thing to ask. We are conditioned to look for classmates we can force into study groups. That's how Diane and I first met, out of need for connection.

"Bio." The material of the envelope feels like velvet as I place it on the table, golden wax seal shimmering slightly under the light from the lightbulb hanging above us.

"Oh, are you pre-med?"

"No, I'm computer science. What is this?"

There are only two exits from the café. One of them leads to the main lobby of the SBS building and the second one is an entrance to the outside patio area, which has metal tables covered by white umbrellas for those students who prefer to eat their six-dollar sandwiches surrounded by the sounds of nature. I make a mental note of these two glass doors lest this turns into an adrenaline-driven chase scene . . . again.

"Look, Ethan, this wasn't my idea. None of it was. If you're going to go fight someone, make sure it's not me."

"Why would I fight you?"

"I'm merely trying to be clear. I'm part of a club. We are pretty normal aside from our induction ceremonies, and they would like me to, well, recruit you."

A good five seconds passes and his face does not move. "Are you part of a cult?"

"Open the envelope and read the letter, Ethan."

Surprisingly, he does, and carefully, breaking the wax seal first and taking out the hot-pressed paper on which the letter is printed. They say the letters are written by hand, and if they are, the person who writes them has perfect handwriting—and I know for a fact that it wasn't Carlos because his scribbles can barely be described as a form of human communication. I'm glad he was born after the invention of computers or he would have had a big problem.

Ethan's eyes sweep over the page before looking at me, then go back to the paper. His eyes slowly narrow.

"What does this mean?"

"Did you not read it?"

"Don't try to joke around."

Sitting back, I resist the urge to mess up my hair. I don't blame him; I'd be asking questions, too, but I have too much homework and too little time to be worrying about these kinds of things. Saint Gemma Galagani, patron saint of students, has failed me. Because yes, while I don't necessarily believe in saints, I wouldn't turn down some holy help with my grades.

"Joking is my coping mechanism," I mumble, straightening up.

"What?"

"Irrelevant. Look, have you tried changing the locks?"

"I did, the day after you broke in." He is far from amused, though who can blame him?

"Then why do you want the key?" I ask.

"If you guys, this club, managed to get it once, what is stopping them from doing it again? I'll keep asking questions until I meet your president. There should be a stop to this nonsense."

"Then join the club."

"Are you listening to yourself right now?" Ethan's on the verge of flipping the table over or slamming his face against it. I surreptitiously take out my phone to record whatever he does.

"Want to see the president and ask her how we work? Great, you already have the invitation—"

"To join your illegal activities?"

"It's your choice, and it's not entirely illegal if I had a key." His shoulders tense. Sass won't get me anywhere with this one. "Ethan, I am sorry about what happened, but they won't let me hand over the key unless you either join or manage to convince my president."

"Aren't you scared of what could have happened if I owned a gun? You could be dead because of a club."

Well, damn, when you put it like that.

"I can't make you another offer. You take it or leave it."

"This is bullshit." He shakes his head, crumples the letter, and drops it on the table. Shouldering his backpack, he struts out of the coffee shop without a second glance at his forgotten drink.

Once I hear the jangling of the little bells by the door, I let my head fall on top of my arms. The fact that I only managed to sleep three hours last night because I was catching up on the readings for my classes does not help at all. On the one hand, I wonder if I managed things as I should have; on the other, I simply cannot gather enough fucks to give.

It's unfair—I *should* care, and there is a pang of guilt in my chest that makes me wish I could take the key from Anna and give it to Ethan, but there is no drive in me to do so.

I used to look forward to the future. I wanted to learn to drive, get into college in a different state, travel, and figure out my life. The kicker is that I could still do all that, but it doesn't feel right anymore. It feels like turning my back on my family, and I'm not sure why it does. Seeing my father sitting in that hospital chair. Seeing Mom at the airport. It's as though the universe was asking me to do something but I couldn't. Everything happened so fast and all I could do was watch in horror.

Last year it felt like my whole life stopped.

But it can't stop, though—homework doesn't stop, my job doesn't, either, and while I'm dragging myself through my life, I can't make myself care for a boy who has already changed the locks to his house.

But that'd make me a bad person, wouldn't it?

Sighing, I look over at the pastry case. A muffin isn't going to solve my problems, but it sure as hell would sit well with my stomach, empty after riding my bike all the way here only to have the letter thrown back at me.

After buying a chocolate muffin and an iced latte, I head out of the café, stopping by the table we sat at and grabbing the crumpled remains of Ethan's letter. Outside, the sun is shining bright and the breeze is nice and cool. WCC is made up of a cluster of buildings that were designed by someone who loved clear windows and concrete. It looks modern, for sure, and the sugar pines bring up the lumberjack-chic aesthetic. It wasn't a bad choice for schooling; Dad didn't even get to go to school.

I'm aware that I am more privileged than some people in my situation. In some cases, people like me don't get to go to college at all, and the fact I am able to get an education and have a job, even with the financial stress in my household, is great. But as I look around the campus, at the students beginning their daily routines, I can't help but feel like things could have been better had none of this happened. As if somewhere in an alternate universe there's another Sol, living her best happy life, and I'm jealous of that. Envious of what could have been.

Of course, this leads back to guilt, and feeling bad, and wanting to look for those people who *are* happy right now. Hence social media and watching internet videos that assure me there are people with perfect lives out there rather than wallowing in my own pity party.

Right now, though, I have to make my way to class, which I am early for, though at the very least I get to enjoy my overpriced food and walk around campus. I grab the small taste of happiness the simplicity of a calm Tuesday morning can bring.

CHAPTER FIVE

Diane's major might be biology, but she watches enough shows and movies for it to be film theory. We've tried to watch TV series at the same time but she always ends up finishing them before I can. So we've started to watch one movie a week on our own time and talk about it once both of us have seen it. However, with everything going on, I have not gotten around to doing even that.

Her coral-colored coat differentiates her among the other students as I come to a halt close to the bike rack outside of the library. It's Wednesday, which means I've had the weekend and a couple of more days to watch what she told me to, but we both know by my lack of messages about it that I have not. The expression on her face as she approaches me is enough for me to assume a defensive stance as I grab my backpack and prepare to shield myself from her wrath.

"Soledad Gutierrez."

"Yes?"

"Did you, or did you not watch it?"

Putting my backpack down and turning fully toward her, I grab hold of both of her shoulders, hoping our friendship won't end the second I say, "No, I'm so sorry."

"Sol!"

"I was busy, okay? Things are kind of complicated because of Ethan. I swear I'll watch the movie tonight, after I finish my essay."

That's a lie. Ever since starting school here I haven't had a lot of time to watch things, especially since most of my waking time is spent doing things at home, at the club, or at school.

"It's the greatest thing ever, I can't understand how you haven't watched it yet. I need you to catch up in time for awards season." We walk into the library as a gaggle of students tries to push their way out the door. This creates an awkward shoving of bodies that is only experienced by those who have camped outside of Best Buy for three days before Black Friday.

I usually don't like coming to the library when I'm not working, but I have to work on a research paper for our history class. It was due a week ago but our professor extended the deadline, so I can't complain. Lenient teachers are a gift from heaven.

The doors of the elevator whine open to reveal the third floor. This area holds most of the computer equipment and the tables that allow groups to meet among the bookshelves and old videotapes. While the place is supposed to be silent, there is a persistent murmur among students that is not allowed elsewhere. It is something of a relief, as most of the time this place is as silent as a corpse.

We set up our study station at one of the tables closest to the floor-to-ceiling windows. I take off my jacket and take out the folder in which I have the notes for the book we're researching: *Twelve Years a Slave*. Rebel men and, especially, women from the past have always fascinated me. Solomon Northup stood by what he knew was right and didn't lose hope, even after being kidnapped and sold into slavery for twelve years. His story is one of many from the mid-1800s when the rising tension between the Northern and Southern states was about to break into full-on war.

"What happened with Ethan?"

If only for a moment, I don't want to talk about Ethan anymore; all I want to focus on is studying, but his name has been haunting me ever since yesterday. Diane has been keeping up with what's happening in the club and at school, and at the moment, she feels like a tether to normalcy.

"I think it's over, but I'm not sure. He left without taking the invitation to the club."

"You're still crazy for joining that club." She takes out a highlighter from her bag, one of those Mildliners that you see on those aesthetic boards on the internet that were the only reason you started a planner before you gave up because your handwriting was hideous.

I shrug, passing her the notes I've written on the story. "True, but I'm already in it."

"That sounds like something someone who is in a cult would say."

"Oh fuck off. I told you Ethan said that."

"He's not wrong."

It's truly annoying how many things are logical about their

arguments. Shaking my head, I take a sip from my nearly cold coffee.

"Here's the thing," I say once I place my cup down. "The school's clubs are shit."

Diane leans back, nodding.

"We have an anime club, for Christ's sake. I'm not shitting on anime, I love my good old *Dragon Ball Z* and *Attack on Titan* as much as that guy in the dark corner does, but "President of the anime club at Westray Community College" does not sound appealing on anyone's resumé.

"When I applied to the history club I didn't know that I'd have to break into the Winstons' house to get in. Carlos went to the middle of town and climbed on top of the founder's statue while only wearing underwear at two in the morning in October. Anna, the president, managed to get on the roof of the school and draped a giant picture of Obama—"

"Wait, that was her?" Diane seems surprised, not that I can blame her. No one knows who does what when it comes to the club until you're in it. Technically, I'm violating policy by telling her, but considering the vice president is also my best friend, I don't have much to fear.

"People have broken into the office of the college president and stolen key documents before. They've skinny-dipped in the fountain at the square, they've—I don't even know how they got the Winstons' keys in the first place." I lower my voice as a small group of guys pass by our table. "All they told me was that I had to get a fork, and I did, and now I'm in this mess."

"You're partly responsible for this mess."

"Diane."

"I'm just saying."

"Yes, I messed up, but here's to hoping that it gets all fixed."

"And that you won't go to jail."

"*Diane.*" I press my fingers to my forehead; we're both aware what she's saying is getting to me and while she is totally in the right, it doesn't help me right now.

"I'm serious, I don't want you going to jail. Who am I going to bother when you're gone?"

"Okay, I get it, thanks! Can we get back to the paper?" Maybe this is all a string of bad decisions that I made because of wanting to be a part of something else, and it will come back to bite me in the ass, but I don't need a reminder of it when there's a time to be a normal student.

Around six in the afternoon on Thursday I get the first message. I have barely finished my shift in the library, and I am more than ready to go home, when I feel the vibration against my thigh. For a moment I think it's Mom, before I realize that it's too early for her afternoon classes to be done.

I reached into my pocket, dread slowly creeping up my spine. It might be Anna with news of the club, or perhaps Carlos asking whether or not we're going to order pizza and hang out one of these days, but I know who it is.

I should have made his notification sound different so I would know when he was reaching out. I unlock my phone and lower the notification bar to see what he sent before I make the mistake of letting him know I've read his message.

Ethan: Where do you guys meet?

Holding back the urge to answer with something sarcastic, I text him our room number and the times we meet during the weekend and then put my phone away as soon as I can.

The air is nice and crisp this time of the year—cool, but not cold enough to require a scarf. I place my backpack in the back basket of my bike and move to unlock the padlock. Earlier today the rack had been so full I had to chain my bike to the very last pole, and I'd prayed I wouldn't get a ticket.

As soon as the chain is undone, though, the bike goes down along with all my precious cargo, including my laptop.

"Oh shit, oh no." I kneel, the air leaving my lungs as I nearly rip the zipper out of the fabric. It's not like I have a MacBook or something like that. Even with a job, I don't have the kind of money that would allow me to get an Apple product, let alone one of their laptops.

My computer appears to be okay, or at least there is no big crack running across the screen. Relieved, I put it back inside my backpack and sling the latter on before righting my bike and finally moving it away from the rack and onto the sidewalk.

I feel a vibration against my thigh. Ethan will have to wait until I get home before I can start worrying about everything else that is going wrong with my life.

Though I restarted it three times, the screen on my laptop says *Your PC ran into an error that it couldn't handle and now it needs to restart.* Sure, I might relate to my computer because of that message, but it still does not fix the fact that I do not have the money to get a new laptop.

Michi meows next to me, pushing her head against my lower arm. When I don't respond she sits on my keyboard and stares deep into my soul with eyes that say, "Feed me."

My parents are going to give me the talk about how I can't have nice things for more than a couple of months before I break them. Which is kind of true, but I don't need them to rub it in. There were a couple of cheap Walmart cameras I convinced them to buy for me when I was younger that could attest to that, as well as a few Christmas presents, but now that I earn my own money, I buy my own things, and I break my own things, which hurts twice as much than if they'd been gifts.

But earning my own money hasn't changed much. Money goes to bills to ease Dad's struggle of taking on all the bills in the house and then sending some money to Mom. With the utility bills and a couple of outings with my friends every month, I'm looking at about sixty dollars I can put into a savings account.

Out of the three months I've worked, minus three weeks in the middle for winter break when the library was completely shut down, that leaves me with about two hundred dollars that I've stashed for going to visit Mom in the future. Money that's now lost because I'll have to get a new computer from what it seems. I'm back to square one once more. It's like the universe loves sticking its middle finger up at me no matter what.

Groaning, I pick Michi up, who meows in protest, lie down on my bed, and place her on my stomach as I pet her head.

I could look for old computers in pawn shops, but my first laptop was from one and it died a month later. While the library does offer a computer lab for the majority of the day, I still need a computer for my online class and the essays I write at two in the morning.

Instead of feeding my cat and making dinner for Dad and me, I grab my phone and text Diane.

> Me: If I give you five dollars, will you run me
> over with your car?

She's used to my morbid jokes. What keeps me going is humor and the reminder that one day all humanity will cease to exist. I put my phone down and stare at the ceiling. Diane answers nearly immediately. One look at my screen nearly makes me forget about my laptop.

"Shit." I sit back up, Michi offended that I dared to move when she was falling asleep comfortably on top of my chest.

I didn't text Diane.

> Ethan: Are you okay?

I begin to type a long message somewhere along the lines of "Oh, well, my computer is dead, and I'm hungry, and my cat won't love me because I knocked her over" before I realize what I'm doing and quickly delete it.

> Me: Sorry lol that was meant for someone else

> Ethan: You didn't answer my question

I'm confused but then I scroll up to the message I had ignored all afternoon. He asked me whether or not we could get together before the club meeting this week.

Me: Sure, I can meet you there with a friend

Ethan: Sounds good

I put my phone down. Michi approaches me as it dings again.

Ethan: Also, bribing people to run you over is a bit dark. Have you tried ice cream?

Me: lmao I'll try some, thanks

This time when I shut my phone I take Michi in my arms, get up from my bed, and walk to the kitchen to get her and myself some food.

CHAPTER SIX

Here is the thing about volunteer work at the History Department main office: it sucks.

You're not superhappy about it, the people in the office aren't superhappy about it, and the only person winning is the dean of the department because he doesn't have to see you or the secretaries sulking. It's a slow death. Arranging flyers, putting out the trash, taking letters to different offices, resisting the urge to play Minesweeper on the old laptops in the department.

Don't get me wrong, I'm sure there's a lot of great volunteer opportunities and people actually driven by passion for them. This simply isn't one of those.

"If I placed a picture of your face right in front of you I bet you wouldn't be able to tell the difference," Carlos says, slapping something against my shoulder.

"What does that even mean?" I remove the sticky note he

pasted on my shirt. It's a badly drawn zombified version of me that looks like it's about to fall asleep.

"If you keep staring at the clock people are going to think you're a statue instead of a volunteer." He tries to stick another note on me but I give him the glare of death and he stops. "You shouldn't let the secretaries see you so bored or they'll start complaining."

"Who are you, the volunteer police?"

"No, but I am your club vice president. If you get kicked out of the department for not doing anything you could get put on probation with the club."

I narrow my eyes.

"That's against club policy and I literally went to deliver a message to the business building five minutes ago." I know what he wants. He has a stack of educational magazines that are supposed to be delivered to the professors' offices and he doesn't want to move his lazy ass.

It's not like I don't know some of the professors; in fact, I'd love to catch up with some of them—after all, some scholars appreciate their students coming by and visiting them outside of office hours to strike up conversations, they're people too. Carlos dragged me into volunteering this morning, though, when he mentioned I was falling behind on my metrics, but my mind is simply not into any of this.

"Why don't I help with the emails you've been going over while you go deliver those academic papers to the professors?" I scoot my chair closer to him.

"I think I'm fine."

"Really?"

"Really."

We stare at each other. Five minutes later both of us have half a stack of magazines and are walking down the hall. The Liberal Arts Building is one of the older ones at WCC, with large windows along a couple of hallways that face southwest onto the square and allow students to see the other buildings across. The concrete floors have specks of white in them and posters for theater plays and upcoming concerts line the walls. The professors' offices are on the third floor, and the sun is particularly bright this morning as we make our way down the hall.

"Think about it, it's faster this way." He places a magazine in the file holder attached to the professor's door.

"Whatever, I'm not talking to you for five minutes."

"You just talked to me."

"Shut up."

"You did it again."

Rolling a magazine in my hand, I approach him like I'm going to hit him when I remember something. I take out my phone, which has been on mute because I didn't want to be that volunteer who is on her phone all the time. There's still about two hours left before the club meeting and a bit of an hour and a half before I meet Ethan outside of the Liberal Arts Building.

Carlos pushes his head against mine, trying to catch a glance of my phone's screen.

"Who you texting?"

"No one." I elbow him away and squeak when he pokes my side. "Stop it."

"Your boyfriend?"

"Shut it!"

"It started out with a fork, how did it end up like this?"

"Carlos—"

"It was only a fork. It was only a fork."

"You know what? Screw you." I drop my magazines on the floor in front of him. "Have fun delivering the rest of these."

He laughs as I walk away.

"You know I'm kidding, Solecito."

"I don't care, I don't like you."

"I'll buy some *raspas* after the meeting if you help me."

There's a little raspas place on the outskirts of town that we like to hit up every now and then. That's how he gets me every single time, that or IHOP. No matter what happens, he knows it'll work and I have cursed him many times over it.

"Will you buy me *el volcán*?"

The volcán is a *chamoy* shaved ice with lime juice, pineapple, and strawberries, and topped with chili drizzle and chili powder, gummy bears, and Airheads. Incredibly unhealthy and heavenly good.

"That and anything else you might want."

I pretend to think about his offer for a second before grabbing the stack of magazines I had dropped and hurrying down the hall, my sneakers making squeaky sounds which are soon followed by Carlos's.

"What exactly does this club represent?" asks Ethan as we walk toward the club room. Carlos is still sizing him up. The neat thing about having Saturday meetings is that there's usually way fewer students than during the week—sure the odd couple of people who like to hang out in the lobbies or come to drink coffee with their favorite faculty member are around, but other than that, the halls are empty.

"I'm sure you believe it's an illegal entity that manufactures drugs and steals candy from children," I say.

"Which is truly a possibility," Carlos adds.

"Really, we're your average school club, but one with a peculiar initiation process," I continue.

"We like to have fun," Carlos points out.

"Breaking the law?" Ethan is far from amused at our banter.

"Isn't that what I said?" Carlos drapes his arm over my shoulders. "Wasn't it, Sol?"

"I didn't hear any difference," I answer.

Ethan looks like he wants to strangle us both, but we have arrived at the club room.

Shaking Carlos's arm off my shoulders, I turn to Ethan. "Don't threaten Anna or the club in the meeting. You're not going to gain any friends by doing that."

When we open the door, we find Alan and Ophelia arguing over a desk on which a tray with two sandwiches rests. Scott is on top of the professor's desk eating what appears to be a third sandwich. Anna is nowhere to be seen. Two girls sit at the back of the classroom, talking quietly, and only turn to look at us for a brief moment before going back to what they were doing.

"What's going on?" Carlos asks, strutting in.

"It's about the sandwich," says Alan.

"It's not about the sandwich," Ophelia says, although the way she says this makes me feel it is about the sandwich. "He's being overdramatic because he forgot to specify what his food restrictions were."

"She's trying to kill me!"

Ophelia throws her hands up at his comment and walks away, taking her own food with her as Carlos approaches Alan and Scott.

I tune out the conversation about Alan being allergic to tuna, and the dark theory of Ophelia trying to poison him. There is also a Shakespeare joke thrown around.

"So, *this* is your cult," Ethan says.

"I told you not to call it a cult."

"Where is your leader?"

"President."

When we met him outside of the building, the first thing Ethan asked Carlos was whether or not he was the leader of the cult I was in, followed by if he was aware that I bribed people to run me over. Carlos was amused by both of those, but yes, he was aware because I'd bribed him in the past multiple times to run me over; what kind of friends would we be if I hadn't?

"And I prefer the title emperor," he'd said to Ethan.

"Pharaoh is better," I replied.

I sit down at a desk closer to the door and Ethan follows me. Carlos and the other three are still arguing about food, but the conversation seems to have shifted to whether or not you can be allergic to things such as salt and pepper.

Ethan takes his glasses off, looks at them, then puts them back on as he sits down at the desk across from me.

"So, Sol? That's your name, right?" he says.

"That's not important."

"You hadn't told me your name."

"I gave you a hint."

"What?"

I can't blame him for not knowing more than one language, but he could have done his research at the very least.

"*Sol* means sun in Spanish—"

"You're Spanish . . ."

"Latina, Mexican, not Spanish. That's a language or it's used to refer to people from Spain, which I'm not."

Ethan lets out a single laugh and holds up his hand. "Sorry, it was the first thing that came to mind. So, why did you join this group?" he asks.

I suddenly feel like I'm in an interview I did not prepare for. But as I'm scrambling for good ideas to deflect any questioning that might lead to me sharing personal information, Anna walks in, blue hair shining over her bright-orange jacket.

"Hello, my children." She's carrying two cases of soda and some bags hang from her right elbow. Every time she goes anywhere it looks like she owns the place, and she has a strut to match. I wish I had that kind of energy. "Sorry for being late, I woke up not too long ago and realized I had to pass by the grocery store for some snacks for you all."

Ethan grabs my arm and hisses, "That's your leader?"

"Our dear leader, yes, Mr. You-live-in-a-cult."

"No, I mean that's Anna Howard."

"Yes, and you're Ethan Winston—"

His eyes widen. "You know my last name?"

"No, I know your grandparents' last name. I'm assuming you go by the same name."

"I won't be getting my key back. Not from her, at least."

Carlos is bringing Anna into the conversation about the poisonous sandwich, which Ophelia, eating her own lunch, is clearly fed up with, and hasn't had a chance to notice me and Ethan huddling together in the corner of the room.

"What? Is she your ex-girlfriend or something?" The drama would be a nice distraction, honestly.

"Not exactly."

Anna laughs and turns around to scan the room, her eyes falling on us.

The room goes silent. This is soap-opera worthy and I wish I had brought coffee or pan dulce to eat as I watch.

A small smile appears on Anna's lips as she says, "Hey, neighbor."

Ethan goes rigid, and I and the other group members quickly look between them. There is static in the air as she beams at him.

"I'll talk to you at the end of the meeting. First, we'll get some things sorted out for everyone else."

He doesn't answer, but the mixture of surprise and simmering anger in his posture tells me that this talk will possibly not go down easy.

The meeting goes over basic club activities. Anna explains the initiation process and answers any questions the newbies might have. She assures everyone the club is normal and harmless and would never put anyone in danger, but avoids any questions about what exactly the dares would be like. Ethan is silent throughout the entire ordeal.

Once the meeting is adjourned, Anna and Ethan talk in the corner of the room. I intend to wait and see if anything interesting goes down, but Carlos pulls me away and out the door.

"Do you wanna come hang out at my place?" he asks. It's not unusual for us to be the first out, and as we walk down the hall I begin to feel like it's another regular Saturday.

Not even a couple of steps later, though, the loud bang of the classroom door being slammed open reminds me today is not a regular Saturday, and as Ethan speed walks past us I get the feeling that his little talk with Anna didn't go quite as well as I secretly hoped it would.

"Actually, I'm going to check out what that's about. I'll message you later about it." I unhook my arm from Carlos's and follow the angry man making his way through the Liberal Arts Building.

CHAPTER SEVEN

"You guys are neighbors. What's the big deal?" I ask, leaning against the side of the monkey bars as I watch him pace around the playground tower.

There is a small park you can cross if you're making your way to the freshman parking lot (the worst parking lot by the way, and another reason why I prefer biking) from the rear of the Liberal Arts Building. I assume the park is here in case some students have children, or perhaps for faculty members who have a daycare close to work, although most of the time it's students who hang around here to eat their lunches when the weather is nice. Today the weather is not, in fact, nice. The sun is high in the sky, warm even though we're nearing the end of January. While the wind is cool, the metal of the playground threatens to burn through my shirt and sear my skin.

Ethan sighs and takes off his glasses as he sits at the top of the slide. We walked here on the way to his car after the meeting; he didn't say a single word the whole way, but he waited for me to unlock my bike and walk with him, so I assume he has something to get off his chest.

"We're not neighbors anymore."

"Then what's the problem?"

He looks at me. Without the glasses his face makes me go: *Whoa, man, he could get it.*

"Never mind."

"Tell me or we'll never get your stupid key."

"He, I mean, she, and I had a thing in middle school, but I might have rejected her."

"She was your girlfriend?"

"No, we never dated. It was before—we kissed once or twice then I moved in with my grandparents and we went to different schools after that." He puts on his glasses, as if having them on will somehow make this clearer.

"You don't think that this is all some sort of plan to get revenge on you, right?" I look down at my phone. Diane texted something about me coming over to her place to watch the movie I never got around to, but I haven't answered yet. I should really pick up around the house and work on that essay before doing anything else.

"Do you think so?"

"No. No one holds on to grudges that long It's been years, and she has a boyfriend from what I know. What did you guys talk about after the meeting?"

Ethan shrugs, sliding down the bright-orange slide. "That you guys need more members to keep the club running and that she wasn't allowed to give the key back because it was policy, unless I was a member."

"Did you ask her how she got the key in the first place?"

"You think I didn't?"

I press a hand against my temple, the ghost of a headache singing "I Feel It Coming" by The Weeknd in my ear. "Humor me, Winston."

"She claims an ex-club member who knew my grandparents gave it to her. I told her that's bullshit but she shrugged and said it was okay if I don't believe her."

That does sound suspicious, but I haven't known Anna long enough to figure out whether she's lying or not. She doesn't share a lot of things, though I can't say I don't do the same. At the same time, she also looks like that cool girl you want to be friends with but don't know how to approach.

I look down at my phone to check how much time I've spent here and not at home, which is where I wish I was. Biking is going to be a pain.

"What will you do?"

"About?" His expression contorts.

"The club. Are you joining us?"

The more times Ethan and I have spoken about the club, the more it really does start to sound like an occult organization where people become enthralled with their members. Although, the club getting dissolved because of a lack of members sounds like a better resolution than me getting prosecuted.

And maybe going to jail.

Jesus, when did I enter this strange parallel universe of my boring life?

"Are you crazy? Break the law? Sol, if someone like *me*"—he gestures at his face—"enters someone's house, I'm getting shot. No questions, just boom. Dead."

I grimace. "Don't say that."

"Am I wrong?"

"Okay, I could ask them not to put you in any situation that could put you at risk of being shot."

"How? Have you seen any amount of news lately? I could be walking down the street and—" He pushes his hands through his hair, shoulders tense as he exhales. There's a part of me that wants to put a hand on his shoulder in reassurance, but not being sure which way he'll react, I opt for offering my best idea. "I can't mess around, Sol, I don't get that luxury."

"I have a good source." Although Carlos, who jumped out of his second-story window with an umbrella and broke his leg when we were younger, is not necessarily the best of sources. "If you don't want to join, fine, but you have to swear not to tell anyone about what goes on in the club. Not to me, to Anna."

"Why does it all come back to her?"

"She's the president, Ethan, everything goes through her. If something happens to one of us, it will all fall on her."

I'm not entirely sure if it was her easygoing attitude to me being found or the fact that she always seems to be on top of everything that told me I wouldn't have been in a lot of trouble if I had been found. She was a lot more public with her initiation, and so was Carlos—it really makes me wonder about the club's involvement with the WCC, or even the city of Westray itself.

"You can't possibly believe that I'll trust you." His eyes narrow as a breeze passes the playground, the trees around us moving slowly in the warm afternoon sun.

"You already do, otherwise we wouldn't be standing here, would we? Besides, I wouldn't have any sort of good outcome by lying to you."

"Then what are you getting in exchange for helping me?"

"A clean conscience, I guess. Life isn't always about what you get and don't get. Now, accept a bit of kindness and believe in me for a minute."

Sometimes a stranger's kindness is all we have, even if the stranger is the person who got you there in the first place. I want to make things right with him, if anything so I can forgive myself. I don't want to be the bad person in Ethan's life, someone who crashes through and leaves the next moment without caring about the repercussions of their actions.

"What's your plan for convincing them not to assign me anything illegal?"

"I can't assure you it won't be illegal, but you won't have to break into any houses or stuff like that."

"How so?"

"Easy. I'll threaten to quit."

"Are you serious? You went through everything to get in only to quit?"

Raising my eyebrows, I push myself off the monkey bars and walk closer to him.

"You're on my side now?"

"Of course not. I'm just saying that it seems ridiculous to me that you would willingly break the law—"

"I never said I did it willingly."

"Were you threatened? Were you forced to break into my house?"

He's right, again, damn him.

"I'm trying to help you, Ethan. If you can't see that then fine, go get your key yourself, but they're less likely to give it to you than they'd be to me. I really am sorry for what happened but

I'm not going to stay here begging you to believe me when you're acting like an ass."

"I—" He shakes his head. "I'm sorry, I guess."

It's shocking to hear him say that. There's this little ray of temptation to record him with my phone so I can present it in court as a way to get out of a prison sentence, but that would be trying my luck.

He's looking at me from under his glasses with his head tilted, and that action alone for some reason makes me want to accept his apology, but I still assume a defensive stance to hold my ground. He has every right in the world to mistrust me, and I do feel like the bad person in this scenario; there's surely something I can do for him.

"Let me help you. I swear I'll get your key back."

"And the fork."

"What?"

"I want the fork back too. If possible."

"Why?"

"Ease of mind, I don't know, man. I don't like the fact there's people out there with my grandparents' shit. They don't deserve anything like this to happen to them. They've never done anyone harm." He sighs. "I want things to go back to normal, Sol."

The trees rustle around us, the wind blowing making the chain links of the swing set clink for a few seconds as the conversation falls silent between us.

While I had been ready to open my mouth to protest once more, I only need to see his face to understand the feeling. The fact that he's been forced into a position he isn't comfortable with, even on a small scale, rings too true and similar to me to even begin to offer other alternatives. I have to get his things back.

But only Anna knows where they keep the fork and any other artifacts that the club has gathered throughout the years, along with the selfies and incriminating data any of the members have given the officials. Even I know what her answer to asking for the fork will be.

"No."

Anna pushes a stray hair out of her eyes. Her hair is up in a messy knot that looks effortlessly easy and yet painfully intricate. Except for the constant humming of the AC pumping through the vents in the roof, the art studio is silent. Her pastel drawing of a bowl of fruit set on a table in front of us is about halfway finished. The shapes and colors are neatly replicated in her sketch pad.

"That's what I thought you'd say." I sigh and push my hands into my pockets as I walk around the room, the horses (or art benches depending on what you want to call them) forming a weird circle around the fruit. The light is dim, making the shadows on Anna's face deepen and lighten depending on where I am walking. Her concentration is fully on the fruit.

"Not only would it be against club policy, but he's asking for this while he's not a member." She finishes a stroke then holds her pastel back to appreciate her work. "Who is to say that he won't tell on us as soon as he has what he wants?"

"He promised he wouldn't, he really wants peace of mind."

"You're easy to guilt trip, Sol."

"What?"

"Carlos mentioned that he convinced you to join because you guys didn't have many classes together."

That was not completely true—while yes, Carlos and I knew our schedules would not align very well once we started college, there were plenty of times to meet in person before he joined the club. It was the fact that I didn't want to meet a lot of times in person that made him pop the question. After all, I had been complaining about not being involved much at school and had started feeling like I was just going back and forth between home and my classes. While my summer had consisted of me and Carlos partying nonstop, when school started it was like my life had fallen apart in front of me once more.

"Think about it, Solecito, volunteer hours, fund-raisers, you can even run to be an officer if you want. It's a group of different people who like the same thing as you. Why don't you give it a shot?" he'd said.

We were hanging out in my room and he was sitting on my desk chair while Michi purred on his lap. I should have known it was all an evil plan the moment he started looking like a character from *The Godfather*.

"I don't know if I'll have time," I'd answered.

It was my first semester in college and I was taking all the classes I could, but one of the things Mom had mentioned from Mexico was that I should join clubs and make friends. According to her, resumés always look more interesting when a recent graduate shows passion that can be reflected into workplaces later on.

I wanted to make her proud, show her I could be a joiner and get good grades even with her far away. Dad had told her about all the time I spent in my room by myself, and she was beginning to worry.

"Then try it next semester," Carlos had said.

"Why are you so desperate?" I'd wanted to know. Apparently

even back then they needed as many members as they could get to stay afloat.

"I'm always desperate for you." He'd winked then raised his arms to catch the pillow I'd thrown at him. "Think about it this way—we'll have more time to chill together. Because you've been so busy, I haven't seen your annoying face in, like, a week."

He had been right, like Anna is right now. There's something in me that doesn't like disappointing people.

"Ethan didn't guilt trip me. I honestly feel responsible for what I did."

Anna puts her pastel down and studies me for a moment. I wonder if she feels as stressed as I do but is better at managing it.

"Would it have made a difference if Ethan hadn't found you that day? Would you care as much if you had been able to come and go?"

"I brought a fork with me that day to replace the one I took because I felt bad about stealing from two old people."

The Winstons were that nice neighborhood old couple everyone loves. Mom would sometimes invite them over to birthday parties. Memories of my childhood living a couple of houses down the road are rose colored, although most memories of my childhood are. My little happy family living in our old wooden home with two floors and an ample backyard, the swing Dad built himself, and the garden my mom kept in the front.

Anna tilts her head, looking mildly impressed. "Clever. Have you told Ethan this?"

"No, I didn't think it would matter to him."

"Have you thought about buying a fork like the one you took and giving it to him?"

That thought had also not crossed my mind. It's the simple solutions that always come harder, apparently. "No."

"Sol, if you want Ethan to stop bothering you, tell him we got rid of the key and give him a fork you bought at Walmart or Dollar Tree. He probably won't think twice about it." She gets up, stretches her arms. "But I would prefer it if he stayed, we really do need more members."

"What happens if the club doesn't get the number of members it needs?"

She gathers her pastels and other pencils that had been resting on a bench next to hers.

"We'll cease to exist. No funding and no ways to participate in activities mean death for a club. We could try to do fund-raisers, but we need school approval for that, and guess what? You have to be a qualified organization to host those, so there that would go. Our sponsors would not be able to give us enough funding to stay afloat either."

"Sponsors?" I didn't think anyone would like to aid a club with such obscure beginnings.

"Most of them are past club members. One is the head of some historical archive up in Portland, there's another one who is some sort of business owner in Tennessee." She shrugs. "I'm mostly the messenger, really."

She doesn't seem too preoccupied with the future of the organization, in fact, she appears to be at ease with everything that is happening. I guess that's her charm—being on top of everything and knowing how to fix things all while maintaining calm is not something every person can do.

Maybe I should bring her my laptop; she would probably know how to fix that too.

"If there's no way of giving his things back, then I'll talk with him again to figure something out," I mumble.

"What are you going to do?" Anna asks.

"I'll try to convince him to stay." As crazy as it sounds, Ethan is kind of growing on me.

"Sounds good." She sets her stuff on the horse, grabs her bright-yellow backpack, and opens one of its many zippers.

"But I have a request."

All it takes is a mere look over her shoulder, and I am somewhat intimidated. "And that is?"

"You can't make him do anything illegal, nothing that would put him in danger." I pause. "If it's too out there, you'll be losing people instead of gaining them. I'll quit."

The room becomes silent as I stop speaking, and Anna slowly nods. "I don't have much say over what kind of challenge the participant gets, but I will try to do my best to keep him safe. I know some of the risks are higher for some of us, and I wouldn't want to bring any harm to Ethan."

"Thank you."

"Like I said, the club will ease burdens. No matter what happens." She smiles.

Nodding, I take my backpack, sure I'm already running late for class. The Fine Arts and Music Complex is on the other side of the campus and I have a ten-minute walk to make it to calculus.

"I'll see you at the next meeting, then?"

"Sure thing, girl. Don't forget to bring your swimsuit."

I turn around. "What?"

"That's all I can say." Anna takes her drawing and heads out.

CHAPTER EIGHT

On top of hiding secret organizations from my parents, work-ing, and staying up all night typing out responses on my phone to my classmates' dull arguments on my political science discus-sion board without going off on the guy playing devil's advocate, I also have a laptop to fix. The blue screen has not gone away even though I promised my girl Mary that I'd begin walking closer to church if she performed a miracle on it. Without much IT experience myself, I turn to the only woman who can actually do the job.

"It's been like that for how long?"

"Four days or so." Diane and I are sitting in front of my laptop, the screen of death still mocking my failed attempts at fixing it.

She crosses her fingers and rests her chin on them. Diane might not be majoring in computer science, but she did build her own PC over the last year or so. She calls it her child, and paid for it all herself through hard work and finding the right sales online. If anyone can fix my laptop—aside from a paid technician, that is—it will be her.

"I'll have to take it apart."

My heart sinks. I grab my laptop and hug it against my chest. "Not my poor baby."

"Well, then get a new one."

"I don't have the money." The door of my room opens, followed by a loud meow and Michi jumping up on the bed.

"Woman, when you dropped your laptop something busted inside. I'm not sure what it was, but it's either out of my expertise or we'll have to replace something that might not be cheap. Besides, at this point I doubt it's worth it spilling more money on your laptop—it would be better to upgrade it."

"Will you come look at cheap laptops with me on Sunday?"

If I take a bit of my paycheck for the next few weeks I'll be able to afford a decent enough laptop. I won't have money to go out to eat or for coffee every morning, but I'll get over it. Besides, I can pay for a new laptop in installments and hopefully that will buffer the pain and allow me to continue saving for future investments like plane tickets to go see Mom.

"Sure, as long as it's before six, because I'm meeting someone that day." She smiles and picks up her phone.

Ah yes, the modern romance. The girl in question being Natalie, whom Diane is still messaging and going strong with. Although they've never met in person, they do talk to each other on the phone or through video chat.

"You're meeting her?"

"Yeah."

"Where?"

"A coffee shop."

I hum my response.

"It's cliché but she said she was going to do homework there and I kind of slipped in the idea that I could study there too . . . and we could get dinner afterward."

"Ooh," I slap her arm. "Smooth bitch."

She pushes her braids away. "You know me."

"What is she studying?"

"Communications." We share a little smile. "She's a sopho-more, and she's cute."

Diane looks through her phone before she shows me a pic-ture of a girl. Her brown eyes are soft, and she has ashy blond hair cut right under her chin. The girl has a tattoo of some sort of constellation on her neck, and her lips are painted a bright red. Not entirely who I would expect Diane to like, but Diane's smile is enough for me to hope this girl is good to her.

"But I'm free all day before that to go laptop hunting." She pauses. "Do you really want a laptop?"

"Yes, I do." She's been trying to convince me for the longest time that I can build my own PC, but I don't see the point when I can buy it as a single unit, although instant gratification and capitalism do not mix well with my wallet.

"Fine, we'll go look for a laptop."

"Yay." I wrap my arms around her, hugging her so tight she nearly has to wrestle me off her. "You're the best."

"You only want me for my car." Not a lie. When all you can do is bike around, your friends become like an older sibling who has to drive you everywhere.

"And your knowledge of technology," I add.

She makes a face and I blow her a kiss, looking down at my phone and wondering what to text Mom for the night.

"My co-worker, Karim, says that they sell these patties that taste really good and are vegan and I wanted to try them." I push the cart through the aisle of frozen products at the grocery store, the concrete floor making my cart jump every now and then, though it doesn't help that I got the "dancing" cart.

"Hmm, I don't know," Dad says on the other end of the line. He sent me to the store to get some hamburger patties and other things to grill tonight. At first we were going for the usual cheese and bacon patties but then I remembered Karim boasting about some delicious vegan patties, which is extremely weird because I rarely get curious about vegan products.

"Well, if you want to try them, bring them home, but bring the ones I like too."

I smile, knowing that was what he was going to say.

"I'll see you in a bit."

"Okay, be careful on your way back."

"I will, bye, papi."

He had offered me his truck to drive to the grocery store—he suggests it from time to time as a nudge for me to start driving again even when we both know I'm not quite ready to do so—but either way, the store is not far from home, and the afternoon is nice enough to bike here and back.

I open the door of one of the many freezers, take out a box of cheese and bacon patties, and then move my cart forward until I find the vegan products. I stare at the veggie patties for a good five seconds before giving in and placing them inside the cart as well.

It takes about ten minutes to gather charcoal, lighter fluid, bread, cheese, ham, and another couple of things before I finally approach the registers. This store doesn't have self-checkout, which means I have to wait in line behind five people because only register eight is open.

Once I'm in line, I take two chocolate bars and add them to the cart. Dad will like that.

Too busy scrolling through Instagram on my phone, I fail to realize it's my turn until I hear a small laugh.

"What are *you* doing here?"

I look up, slightly startled to see Ethan—in a bright-green shirt with the store's logo on it—staring back at me. It's jarring seeing him in a place I've been to multiple times. How could I have missed him before?

"Shopping?" I say placing my stuff on the belt. "I didn't know you worked here."

Ethan grabs the first item and quickly scans it. "I've worked here for a while actually, nearly a year."

Okay, I am the worst at recognizing people.

The problem is finding a topic of conversation that doesn't involve the club or the key. It'd be strange to comment on the weather or ask about his day at the supermarket—it would feel too normal, and my relationship with Ethan has been anything but normal so far.

"Night shift?" I finally manage.

"Yup, the only one that allows me to go to school in the morning." He's nearly done, thank the heavens. "Making burgers tonight?"

"How do you know?"

There is a box of burger patties in his hands.

"Oh! Yeah. I mean, I could be saving it for another day, but yes, we're making burgers tonight."

Think, Soledad, make coherent sentences.

"Thirty-seven fifty-five."

I insert my card, quickly type my pin, then look up so I can get my receipt. He makes direct eye contact while he hands it to me, and as he does, our hands brush. His skin is warm, and softer than I imagined, and for a second I feel out of place.

"Thank you, have a good night," Ethan says, and my throat feels sandy.

"You too."

I hadn't even noticed there was someone bagging my stuff and putting it back in my cart until now. As I'm making my way outside all I can wonder is whether or not he still thinks I'm weird. Not that I care . . . much.

When we moved to the apartment, Dad had to sell his old grill, but we found one small enough to fit on the balcony, as well as a small table and one plastic chair. Dad usually eats standing by the grill while I sit and maneuver around the table to see which way my phone would fit the best for a night call with Mom. It's a ritual that is as difficult as it is sacred, and happens many a times throughout the week.

"¡*Hola*, mami!" I call as soon as the screen turns from dialing to my mother's beautiful face.

Mom waves at me from her table. The small replica of my

face manages to show Dad in the background flipping one of the burger patties before looking over and waving as well. The lightbulb hanging over us does not give much light, but at least helps us see where the burgers are on top of the grill.

"Hola, *mis amores.*" Mom looks tired, not that she has ever looked full of energy on a good day. Ever since I was little, she has always worked hard.

She used to work with her parents in the fields, picking all sorts of fruits and vegetables. From Florida to Oregon, my grandparents used to take her on the road—she started working when she was about eight years old and her dad used to say she was twelve to stay within the laws. The people who hired him believed him—work is work. Once her parents actually settled in Texas she started cleaning houses with her mom and attended a public high school, and once she graduated, attended a community college and got an associate's degree in English so she could work as a teacher's assistant. Mom wanted to be an ESL teacher and help kids who came from different countries learn English, since she struggled a lot as a young child after only being spoken to in Spanish by her parents and peers. I don't think Mom ever outgrew overworking; it's in her genes.

"How's dinner?" I ask, balancing my phone on top of the table, using the salt and pepper shakers as a sort of stand so that we all are in a very long virtual table, together again, even if it's for a short call.

"*Bien.*" She lets out a yawn. "*Caldo de pollo* I made earlier this week."

Caldos are not exactly like soups; they have a lot of veggies and are often made on sweltering summer days by Mexican mothers when the last thing you want to do is have steaming hot soup. What I wouldn't give to eat that with my mom right now.

"Did you get the money I sent you?" Dad asks, taking his attention away from the grill.

She nods. "I put it in the savings account. I'll have to take out a loan if I get a cheap car since commuting is not the best."

"Traffic in Monterrey is so bad, though!" Dad takes a swig of his beer.

Mom makes a face, pushing her dark hair away from her neck. "It is, but it would still be faster than taking the bus every morning and afternoon."

We carry on chatting back and forth in Spanish, and I wish I could tell her that she won't need to buy a car in Mexico because I'll get her papers, but I can't do anything until I'm twenty-one. Dad and I have met with a couple of lawyers to see if anyone could take our case pro bono, but they've said there's not much we can do until I am of legal age. I won't turn nineteen until September, so that won't happen for another three years, and even then it seems like a long, slow battle, considering the grounds for deportation.

But because Mom willingly left the country they gave her a light sentence of ten years.

Light.

Mom, who had lived in the United States since she was six years old, is now thousands of miles away from me. I am still trying to find out how these things work. If Dad had been in the same position, I would have lost them both, and I'm still not sure if I would have been able to deal with a loss like that.

There are people who have it way worse than me. I have heard the stories and seen the news. Mothers and fathers of large families being caught over minor issues and being deported within a week of being turned over to ICE. People who lived in the United States for ten or twenty years, sometimes even more, being deported in a matter of days, to places where they have absolutely no one waiting for them.

In a strange, bitter way, Mom was lucky that she had extended family left in Monterrey, but it still hurts, and I can't help feeling like the universe decided to kick me in the stomach. The physical injuries of the accident have faded, and while I still wake up in the middle of the night gasping at the sound of metal and glass slamming against my body, the pain of having my mother ripped away from me somehow hurts more.

I take a sip from my glass of soda. The weather is nice enough to wear a short-sleeved shirt and a pair of yoga pants. My massive amount of hair is wrestled into a weird ponytail that lets the fresh breeze cool my neck. If I close my eyes, I can nearly ignore the static edge to her voice and pretend she's still here, that tomorrow morning she'll be up before me, making breakfast for Dad and giving me a look that says I overslept again when I walk out of my room.

But I open my eyes and she's on a small screen. So far away.

Dad said the woman from the crash had called me and Mom illegals when he arrived at the scene and they were loading me onto a stretcher. He had to see the officers coming from Mom and the paramedics taking me away, all the while a woman was complaining about her being in the right to merge, and how some wetbacks had cut her off. He watched his family being torn apart.

ICE is not very nice, even if you've lived here all of your life, even if your daughter is a citizen.

"How was your day, Soledad?" Mom asks.

I'm gripping my glass so tight my knuckles hurt.

That call lasts about two hours, and that's how long it takes for me and Dad to eat and wash dishes. By the time I go back to my room it's nearly eleven thirty at night. Michi is sleeping on top of her tower, next to my desk. The fairy lights I strategically placed around my walls flicker lightly as I make my way in.

When we moved in April last year, Carlos helped me decorate my room. In fact, he helped us move a lot of the stuff we brought over to the new apartment. Dad was extremely grateful for the extra muscle, and while we spent so much time making it as cozy and "me" as possible, it still doesn't feel like mine. It's only four walls that holds all of my stuff.

I miss my old house, my room that had a view of our large patio, and the swing on the old oak tree. I miss being able to run through the house without fear of waking up the neighbors, and having my own bathroom. It wasn't the fanciest of homes, but it was something my parents had worked for, and I had been raised there.

Sure they were renting it, but they wanted to eventually own it. A far-off dream that would have become more possible once I was financially independent from them and could help. A possibility that didn't seem too far away back then, but that now feels like a completely different life.

I miss when things were easy.

CHAPTER NINE

It turns out not having a reliable computer when you are a college student is a very bad thing. So instead of waiting for Sunday to roll around, I whine to her enough during Thursday's lesson that she agrees to take me laptop shopping Saturday before the club meeting. While we did go to a pawn shop and used her all-seeing eyes on the laptops they had there, we still end up at good old Best Buy.

"It's out of my budget."

"It's only six hundred dollars," she says, hands displaying the laptop in front of us. There is a worker who keeps eyeing us and walking around the perimeter, but they haven't asked us if we want to get anything yet. It might be Diane's energy, which simply radiates confidence in what she's doing at all times.

"It's out of my budget."

"But look at the dedicated video RAM!"

"Diane." I grab her face between my hands, nearly resting my forehead against hers. "It's. Out. Of. My. Budget."

"Fine, get lower graphics then." With a huff she turns away and walks toward the other models in a section that is clearly marked FOR STUDENTS!

Diane and I clicked in a strange way, like Carlos and me in middle school. We met in class but found ourselves spending time around each other because we enjoyed each other's company. I met her ex only once before they broke up, and in the aftermath we hung out even more. She has such a relaxed and no-fucks-given attitude to life that it's easy to tell her what is on my mind.

The first time I invited her over to my place she noticed that only Dad and I lived in the apartment.

"Divorced parents?" she'd asked as she petted Michi.

"No, Mom got deported," I'd said. We were in my living room, ready to start watching a show on my then-working laptop.

She paused, holding a finger toward me, and added, "Yikes. My parents are on their second marriages, so I was going to say I understood if yours were divorced. But I'm here, if you need to talk about that sort of thing."

"Thanks, dude." It felt genuine, a comment not made out of pity. "I'm here, too; must be rough."

"It's good, I don't live in my mom and stepdad's house anymore. I love them but I couldn't live with them any longer." She waved her hand as if dispelling memories. "We're fine, though; even my mom knows I'm gay."

I've never felt pressured into being someone I'm not or hiding anything from Diane, because I know she can see right through that, and respects my desire to keep some things to myself. While I know her relationship with some of her siblings is still rocky, I can tell she really loves her family and would do anything for them. If we ever do need advice or thoughts on a subject, we'll be there for each other.

"It's not all about graphics," I say.

"I never said it was." She pushes past me. "It's important in general. How are you going to marathon new shows if it looks like you're watching something straight out of Super Nintendo?"

"Hey, those were good games."

"Did you even play them, child?" She pulls a hand up to her shoulder and gives me a look.

"Of course I did, you old woman."

"Whatever. What's your price range again?"

"I'm not getting anything over three hundred." I bump her away from the laptop she's staring at, the card next to it clearly indicating that it is $130 over my budget.

"You're gonna kill me, girl."

"I know." I wink. "That's why you like me."

We leave the store without getting anything. I wasn't planning on getting something today; I still need another week before my paycheck. And I haven't told my parents that I will be getting a new laptop. It's not like I need their permission, but it will raise questions if I arrive with a box and I haven't discussed it with them. They want me to make good financial decisions, as impossible as that is.

It took me about a month to convince them to get me a phone when I was a freshman in high school, and even then I got one of the cheapest ones that were around at the time. Mom and I had a small argument about whether or not I could update it a year later, and when I look back on it, those little petty arguments seem so stupid now. I'd give all my possessions away just to have her back.

"How's your brother by the way?" I ask, putting on my seat belt as Diane starts her car. The engine comes alive with a bit of a strain, sending vibrations through the whole vehicle.

"Being an idiot, as usual, but he's good." She shrugs and fidgets with the radio until she finds the station that can connect with her phone's Bluetooth. "He's thinking about dropping out of school again, but Dad will kick him out if he does, and he knows I can't help him much since I live in a shared apartment."

"Aren't you worried about him?"

"I said all I could to keep him from dropping out. He might go to Mom and my stepdad, but whatever he does, it's up to him." That's the way Diane functions—she gives you the facts and then leaves you alone. She believes liberty is doing whatever you want with your life, even if that means screwing things up.

"You're such an old woman for an eighteen-year-old," I say, looking at her profile while she drives. Her braids fall over her shoulders and the sun shining over her brown skin accentuates her features and brings out how beautiful she is.

"Shut the fuck up." Diane laughs, but it's true—she's very patient and knowledgeable when it comes to life topics. I wish I could set my eyes on the future like her, and not let the past drag me down as it so often does.

"You're my favorite old woman, don't worry." Before she can answer, I lean forward to turn up the volume, singing along to the soft R & B song playing even though I don't know the exact lyrics. She flips me off, slows down at a red light, and lowers my ear-crushing music.

I let my head fall back against the seat. The sun is high in the sky, making the shadows stark against the pavement, and the trees around us move slowly with the breeze. If I had my camera with me, I would take a picture—perhaps one of Diane concentrating on the road. There are countless moments I sometimes wish I could capture, not with my phone, but with a real camera. Little pockets of memories that you won't remember later on but that are mesmerizingly perfect in the space of time in which they exist.

"Okay, if this isn't shady I don't know what it is." Ethan hands me the note that was taped to the door of the club room. I was surprised when I saw him waiting outside the room before anyone got there. I'm usually late to the meetings, but today Diane dropped me and my bike right outside the building.

> Morning meeting is canceled. Please meet at the
> back of Motel 6 by Main Street at 7:30 p.m.
> —Anna ♡

I narrow my eyes. Anna had mentioned something about a swimsuit the last time I saw her, but I can't remember whether or not Motel 6 has a pool, or where it is even located. There are a handful of hotels and motels around town, especially on the outskirts close to the highway.

"Hey, guys, what up?" We turn to Scott, his backpack half falling from his shoulder. He has a somewhat messy American style, with his jean jacket and dark-blue shirt underneath; his pants are tattered and he wears brown combat boots. Today his hair is undone and it spills in golden locks past his shoulders.

"Do you have any idea about what this means?" I pass him the note.

He pushes his hair back, scrutinizing the piece of paper for a second before shaking his head.

"Nah, man, I don't know what's going on." He gives me the note back. "But I know that place, hooked up with a guy there once. Kind of a creepy place, but it was fun."

"Why hold a club meeting there?" Ethan asks.

"Beats me." Scott shrugs. "But that gives me enough time to take a nap, so I'll see you guys later." He gives a salute before turning on his heel, steps sure and fast as he marches out.

Ethan and I exchange a look before we stare again at the note in my hand. There are nine hours before the meeting starts, and I don't have a ride to get there, aside from Carlos, who hasn't answered the text I sent him earlier today asking him what the meeting would be about.

"Are you going to go take a nap too?" Ethan asks while I tape the note back on the door, in the case other members come by. Thinking better of it, I take a picture of the note with my phone and quickly send it to the group chat.

"No, I have to work and a class to attend. I'll probably hang out at the library when I'm done with that."

"Ah, that's right." He pauses. "Wait, do you have a ride to the motel then?"

"Ethan, there's better ways to ask me out." It's an offhanded, playful thing I'd say to my friends, although he doesn't appear amused by it.

"You know Main Street is, like, six miles away, right?"

I don't even know where Main Street is, but Ethan seems to be pretty sure. Most of the time I navigate by places rather than street names since Westray is small enough to know where in the area you are.

"I can make it." This me speaking while typing a message to Carlos.

He's not answering. Ethan looks at me. Why am I nervous?

> Me: Carlos pls

No answer. Dammit.

"You know, I can give you a ride." Ethan fixes the strap of his backpack. "I have a class before the meeting, so I'm going to be around campus, and my car has a bike carrier."

"I don't want to be a bother."

"It's not a bother, text me if you need a ride." He pauses. "I don't hate you, you know."

My fingers hover over my keyboard, the intricate message I was about to send still half-typed on my screen. I hadn't expected that comment at all, and I'm not too sure how to handle it. "I never said you did."

"You sure act like I do. But that's partially my fault, I guess." He gives a short tilt of his head. "I'll catch you later, Sol."

Ethan doesn't have a jump to his step as he walks away like Scott did, and yet he stands out from the other few students who are at the small tables in the lobby of the building. Maybe it's his height, or his forest-green hoodie, but I follow him with my eyes until he's out of the building.

Me: Heyy

Ethan: Yes?

Me: I don't wanna bother you

Ethan: It's not a bother

Me: Let me finish

Ethan: Sure go ahead

Me: I don't wanna be a bother but like Main Street is farther away than I thought . . .

Ethan: I told you it was

Me: Ethan I'm TRYING to ask nicely

Ethan: You don't have to ask nicely, just say it

I press a hand against my temple. He's not going to make this easy at all.

Me: Can you

Me: you know

Me: give me a ride to that thing?

Ethan: Sure, where do I pick you up?

Why does he have to make things so simple? Do I like that? Yes, of course I do, but I don't want to. By the time I had caught up with my class, shift, and homework, I realized it was too late to simply ride around town until I found the meeting place.

Where am I? I look around. After studying at the library for a couple of hours and not getting a response from Carlos, I walked around the school while wrestling with the idea of asking Ethan for a ride to the meeting. I'm by the mathematics building, and that's close to Parking Lot C, so I text that and put my phone in my pocket. It buzzes.

Ethan: I'm close to where you're at, give me like three
minutes

Me: Ok

He wasn't lying. Ethan pulls up in a shiny black Honda
Accord moments later.

There's a click as he opens the trunk and then takes out the
previously mentioned rack. After closing the trunk, he sets up
the rack while I get my bike from the building I was leaning it
against, the full realization that I'm actually getting in his car hitting me now. I'm trying to grasp how we've come to this point in
a couple of weeks. *Time is an illusion.* After securing my yellow
bike to the back of his car, I climb in, mildly surprised at how
clean the inside of his car is compared to Diane's or Carlos's. The
dark leather seats and a single, dark-blue pine freshener make it
look as sleek as his usual fashion style is.

"Please don't kill me," I say as he drives out of the parking lot.

Ethan laughs. "I'm a good driver, I promise."

"I never said you weren't, I asked you not to kill me."

"Okay, I'll try."

Indie music is playing as we make our way to the motel, and
I'm restraining myself from tapping my fingers or singing along.
It's like the time you go to your friend's house for the first time
and you're trying not to reveal your inner weirdo.

"Why do you bike to school?" He puts the signal on and then
turns onto a less busy street, the dying sun hitting his face from
the side of my window.

I move back in my seat; he's calm, and it's nice to see. I've
noticed his really nice features—in fact, if it wasn't for the way
we met, and we had had class together, I'm sure I'd be texting Diane or Carlos about him, like I would any cute guy or

girl from whatever class the universe would have placed us in. Ethan's cheekbones are high, and his nose is cute and wide. The way his glasses frame his features the right way makes me hold my answer until he looks my way at a stop sign.

"I like to save on gas." It's the most believable lie. What student wouldn't like to save the fifty dollars they spend on gas a week? I don't like opening up about my situation to other people; it's too personal and feels like I'm asking for sympathy.

It works. He gets it, but that comment seemingly kills the conversation until Ethan pulls into the parking lot of Motel 6, a shady-looking building with a pool outside.

"Are you sure this is the right place?"

"I'm afraid it is." Ethan takes off his seat belt. "Let's hope they're not pranking us and we came to this side of town for nothing."

There aren't many other people around as we approach the building. Anna said in the message they would be waiting for us at the back of the motel, but it's hard to find the back since the building is surrounded by a parking lot.

"Don't you think security will get suspicious of us?" I ask as we pass some bushes. "Hopefully they won't call the cops."

"Now you're worried about that?"

We slow down as we hold each other's gaze for a moment. "You could sound more concerned."

"After spending some time with you, I feel like that word is not in your dictionary."

"Concerned?"

"Yes, along with self-preservation and—"

"You guys made it here alive, I see."

Carlos leans against the building, wearing a green and orange club-logo T-shirt and a pair of swim trunks. I march over to him and smack the side of his head.

"Ow, Sol!"

"That's for not answering my messages."

He covers the top of his head against my continuing assaults. "Anna told me not to!"

"Is Anna your mother?"

"No, *pero* you surely sound like it."

I hit him again.

"*Ay*, I'm sorry, stop."

"You're not sorry." Growing up with him has made me keen to when he's actually apologizing or not, and him not answering my texts was totally a way to mess with me.

"I really am. Stop, you're going to mess up my hair." It's only when it comes to his hair that he sounds apologetic.

"You two look like siblings," Ethan says.

I look at him like he has just offended me and my entire line of ancestors.

"Oh my God, don't say that."

"It wouldn't be that bad," says Carlos.

"You really want me to beat you up, don't you?"

"You know you love me too much to do that." He takes my hand before I can do anything else, even if playful. "I couldn't answer your messages. They made me put my phone away. I'm sorry. I'll buy you ice cream later, I swear."

"It'll be a whole banana split this time, boy."

"With extra sprinkles if you want."

I step away from him, pushing my hair out of my field of view. I really wish I hadn't gone crazy on Carlos in front of Ethan; now he must think I'm a psycho for reals.

"What is happening here?" Ethan asks as I step back and finally focus on the spot my friend is guarding.

Carlos is standing next to a fire exit propped open by a rock. "Nothing much, we're throwing a small party for you right here, and the other newbies who decided to join the club. We have a contact on the hotel staff working today, and they pulled some strings so we have access to the pool all evening."

"We didn't bring swimsuits," I say.

"She's right."

Carlos sighs, then pushes my shoulder toward the door.

"Go inside, room 154, and don't bother the hotel staff. Anna will get you anything you need."

It doesn't take long to find the room as it's only a couple of doors down from the fire exit. The carpet under our feet is an ugly dead green with some blue rhombuses that I stare at as I knock on the door.

"What's the password?"

Ethan and I exchange a look.

"There's a password?" he asks.

I perk up. "Cornbread!"

The door opens to reveal Anna in a black swimsuit and a red kimono.

"You got it. It's always fun to see who remembers. Come inside, you two."

Inside are two beds I'm slightly scared of sitting on. The walls are gray-ish beige and the carpet is an extension of the one outside. Alan's watching a random cooking show on the old TV in the corner. He is wearing a pair of swim shorts like Carlos was, except his are bright purple.

"I wanted to make this a surprise, so I didn't tell anyone but you." Anna points at me with a wink. "But I still got swimwear for everyone in case you forgot."

She ushers us to the bed next to the window, where Scott is looking at a pair of trunks. He gives us a nod as a "hi again" before going back to his search. Spread out on the bed are a variety of swimsuits for men and women in different sizes.

"They are from Goodwill so don't worry about the money, and I washed them last night, so no need to be scared. I used the sizes you guys provided for the club T-shirts to figure out what to buy, so if you find something you like, try it on." She gestures to the dilapidated table in the corner, on top of which are a couple of chip bowls, salsa, cheese, and all that good munch-worthy kind of food. "We have some snacks and we're going to wait a couple of minutes for the rest of the members before heading to the pool. You two make yourselves at home."

"All of this is because of the new members?" Ethan asks, walking over to the bed and grabbing a pair of the swim trunks but showing the same distrust a child has of broccoli.

"Yes, and because we like to have fun," Anna says, "you're getting baptized into our cult today, Ethan. At the end we're going to tell you what your sacrifice is going to be."

"That's a bit dark," Scott interjects.

"Anna likes to make dark comments from time to time, you know that," Alan says from his spot. "It's her thing."

"I'm not going to disagree with either of you." Anna shrugs and picks a bottle of water up from the nightstand between the two beds. "You guys worry about finding something you like. The meeting will start soon."

There is a large one-piece black swimsuit with white polka

dots, and while the design is a bit dated, it appears to be close enough to my size to try on. Once it's on, I feel comfortable enough to grab one of the towels provided for us and drape it over my shoulders.

Ethan and I make eye contact when I walk out of the bathroom. A pair of shorts hangs from the crook of his elbow, but we each turn the other way as I let him enter the bathroom so he can change out of his clothes.

Once more members arrive, Anna calls Carlos back in and we all head to the pool. The sun is already gone at this time of the evening in the middle of winter, but the weather is mild enough today that it doesn't truly feel like the end of January. All there is to hope is that the water is heated enough so that we all don't get hypothermia in the cool night.

A couple of tables and lounge chairs surround the pool, as well as a lifeguard chair and a single rescue buoy. A large sign behind the chair states the pool hours, and in bright bold letters says No Lifeguard on Duty. Swim at Your Own Risk.

"Everyone front and center!" Carlos calls out.

"The history club was founded by five Westray students thirty years ago." Anna paces in front of the pool, the blue light from its water shining over the members. Surprisingly, no other guests of the hotel are out and about tonight. "They didn't want something that would feel too formal as they were all friends. Of course, they wanted recognition and something they could proudly write home about."

"Nothing very historical about it," Ethan, who is standing right beside me, murmurs.

"But for people to become part of the club they had to do

more than get a bunch of recommendation letters and have perfect academic records."

"So they opted for breaking the law," Ethan whispers.

I shush him with a look, and he shrugs. It's kind of difficult being stern with him when he's wearing swim trunks. The boy works out. His bicep game is strong—hell, his whole body game is strong, but I never noticed because he always has at least two layers on.

"While we already had our induction ceremony . . ."

I realize Anna has been talking while I was trying not to stare at Ethan.

"I thought it'd be fun to have a pool party to celebrate that we have all the members needed to keep the club afloat this semester."

A round of applause is followed by her holding up her hands for silence.

"Please introduce yourself, your major, and what year you're in, and then jump in the pool as we welcome you into the club. Once this is over, I'm going to give the newbies their assigned initiation dare and after that we can all go home. We have some floats here, and a couple of water guns, but we have to keep it down in case someone comes in." She clears her throat, steps forward and shakes her shoulders. "I'm Anna Howard, the club president. This is my junior year in college, and I am an art major with a minor in history."

Then she jumps and from what I can tell the water is colder than I thought because she emerges with a squeal that quickly turns into laughter before she shouts for someone to continue.

"I'm Scott Miller, a junior-year history major with a minor in architecture." He takes a deep breath and jumps in, his long hair flying in the wind before he splashes into the water.

"I'm Carlos Oslo, engineering major and history minor and *this* lovely lady here is Soledad Gutierrez, a history major and political science minor, and we're both freshmen."

I whip around, panic rising up my throat as I see him running toward me, shades on, with no intention of slowing down. "Wait, Carlos, *no*—" His arms wrap around my waist and the next moment we're submerged in icy-cold water. I push him away, kicking up until I've broken into the surface. "You jerk!"

Splashing water his way does nothing, Carlos doesn't care, he's laughing too hard and swimming away from me.

Ophelia, whose red hair fixed in a braid wound around her head like a crown, is the next one, followed by one of the new girls who says her name is Melina. Alan is next, and then after that the other two girls, who look nervous about the whole ordeal. Ethan nears the edge, hands balled up at his sides.

"My name is Ethan Winston, I am a junior with a physics major and a computer science minor, and I don't know how to swim."

I and a few others scream, "Wait!"

He looks directly at me, winks, and jumps in the water. After a second, he emerges, smiling. That makes me lose my train of thought more than seeing his biceps because I'm used to seeing him when he's grumpy or serious.

"Hi, my name is Angela and I'm a freshman and a chemistry major with a minor in forensics." She jumps in, followed by the last member, Xiuying, who quickly says she's a freshman pre-med with a minor in business, and then covers her face before jumping in.

Once everyone is in the pool, it's like a weird social seal is broken. It's easier to talk to people when you're in a certain environment. Being an introvert by nature, I swim to a place that is not too deep for me and hang. Anna gets out of the pool to put music on and throws some floats in for the members.

It's relaxing watching other people interact, the way their facial expressions or body language changes. Like the way Mom would look at Dad when he didn't notice, or how he'd lean toward her at the table after we were done eating. That's why I love candid photos—people's personalities really shine in them. Scott is shooting Alan with a water gun, Ophelia lies on top of one of the floaties, even though there is no sun to take, Carlos and Anna are going over something on her phone outside the pool, and the two new girls whose names I have already forgotten hang by a corner, talking to Melina.

"What are you thinking about?"

I blink, not realizing Ethan had made his way over to me. "About how people behave around other people."

"Very psychological."

"It's a human thing, that's all. We only know what others are willing to show us."

He moves closer to me, his steps slowed down by the water. Our eyes meet for a fraction of a second before I look away.

"The way we talk to each other and act around each other varies depending on the situation," I continue.

"Like when we first met versus right now?"

"Thanks for bringing up bad memories, but yes." I sink into the water to keep my hair from drying up and becoming a human-size sponge. When I surface Ethan is still there, his arms crossed over his chest as he looks at me. "Why are you hanging around me? You should go meet the other club members."

"I will, I was just checking on you."

"Oh, I need to be checked on?"

Ethan sighs and moves away. "No, I was wondering why you were in a corner by yourself, you're usually livelier. And after your friend tackled you into the water, I thought maybe you weren't having so much of a great time."

I pause. I'm fairly shy when it comes to large groups of people. Ethan has only seen me be extroverted, mainly because when I'm with him, it's a one-to-one encounter.

"I *am* having a good time," I assure him. "Are you?"

He studies me for a second, and smiles. I have the sudden urge to smile back.

"I am too."

"Okay, people." Anna gets closer to the pool, her black one-piece bathing suit contrasting with her hair. "Stay where you are, I have a few more announcements before we can relax and wrap things up in an hour or so."

"She's going to give us the assignments, isn't she?" Ethan moves once again against the side of the pool next to me, our arms touching. I don't move away.

"I think so," I whisper back.

"I'm not giving details for what you guys are doing, that goes against the rules." She walks over to a lounge chair where she had placed her bright-orange backpack. "For details you're going to have to pick up one of these." She holds up some envelopes with names written on them.

My instruction sheet included directions on how to enter the Winstons' house from the back, which specific door the key provided would open, and a sloppy drawing of the floor plan of the first floor. Their tests are not about stealth or intelligence—they provide everything for you—they only want to know if you're brave or stupid enough to go through with it.

"All I will say," Anna says, putting the envelopes down, "is that Melina, I hope you're not scared of heights. Angela, I hope you aren't scared of getting your hands dirty. Xiuying, that you're willing to lie to someone important. And Ethan"—Anna turns to us, shaking her shoulders a bit as she does—"I hope you're not scared of the dark."

"What do you think that means?" I try not to shiver too much in the passenger seat as Ethan drives us back from the pool party. It's already ten and I didn't think much when he asked me if I needed a ride back home; after all, my backpack and bike were still in his car.

After her cryptic messages, Anna told everyone to go back to enjoying the party and refused to give me any information when I asked. Carlos, damn him to hell, was also not been very helpful. He also offered to give me a ride back home, but after the little stunt he pulled on me today, I lifted my finger at him and marched away with Ethan behind me.

All Ethan had gotten at the end of the party was a small envelope with the instructions. He was told not to open it until he was home.

"I don't know," he finally says, eyes focused on the road, two hands on the wheel. "You're sure she promised not to involve me in anything dangerous?"

"She said she would try to make it as safe as it possibly could be." The streetlights flash by the window, making neighborhoods and small businesses come to life in the night.

"I still have a bad feeling about this."

I do too.

"By the way, where is your house?" He slowly comes to a stop at a red light.

For some reason I thought he was going to drop me off at school. But once I actually pay attention to which area of town we are in, it becomes clear that Ethan is driving around the perimeter of the city instead of cutting back through WCC to get home.

"Um, you know where your grandparents live?"

"I live there, yes."

The light turns green.

"I live, like, three streets past that." I get the feeling that if he was not driving he would be glaring at me.

"You bike to school every day from that far away?"

"It's not that far . . ."

"That's at least five miles."

"People take morning jogs that are longer than that."

"True, but that is still insane." He sounds impressed. "I wish I could do that. Wait, what do you do when it's colder outside?"

"If it's below the forties I ask my dad for a ride to school. It gives me time to do homework." In the beginning, Dad wanted me to drive the car to school. Though the back door was nearly falling off, it was still drivable, but with my broken arm, bruised sides, and fragile emotional state after literally losing my mom to the US government, I could not drive the death machine. Every time I got behind the wheel I found myself shaking and being overly scared of what other people could do, especially around the freeway. Dad says it's something that goes away the more you drive and offers me his truck from time to time, but it's not the same.

There'll be a point in my life when it'll no longer be an option to simply not drive, and I'll have to get over it, though I'm aware I'm not there yet. Besides, with the cut in income and having to downsize in the home department, we figured selling the car was the best option for our family.

So I chose a bike, because bikes are easy. With a bike I don't have to worry about someone else's life. If someone decides to hit me, it's all me.

"If you ever need a ride to school you can message me," Ethan says, slowing for a yield sign.

"You're being nice. Why?"

"Can't I be?"

"It's weird." I lean against the door. My mother's voice rings in my head telling me the door could fly open and I could fall to my death, so I straighten back against my seat. "I've been an ass to you for the past few weeks."

"You're not an ass, you're just—"

"A bitch?"

"Would you quit insulting yourself?"

"I'm trying to give examples of things people might have called me in the past." In reality, I'm trying to make him laugh. He's been tense since Anna gave him that envelope, and part of me wants to see that flash of playfulness he showed before jumping in the pool—it was a breath of fresh air.

"Those people are the asses for calling you that." He slowly turns the car onto the street that goes to his neighborhood. "You seem to be under the impression that I hate you when I'm annoyed *around* you half of the time. Ninety percent of *that* time, you're the one who places yourself in that situation."

"What is that supposed to mean?"

The neighborhood around our place has a few speed bumps scattered around. He takes them slowly, and as he's driving by his grandparents' street, I sit up a bit to see my old house. There it is, still there. Someone painted it white instead of the pale-green color it used to be when I was growing up. They took out the orange tree my mother planted and the rose bushes have been replaced with hedges, it looks . . . modern. Whenever I go to school I always avoid this street for fear of seeing how they've changed it.

It looks nice, nothing wrong with it. It's simply not my house anymore.

". . . that even when I'm trying to be friendly, you constantly push me not to be for some reason. Do I turn left or right?" Ethan's voice pulls me back into the conversation.

"Left, and then keep going straight for three blocks, then turn right. I'll tell you which apartment building when we get there." I lift my hand to bite my thumbnail, but quickly move it away. It's an old habit I'm trying to beat, but it's hard when I'm under stress. "I'm sorry that you feel like I want you to hate me."

"That hardly sounds like an apology."

"I'm not entirely good at apologizing." Looking out the window as we move across the neighborhood, I can't help but notice how close we live to each other. I could literally walk to his house if I wanted to. Hell, I could have told him to drop me off at his house and I could have biked home, that way he would never know my address. "I guess part of me wants you to be mad at me. I feel like I deserve it."

"Because of the whole breaking and entering thing?"

"Obviously, but also because you're so nice. You let it go too easily, or at least it felt that way to me. I guess I was never okay with the idea of breaking into someone's home. I should have said no—then you would have never met me and I would not have to worry about you calling the cops on my ass. But you're too nice for that, and that makes me feel worse." The music that has been playing on his radio slowly fades away and it takes me a moment to notice that he was lowering it as I spoke.

"Soledad." He says my name weirdly, opening his mouth too much on the "le" part and saying the "so" like the English "so," but I don't mind. He says it better than most baristas. "I was furious the night I found you at my grandparents' house. They were on vacation, and I had come back from visiting a family member that same night. I've lived with my grandparents since I was young and never before did I feel so vulnerable in my own home. I thought you had stolen something valuable, and they mean the world to me. I wanted to catch you and make you face the consequences. I probably would have if you hadn't jumped out the window."

I had no idea Ethan has lived with his grandparents since he was young. While I want to ask more about that fact, I know this isn't the time. It only makes me wonder if we went to the same high school; he's only two years older than me, though those years sometimes do make a difference in friend groups. Mom always drove me to school, too, so I didn't take the bus, so we wouldn't have met there either.

I push the thoughts away.

"You're not making me feel less guilty. You can park here, I live in the next building." Only the light in the living room appears to be on, which means Dad has already gone to sleep. "Since you assumed I was dead, did you feel bad for me?"

"I didn't think you would die, I thought you might have broken a limb or two."

"Lovely."

"I'm not saying this to make you feel better, I do think there should be a sense of guilt for what you did, *but* my night had already been pretty shitty before I saw you. You made it worse and I took it out on you by chasing you." He laughs and stops the car by the sidewalk near my apartment. "You might think I'm crazy, but after I saw you limping off, I felt better because you made me laugh."

"I aspire to be the comedic relief of this story." His expression makes me breathe a little easier. "So you don't hate me? Really?"

"I don't, you just annoy me from time to time. You'd be way less annoying if you stopped being so self-deprecating."

"But that's what I do best." I rely on self-deprecation like a crutch. People can't insult you when you've already insulted yourself.

"I'm sure you can find another hobby. You're a resourceful woman." He sits up, then reaches into his back pocket and pulls out the envelope. "What if we read this now instead of waiting till I get home?"

"For sure."

Ethan reaches for the light and turns it on, then opens the letter and reads it out loud.

"*To Ethan Winston,*

"*The Westray Historical Archive is a museum located in uptown Westray that has been a part of the community since April 1963. We are sure that as a history enthusiast you might have visited this historical archive more than once. It is open from ten in the morning to ten at night, holds different exhibitions depending on the time of the year, and has a fee of three dollars for college students. The museum is a Catholic church that was abandoned and restored many years ago, and still holds a fully functional bell tower, though this part of the museum is not open to the public.*

"*Your mission will be to ring the bell at the archive at midnight. Of course, it is not an easy feat, and you will not be alone. To do so you will have—*"

He stops, looks at me, clears his throat, and continues, "*Soledad Gutierrez's help in order to complete this task.*"

"Wait, what did you say?"

"It says you're going to be helping me."

"No, it doesn't. Give me that." I take the paper from his hands and skim through it until I find my name. "What in the hell? *You will have Soledad Gutierrez's help in order to complete this task. The two of you are to stay one hour and a half after the museum closes without being detected by security, and make your way to the forbidden area. At eleven thirty there will be a power outage that will last thirty minutes so all security footage will be lost. You two will climb the bell tower. While Soledad takes a video of you, you will ring the bell to signal midnight. There will be an open exit door for you two to get out safely, and a vehicle will be waiting outside of the museum's main garden.*"

I flip the page around, trying to find any indication this is a joke, but all I find is a detailed floor map of the museum, all three levels. The bell tower is the fourth floor. This is the *opposite* of safe.

"This is unreal," I say. Ethan stares out of the windshield. I put a hand on his arm. "Hey, don't worry, I'll fix this."

"You don't have to fix anything, Sol."

"I understand that you might not want to become part of the club, but I swear I will get your key back. I can't promise the fork, but I will—"

"No, it's okay." His eyes shift to me, a streetlight reflecting off the rim of his glasses. "I'm going to do it, if you're fine with helping me."

"You are?"

"I've come this far, haven't I? Jumped in the pool and all."

"I don't think this is a good idea." The only sound following my comment is the hum of his AC. It shouldn't be a surprise that Anna would get creative with the dare, but this only makes anger crawl up my spine.

"Me either." He takes the paper from me and slowly folds it back up. "But I don't think Anna is going to change her mind, and I am tired of waiting around to see if she does."

"Then I'll help you. I got you in this mess so I will help you get out of it." I hold my hand up. "Pinkie promise."

"I—seriously?"

"I'm always serious when it comes to pinkie promises."

He locks his pinkie with mine. "Pinkie promise, Sol. We're in this together."

"Like *High School Musical*."

He laughs again. It's nice. "Get the hell out of my car."

"That movie deserved an Oscar."

"Out of my car, Sol."

Huffing, I grab my bag and the plastic bag containing my new swimsuit before opening the door of his car. As I take a few steps along the sidewalk, I notice my bike still hooked up to his car. I point at the back to remind Ethan.

"Oh right."

He helps me take the bike down. The neighborhood is silent at this time of night, the streetlights the only source of light for us to see as he puts the bike rack into his trunk. It's a nice car, nicer than the one I lost last year, and he keeps it really well.

"Thanks for the ride, I really appreciate it."

"Like I said, if you ever need a lift you can message me."

He lingers a bit and I do too. Then I give him a half hug. Later, I will most likely regret it, but it's something I do with all of my friends, and it feels right at this moment.

"See you later, Ethan."

He gives me a small salute with two fingers to his forehead as he moves back to the driver seat of his car. "Good night, Sol."

I wait until he's gotten back in and done a U-turn in a driveway before I begin walking home. The night is nice, and everything that happened today feels almost like a strange dream. I'm going to be spending more time with Ethan than I first anticipated, but for a strange reason, that doesn't seem like such a bad thing anymore.

CHAPTER TEN

I'm dying. It's eight in the morning and the professor is droning on about the complexities in the behavioral studies performed after World War II. He has a point, and it is somewhat of an interesting and intriguing topic, considering how much the world was changing at that time, but even then I don't have enough energy to keep myself fully awake to process half of the things he's saying.

I blame Anna because of the stupid dare. It's unfair that I have to be a part of it, considering that I am already in the club. I want to ask her why she'd do this, to stomp my foot on the ground like an angry eight-year-old and demand a refund because I did not sign up for this—unlike my class, which I did sign up for and for which I *am* paying.

"In consideration of Merriam's and other political scientists' approach to looking at the individual rather than focusing sim- ply on the government . . ."

At the very least there are the notes I wrote last night while reading the chapters that I can still highlight during class. Bless Dr. Barton's soul, he always tries his best to keep the class involved, and it kills me slowly when he asks everyone a question and no one dares to answer it.

I blame Ethan, too, because of what he said. How I put up these walls and push people away. He's not wrong. I let my guilt take over and try to fix everything on my own.

That's why Tyler broke up with me.

"Now, we get *post*-behavioralism, which was a reaction to behavioralism when scientists started going 'Wait a minute' . . ."

There was also the pinkie promise and the hug. I don't want to dwell on that because it's way too easy for me to develop feel- ings for someone. Whenever I develop a crush on anybody I feel physically ill, like at any moment when I'm around them I am going to throw up or faint.

It's not like this is the first time. I've had one actual relation- ship in the past, as well as some "encounters" as Carlos likes to call them, since he was the one who moved the strings for most of them, but the feelings never change. My body won't let me function normally while I'm crushing on a person.

It's silly, and I delayed dating Tyler in high school because it felt strange. Blame it on my vaguely religious parents and the fact that I wasn't aware Tyler liked me until he stopped me on the way to second period and asked me if I wanted to be his girlfriend. I had to go to the nurse's office right after, and he took it as me being grossed out by him, but in fact, I was so shocked by my own undiscovered feelings that I simply couldn't answer him. A week later I kissed him after school. I couldn't concentrate—I liked this boy so much and so quickly that I was second-guessing my emotions.

In a way, my emotional side is what caused us to break up. I don't really blame Tyler; he couldn't handle me being emotionally and physically broken after what happened. I ignored him a lot and became a different person from who I was before the accident. He told me I needed to get over it and keep going with my life, and while now I think I understand what he meant, back then I took it as a direct insult. There was no way to figure things out after that.

It took an entire summer of meeting strangers and having mixed emotions to realize that maybe I wasn't meant to meet someone until I figured myself out first.

The thing is, I am far from figuring myself out, and while I know I don't have a thing for Ethan, it feels nice to be around him—and he's good looking, no one can deny that. It's hard not to develop a crush on him, and I can't really explain why. It feels good that I've met someone who doesn't know about what happened and isn't judging me for it, even if this relationship will only last until he has his belongings back.

I look up at the board, at the Word document with the key words from today's lesson, trying to figure out what topic we're on. I wish he would jazz things up with PowerPoint slides, but Dr. Barton believes in the old type of lectures and I've been staring at him move his mouth without retaining any of the information he's trying to give.

"For the next class we'll be looking at chapter three and the components of political science, and then we'll have our first exam, so I hope you're all keeping up with the reading material."

God, I promised myself that I would pay attention to class this time; I have failed Dr. Barton.

"What did you think of the lecture?" Diane asks as we exit the classroom, the hallway slowly filling up with students.

"You mean how my nap was?"

She hooks her arm through my elbow so we don't get separated by the crowd.

"Yeah, I totally saw you spacing out. I'm pretty sure Barton noticed, too, but he's too nice to say anything."

"I couldn't help it. With the way things have been going recently I hardly get any sleep at night."

"Whose fault is that?"

"I don't need your sass right now, thanks."

We step out of the Liberal Arts Building and onto a concrete path leading to the student union, where we are planning on grabbing lunch. It's milder today, so some students hanging by the square are wearing what I like to think of as it's-cold-right-now-but-in-a-couple-of-hours-I-might-be-sweating-my-butt-off-in-cold-weather clothing. The fountain in the middle of the square is on, shooting up splashes of water every now and then as people gather on the grassy areas between the buildings, studying or eating before the next set of classes start. I tell Diane about the next "task" the history club has for me and Ethan.

"They're asking you to break the law again. One day someone is going to sue their asses and then all hell will break loose. Not to mention what might happen to your family. You don't need that kind of heat, Sol."

I grimace and let her arm go. "Don't say that. Even if what they're doing is stupid, I'm still a member. If something happens it'll affect me too. The club wouldn't do anything to truly put me in danger."

"That's what I'm saying. But I hope nothing happens to you, or Carlos, or Ethan." Diane sighs.

"I honestly feel bad I got him involved."

"Don't." She grabs my shoulder, stopping me in the middle of the walkway. "He did it to himself. If he didn't want to get involved he would have called the cops on you."

She's right—in a way I know this, but it still doesn't feel right. It never felt right from the very beginning. When I was given the assignment I told Anna I wouldn't do it. The Winstons didn't deserve it. They're a nice older couple I didn't know much about, but who always seemed like the perfect image of grandparents—those I never got. After Mom and Dad eloped and moved to California, I heard very little from either set of grandparents. I know Dad's mom lives in Texas, and is also an illegal immigrant, and while he's mentioned we should visit her, we never have.

The Winstons were that picturesque old couple who would wave back at me if I waved at them when I walked home.

And yet I did it, telling myself it'd be okay because it wasn't really breaking in if I had a key. It wasn't really stealing if I left a fork for a fork. I wasn't really there in the first place if no one caught me.

Even now I'm not too sure why I did it. I tell myself it was because it was a requirement for a club that aligned with my major. Sometimes I think I only wanted some excitement back in my life. Anna asked me if I would feel guilty if I hadn't been found out by Ethan, and honestly at this point I'm not even sure, but when Ethan said his grandparents didn't deserve it, I completely agreed. They didn't, and I feel responsible. Perhaps it's because I'm Catholic and think all my sins follow me around like some sort of emo backpack.

"It's strange that after everything that's happened he's still putting himself at that sort of risk when he had nothing to lose but the key," I say as we resume our walk, the double doors to the union offering the AC and food we're craving. "He changed the locks so the only reason he's going through with this is because he's stubborn."

"Like you."

"Hey." I stop, looking at her. "Whose side are you on?"

Diane drapes an arm over my shoulders and pushes us forward.

"I'm on your side. All I'm saying is that maybe he saw something in you that reminded him of himself. Who knows? Maybe the boy is into you. What if all of this is an elaborate plan for getting laid?"

"He could have asked, I wouldn't have said no."

"What?"

"He's a ten when wearing a swimsuit." I wink. "Daddy material for sure."

"Ew! Don't say that! Gross me out."

I buy a burger combo at the McDonald's in the union, Diane gets a vegan burger from a vegetarian and vegan restaurant the college added after enough students petitioned for it. We eat by the big floor-to-ceiling windows that look out onto the garden that separates the building from the library, which is my next destination, since I work until five today.

As we're eating, I send Mom a message, telling her what my plans are for the week and all that good stuff. Sometimes she sends me little videos about mothers and daughters, or puppy compilations she found on Facebook—little things that keep our conversations as lively as possible. Sometimes I forget to message her all day and I feel bad when she asks me if everything is all right when nighttime comes around. I can't help feeling like a bad daughter whenever I forget to talk with her; I feel like I'm hurting her without meaning to.

"If you guys do go through the whole museum thing, when will you be doing it?" Diane takes a bite out of her burger.

I swipe away all my notifications, trying to declutter the bar at the top of my phone.

"Next Saturday, the day the club meetings are held."

"Are you ready?"

"I've never been ready. I don't think Ethan is ready, either, but what can we do?"

"Quit?"

"Hilarious."

"Hey, at least I try to lead you onto the right path." She holds up her food. "You might thank me one day when you're out of this mess."

"Quitting isn't easy, Diane."

"That sounds exactly like something a drug addict would say—what are you doing this weekend?"

Waiting for a few students to walk by us with their trays of food, I take a bite of one of my fries before responding. "You mean aside from illegally overstaying at the museum and ringing the bell at midnight?"

"Yes, aside from that."

"Studying for the exam we have next week."

"Come to the bar with me and my lady friend."

"Are you guys sleeping together already?" I notice she avoided using the *g* word.

"No, of course not. I don't want to rush things, but I told her about you, and we were planning on going out this weekend. You could bring Carlos."

"I can't drink, Diane."

"You don't have to drink at a bar." I give her a look. "Or we could do something else. I need you and your relationship-sensing eyes. Come on, Sol, you're my friend, you should meet the girl I'm talking to."

I once told Diane that I could sense when a couple would stay together or not. It's not witchcraft—it's easy to see by the way they interact—but she has called me a *bruja* ever since.

"Sure, if I don't end up in jail this time. I'll bring Carlos so I don't have to be the awkward third wheel." She beams at my comment as we continue to eat in the midst of the chaos of the food court.

"How was your day?" Dad asks, spreading some salsa verde over the eggs I made him for dinner. I scoop some refried beans onto my plate and sit down next to him on the couch. We bought two little foldable tables we can place in the living room that are more space efficient than our actual kitchen table in the corner. In fact, we've mentioned getting rid of the kitchen table and the two remaining chairs to each other, in order to have more space in the apartment. We just haven't gotten around to it.

"Bien," I answer, reaching for the *tortillero* and grabbing a corn tortilla. "Tiring, as usual. How was yours?"

Dad sighs, shaking his head as he scoops some food up. "You know how it goes with my boss."

"I'm guessing the project is not going well?"

"The project is going well. We're actually looking to finish by the end of the month. The problem is the money and how they don't want to pay some of the workers what was promised to them."

"Are the workers they don't want to pay the same illegals?"

"Of course."

Dad gets paid well and on time because he's a resident. It's the reason he has stayed in the construction business for so long, but some of his co-workers are working long hours under the sun and rain and not getting paid what they're promised because they don't have papers and can't tell anyone about the unfair treatment. People seem to think that the moment one of us gets paid more than the minimum wage it's a personal attack on their livelihood.

We eat for a moment, listening to the news anchors speak among each other on Univision.

"I was thinking of visiting Mom over Christmas."

Dad looks at me. I sigh, sitting back to drink my apple juice.

"Look, Soledad, it's not that I don't want you to go . . . things are getting ugly right now, especially on the highways."

"Things have always been ugly." It's unfair that classmates go to Mexico and come back unscathed, and even share wonderful pictures of their time there. Carlos always asks if I want snacks or presents from his trips, and mentions taking me in his luggage the next time. I feel so disconnected from an entire country because of my parents' fear. "Mom is living there fine."

"Your mom lived in Mexico when she was a little girl, she knows some things you don't, especially because she was raised by your grandparents. Anyone can see you and tell right away that you're not from there." I sit back, my appetite gone. "If things simmer down we can think of doing a family trip, but I don't want you traveling by yourself."

It's frustrating, not truly feeling accepted in one country or the other.

"Just yesterday one of my co-workers told me an entire family disappeared outside Monterrey about two weeks ago. They haven't found them yet," he continues.

"It's ugly, I know" Similarly to my appetite, my mood has faltered, but I have to eat or Dad will feel bad. "I miss her, though."

"I know, corazón." He places his hand over mine. "She is with us in spirit, and we want to make sure you are safe."

I push my food around, thinking about Mom living in Monterrey. How she says it's beautiful. It has its downsides, of course, and her pay is so small that she wouldn't be able to afford her apartment were it not for the monetary help Dad sends her each month, not to mention the cost for public transportation and the traffic. She's also been followed to the bus station before, and she suspects someone tried to kidnap her once.

But she says it's beautiful, and enjoys seeing the Cerro de la Silla from her window in the morning and grabbing a coffee on her way to work. Says she's gotten somewhat used to the lifestyle.

Safe.

I wonder what Dad means by that word, because it doesn't feel very safe that I am risking my academic record, reputation, and their trust to stay in a stupid club.

CHAPTER ELEVEN

The van is deadly silent as we make our way down the highway. Ethan and I sit in the back. Scott is driving and Anna is in the passenger seat reading through some messages on her phone. I feel like I'm sweating but I know I'm not, or at least I hope I'm not. I press the back of my hand against my temple, but it doesn't feel wet.

"Hey, you guys mind if I listen to some music?" Scott says.

I clear my throat before answering. "Sure, man, go for it."

Within seconds Lionel Richie's "Hello" starts playing. I love this song; I would be swaying and singing along to it if I wasn't sitting in a van driving to another location in which I'm supposed to break the law. Not necessarily the definition of a fun school field trip in my opinion.

I turn to Ethan and notice he's watching me.

Lionel's voice soothingly plays in the background and it's

then that I notice how strangely close Ethan and I are to each other. My face feels hot and my stomach twists as the headlights of the car behind us softly outline his features.

"Are you okay?" Ethan whispers.

"Just nervous." My hair is in a tight bun so I can't play with it to distract myself from the close proximity we're in. "I hope this all goes well."

"It will."

"And I should trust you because?" I want to make it sound playful but the tension in the vehicle makes it difficult.

He shakes his head. "Don't trust in me. Trust in us." He reaches over and takes my pinkie with his. "We're in this together, and we'll get through it."

"Are they going to kiss?" Scott asks, and it takes me a second to realize he can see us in the rearview mirror.

"I think they were before you interrupted them," Anna responds, leaning over the console and smiling at us. "Don't worry, you guys will have more than enough time to bond in the museum, but make sure to keep it quiet."

"How is this really going to work?" Ethan moves back against his seat, disbelief in his posture.

"I thought you both read the letter." She smirks.

"It wasn't very good at explaining what we are supposed to do, especially how to find the forbidden area of the museum."

"Oh that," she huffs. "It's easy. You guys will enter the museum through the back, with passes of course, so if they find you, you lie and say you got lost. The closest exhibit to the bell tower is going to be east of where you guys first enter. It's still under construction, so when you see posters for"—she looks something up on her phone—"*Mexican Culture from the Late*

1800s, you'll know you're near. It's off limits to the public but you two are lovebirds who feel adventurous." She winks. "Get creative, you'll have to hide in an office or somewhere dark until the lights go out at eleven thirty."

"That's a whole hour and a half after the museum closes," Ethan protests.

"You wanted something safe, didn't you, Ethan?"

He's glaring so I take his hand, lace my fingers with his, and give him a squeeze of reassurance.

"We'll be okay," I mumble, though even I am not too sure about that.

Westray's historical archive originally commemorated veterans of World War II, but eventually became a museum for all things related to the city. Slowly but surely it acquired different exhibitions that went around the country, and thus became a source of civic pride. It was built on top of a Catholic church that was left ruined and abandoned after a fire.

I have fond memories of the archive—whenever my parents didn't know what to do on the weekend, they would bring me here to see the new exhibit or explore the galleries. Later on, in high school, I'd come and volunteer from time to time; teachers always said volunteer hours were good for college applications. It's the type of place that you can always go to if you feel stressed or anxious. When Carlos mentioned I could volunteer here for community hours for the club it only seemed another incentive to join.

Time does not pass in the archive. There are things that always stay the same—artifacts from the town that will never leave and offer a sense of reassurance that some things don't change. For example, the mining and precious metals exhibits, the classes on the geology of California, different eras throughout time in the area, and the like. The archive even host shows and exhibitions for local artists.

At this time of night there are few people left in the building. My heart beats quickly in my chest as we slip in through the west fire exit. On this side of the building the history of Westray is explored, from its humble origins as a mining town, to the resources used throughout the twentieth century, to the materials it provided for World Wars I and II, to the expansion of technology.

We walk around a train car in the dimly lit room. The echo of a record playing fills the halls as we make our way around the seemingly empty building. I can't say the archive attracts a lot of visitors, so it does have an eerie vibe this late at night, with the music playing in the empty natural resources area.

"Remain calm," I whisper to myself, taking a few steps toward the hallway.

"I am calm," Ethan whispers behind me and I nearly scream. I knew he was there, but I didn't expect him to be close. "Remember we have a pass, and that we entered through a blind spot."

"Yeah, I know."

It's hard not to look suspicious when both of us are wearing black clothes, in case we have to blend in when the lights go out. My jeans have fake pockets on the front and it's annoying that I can't carry anything in them (but they were cheap and looked good when I first got them), so I slip my phone inside my jacket pocket and pretend I'm looking at the train. Ethan walks near me, his shoulder brushing against mine.

Anna told us to look like a couple. As a volunteer, I've been on the last shift and know they announce that the archive will close about thirty minutes beforehand, then at fifteen, and finally at ten. We plan to hide until the guards and guides stop doing their rounds.

"I didn't know there were mines around here," Ethan says as we casually walk together along the exhibit. There is a film about mining somewhere close to us, the voice of an older man filling the hall as we silently make our way across.

"Copper. There were a few good spots in the late nineteenth century, but it either ran out or the government stopped funding it, I can't remember." I stop in front of a chunk of natural copper covered in patches of rock and green patina, encased in glass. "The mining didn't last long in this area since there was an influx of gold farther up north, so I don't think a lot of people remember or even know it was a part of the town. There must still be sites on the mountains to the west, unless they were covered."

"It'd be a nice place to shoot a horror movie." Ethan laughs. "Getting lost in a hundred-year-old mine, being chased by dead miners."

"Thanks for giving me a reason to have nightmares tonight."

There is an arch at the end of the hallway that leads to a different room, this one filled with artifacts from the late nineteenth and early twentieth centuries. It's the following room—with the postwar and nuclear ages—that is my favorite, though. There's something interesting about the 1950s, how perfectly imperfect it was. Not to mention the social expectations and injustices people suffered during those years. Everything dark was covered with a glittering mantle and proclaimed fixed.

"The town has a very rich historical background," I mention as we make our way through the gallery. "But they always seem to bring new things in instead of talking about the things that happened here."

"Like?" He turns to me as we walk.

"Like the Indigenous people who had a town here before the area was colonized, or the impact different wars had. It's nice to learn about other places for sure, but sometimes I feel like as a community we fail to see what got us here in the first place."

"Do you know about this?" Ethan says, pointing to an old, rusty axe.

"It's an axe," I say, shrugging.

"What if it's made out of vibranium, like in the Marvel films?"

I elbow him away. "Sure thing, buddy. I'd like to see that."

"Come on, Sol, it's funny. Besides, you can never be too sure."

"And I'm a superhero trapped in the regular world." There's probably a good reason why humans don't have superpowers, aside from science and stuff. As a society we already do pretty shitty things to each other without having eyes that melt metal or strength that can break through brick walls. God knows I wanted to do something violent to the officer who escorted my mother away at the detention center, even if that was his job.

"You could pull off being a superhero, they're always breaking into high-security facilities."

I elbow him again as he laughs. It's then that I realize how easy it is for sounds to carry here. "How much time is left?"

"F—"

"Dear patrons, the Westray Historical Archive will be closing in

fifteen minutes. Please make your way to the main lobby. Thank you for visiting us."

"Time for us to find that forbidden part," I say.

He links his arm with mine, and we walk in the general direction of the lobby. To the right there is a large poster with a photo of Porfirio Díaz, a Mexican "president" and dictator in the late nineteenth and early twentieth centuries, and the title "The End of an Era: Mexican Culture in the Late 1800s." The exhibition room is not open yet, and many of the display boxes are covered with sheets, but at the end there is a small hall that leads to the bathrooms and a staircase that is roped off with red cord.

"Whisper something to me," Ethan says, getting very close to my face.

"We are so dead," I mouth, the smile on my lips a nervous reaction that I can only hope translates as a love-struck gesture on camera.

My throat dries as we walk toward the camera at the end of the hall, pretending to be talking until we're right underneath it. Ethan, giant that he is, reaches over and turns it to a different angle, facing a wall to the right.

"This feels too easy," I whisper.

"It's not. They might notice, let's go." He pulls my hand, and our steps nearly become a sprint until we're by the staircase, then he removes the rope so we can walk up the stairs. This area is closed off, even to volunteers.

"Wait." I stop him before we reach the second floor, a few steps away from another well-lit hallway. "There might be another camera—"

"Dear patrons, the Westray Historical Archive will be closing in

ten minutes. Please make your way to the main lobby. Thank you for visiting us."

"We need to keep moving. Maybe they'll be distracted with visitors at the front."

I believe him. I have to because otherwise I will have an emotional breakdown.

We begin climbing again, turning at the end of the first flight of stairs and going up to the third floor. I know the next staircase up will take us to the bridge connecting to the bell tower, so we'll have to wait in this hall. With a quick look at the door, Ethan and I enter the hall connected to the stairs, which is lined with doors and at the far end there is a camera looking toward another connecting area. This and the fact that the camera will possibly soon turn to us makes me push Ethan to the first door and try the handle.

It's locked.

"Shit, shit, shit, shit." I move past him and try the next door only to find it bolted like the first one.

Turning the opposite way, I try the first door on the left, nearly falling down when it actually gives.

"Easy there." Ethan tiptoes after me, closing the door behind him. We're in a supply closet. There are a few posters as well as other marketing materials stacked on some shelves. A broom and a dustpan rest in a corner, and the door Ethan just closed holds a large infographic of the different animal species at the local lake. "Are you okay?"

"I'm fine," I say, sounding not fine, and push some strands of my growing fringe out of my field of view. "I panicked."

"I noticed." He moves around me. A couple of chairs are stacked at the side and he takes one out and pushes it to my side.

"What are you doing?"

"By panicking you found the perfect hiding spot for us." He sits on one of the other chairs. "All we have to do now is wait an hour and a half for the blackout."

I look around once more; it's not a large closet, but there is sufficient room to walk some five steps between us. Deciding this is better than going out once more and finding a larger office space, I sit down on the chair he pushed to me and quickly look for some moral support from my friend.

Me: I feel like I've made a terrible mistake

It doesn't take Diane long to reply. She knows what's going on right now and there's a possibility she was expecting a message like this at any given point tonight.

Diane: Have you guys gotten caught?

Me: No, but I have a bad feeling

Diane: You always have a bad feeling, you did the night you met Ethan too

Me: For a reason, I wouldn't be here if I hadn't met him

Diane: Touché

Diane: Well concentrate on the mission and tell me if I need to come bail you out

Me: I hate you but also love you

Diane: ♡

"I can't believe they're making us wait a whole hour and a half before the lights go out." I groan, moving back on my chair and taking out my bun, which feels like it's cutting off too much blood from my head. "Whose idea was this? I'd like to personally fight them."

"Maybe Anna's, who knows? We're already in the middle of this."

"What was the deal with you guys back then? If I can ask." He mentioned it briefly before, but I don't know much about their past aside from that. Anna keeps a lot to herself, and Ethan is fairly similar in that respect.

My question makes him turn toward me.

"Look, here's the thing. I used to live with my mom when I was younger. Some things are complicated in my family and Dad lived in a different place. Anna was my neighbor so we'd take the bus and get off at the same stop. In eighth grade I think we had the same math or science class, so we got together to study from time to time and"—he shakes his head—"it's strange telling the story now so long after. It was before Anna was Anna. I thought he was gay back then, and I was dealing with my own stuff, so we ended up sharing a kiss. I got self-conscious and bolted. I think I hurt him."

"Her," I correct softly.

"Her, I'm sorry. I think I hurt her because she didn't talk to me for so long after, and I couldn't look at her the same. I felt like an asshole and didn't know how to ask for forgiveness for running. That year Mom got a job that required her to travel a lot, and again Dad was out of the picture, so I spoke with my grandparents and my mom and decided the best way to go about it would be for me to move in with them while I was in school. So I never got to see Anna again until college. When I realized she was the president of the club, I panicked, I don't know why. I know it sounds so stupid now, but I thought: What if it's revenge for what happened six years ago?"

"No one holds grudges for that long, though, especially for a small thing like a kiss."

"I know, and I feel kind of dumb for it, but it still doesn't make much sense in my mind that all of this is connected to my grandparents." He shrugs. "I mean, it's cool that she got to a place where she's comfortable, I really am happy for her in that regard, but I wish she could tell me more about my things, or how they got them in the first place. All of this just doesn't add up."

I move my legs up on the chair, trying to find a comfortable position while we wait. "Mind if I ask you another personal question?"

Ethan looks at me from the corner of his eye. "We have a lot of time to kill, you might as well ask, Sol."

"You mentioned you thought Anna was gay and that you were going through some stuff back then. I ask because last summer I had a personal encounter that made me question my own sexuality, and while I am still figuring that out, I wanted to ask if you're bi, or what quote unquote label you prefer." I'm not usually this forward, but I am attracted to him and sometimes I feel like he might also feel something for me—though it's hard to figure things out with Ethan; things have happened so fast and I barely know him.

He makes a face, and I'm about to take my question back with a quick apology when he begins speaking.

"Labels are . . . difficult, Sol. Growing up as a black guy is not something I can really put into your perspective. I have these expectations from society that are different from some expectations from society that affect you. I had feelings for both boys and girls, and for a long time instead of confronting my own feelings, I ran from them.

"To answer your question: kind of? I find some guys attractive, depending on the man, but most of the time can't see myself dating them over the long run, so I don't want to label myself as anything other than straight, but if you got it, you got it, you know? It's hard to answer if I'm bi when there's such a wide range between that and—"

I smile when he tosses his hands in the air. That was not the answer I expected at all; it seems so honest.

"I feel that."

"Like, I've only slept with women before, but I've made out with other men. Does that make me bi? Probably yes in the books of most people, but why do people care as long as I'm confident and happy with who I am with? Really, as long as someone isn't an asshole and I'm attracted to them, what's the matter with trying? I'm sorry for oversharing."

"No, you're completely fine. I like how open that was, after all that's happened between us."

"What about you, though? What happened in the summer?"

It's only fair after his answer—there's no way I can brush him off, and besides, it feels good to know more about him.

"I met this girl at a party, her name was Taylor, and she was gorgeous. A lot of things happened earlier last year, one of which was breaking up with my boyfriend, and Carlos and I were partying a lot to forget about things. Taylor and I kissed while music was playing in the background, and the lights were low, and she gave me her number, and it was magical." It had felt right out of a movie. She had jet-black hair and boots that made her exactly my height, said she was a freshman in college, and in that single night I felt so high in how the crush feels and yet so nauseated when we made it back to Carlos's place. I should've known my good old crush allergy would kick in.

"But then a week later she ghosted me, and for a good week or so I asked myself if I was a closeted lesbian. Then I met my friend Diane, who is a lesbian, and had this deep talk over gas station taquitos after studying all night for an exam. After that I thought: okay, maybe I'm not just attracted to girls, but am I bi or was I simply trying to spice up my romantic life after my breakup?"

He looks a bit impressed, and a couple of seconds go by before he breaks the silence.

"What did you figure out?"

"I figured that I'm not fucking sure, honestly." We both laugh, and just as quickly cover our mouths in case someone can hear us. I press a finger against my lips before continuing on. "I have too many things going on to worry about who I like. It's exactly what you said, though, if you got it you got it. I don't care as long as you're not an asshole. Life is about figuring out things as you go."

"We're in the Who Knows? Club," Ethan says.

"Who Knows? Club. I like that. I'd prefer it over this club."

"Sol, what made you join the club?"

Stretching my legs back out, a couple of excuses fly through my mind before I notice that there aren't very good believable answers. "I wanted to fill in more spots on my resumé, but . . ."

"But?"

"Well, it's not ideal." I motion around. "Risking my reputation for a stupid gap on my resumé."

"Isn't that what students do, though? We kill ourselves for a diploma only so we can be rejected when we get out of college. A spot on our resumé can make a difference, as sad as that sounds."

I wonder what his background is; after all, he's living with his grandparents for a while but also mentioned he used to live with his mother before. The air around him is tense but when our eyes meet I don't feel the same strain that was between us when we first met.

"Why are you so wise?"

He scoffs. "At our age if you're not in debt or depressed you're either lucky or come from a very good background. Sometimes things don't seem to be fair and you get angry."

"At who?"

"At everything, Soledad." Ethan pauses, closing his eyes. "How much longer?"

"Forty minutes."

"God, this is going to take forever."

And it does. I play a few games, text a few people, but the time slowly drips through the corners of the room. Ethan and I talk about the weather, our pets (he has a fish named Nemo and his grandparents' cat is named Muffin), our favorite color (yellow), our classes, and our upcoming exams, and yet there is still fifteen minutes left.

"What made you really want to join the club?" I ask not only because I'm running out of topics but because something tells me there's more to it than a key and a fork. Something that doesn't fit right in the larger puzzle that is Ethan Winston.

He turns to me, his hair messy because of the many times he has passed his hands over it, a few curls touching his forehead. "You."

"Me?"

"At the beginning I wanted the key, even though I changed the locks. I felt insecure, like at any moment someone could come into my house and steal something else. It's really nerve-racking, Sol, to live like that."

"Thanks for adding to my baggage of guilt."

"But spending time with you made me realize you're not a bad person. Crazy? Yes. A bit reckless? Absolutely, but not bad. I kept wondering what would make you want to join *this* kind of club—I wanted to see it for myself. Given where we are, I don't think I have found the answer to that question."

"I'm surprised you're still here. If I was you, I would have bailed a long time ago."

Ethan points at the door. "If we want to we can barge out of the room and tell everyone everything about the club."

"Or get arrested."

"That would be our choice, but do you know why I'm not doing it?"

"Why?"

"Because I know you're a smart woman, Sol, and a smart woman does not join a cult-like club simply to fill a space on her resumé. There must be another reason."

I think of my mother, of the immigration officers taking her away, of me talking to her through a thick sheet of glass with a phone against my ear. The wrongness of seeing her being treated like a criminal, detained and away from me. The memory of her telling me to be good and pay attention in school, to join clubs and keep my grades up because in the United States education is a key factor for your future, and she wanted my future to be bright and have the things she and Dad couldn't have.

"Or I could just be stupid," I say, redoing the bun in my hair as I speak. "Everyone makes impulsive decisions."

Ethan nods, getting up. "I've been there too."

I want to ask him what he means but my phone vibrates, telling me the wait is over and that the lights are going to go down—if everything is going according to Anna's plan.

"What if it doesn't work, what if the lights don't go out?" I say.

Ethan gets up, flexing his legs, which, if they feel like mine, might have become numb.

"Then I guess we'll have to sleep here all night."

Apparently, we won't have to sleep in a small closet some-where inside Westray's historical archive because after Ethan finishes speaking, our cramped little room goes pitch black. Even while being fully aware this was going to happen, I still gasp, bumping my arm against his as I try to reach for the door.

A hand grabs mine in the dark, which honestly is terrifying, but I won't let Ethan know that.

"Shh, even if they can't see us they'll hear if you storm out."

"Who, the ghosts?" I hiss back.

"Oh, half of the things here are probably haunted. Don't try your luck, Sol."

Look, I'm atheist-ish as hell (and yes, I recognize the irony of that statement), but I *was* raised Roman Catholic, so the idea of ghosts, demons, and possession has been ingrained in my mind since I was young. "You know I'm kidding, right?" His hand leaves mine and grasps the doorknob.

"If you get possessed I ain't saving you. I could, I've watched *Supernatural*." I move past him into the dark hallway.

The hall is darker than most of my jokes, so I take out my phone and raise the brightness as much as possible. I'm not crazy enough to turn on the flashlight since any guard would make a beeline for that.

"We should have gone full-on *Strange Encounters* and brought night vision goggles," I say, walking slowly down the hall. The tower is a floor above us.

"We don't have the money or the time, let's move on." He walks ahead of me, finding the door that leads to the stairwell and surreptitiously making his way up.

I follow, glancing behind me as we go, the feeling of someone or something watching us leaving a chill against the back of my neck. Large buildings like this, *old* buildings like this, seem to carry a spirit of their own, as if the halls themselves are filled with memories. It's good we didn't have to navigate the entirety of the archive with the lights out or otherwise we would have been hopelessly lost.

Of course, there are rumors from the workers at the archive that the building is haunted, especially the church area. La Parroquia Nuestra Señora de los Dolores was erected in the early 1800s on the backs of minorities, mostly Indigenous people, who built the church stone by stone. It is, quite possibly, the oldest standing building in the entire town. Which is why, when it was abandoned after the fire, city officials decided to make it part of the archive.

"Sol, let's go, we're losing time."

"Sorry, got distracted."

The third floor is the last one the stairs reach. At the middle of the hall there is a small bridge that leads to the bell tower. If Anna is not wrong, the security door that separates the main building from the tower should have been unlocked with the outage. Ethan is currently looking over the keypad on the door.

"Come on, open the door. I want to get out of here sooner than later."

He sighs and tries the lock. It gives, and the door swings into the small hall. The moonlight fully shows through the glass windows, our shadows becoming highly contrasted on the stone floor under our feet. Ethan holds the door open for me.

"This feels too easy—"

He holds a hand over my mouth, turning slowly and looking at something over my shoulder.

Ghost, ghost, ghost, ghost.

"I thought I heard something. Let's get this over with."

Ethan closes the door behind us so slowly and quietly that I give him a sharp look to get it over with. Once it's closed we make our way across the hall, which stretches for a seemingly impossible length during which we are crouching and stealthily trying to be on the lookout for any cameras that might have stayed on even during the blackout. A distance that should be crossed in under a minute thus becomes a five-minute ordeal.

"We must look so stupid right now."

"Speak for yourself," I hiss. "I look like a spy."

"Sure, Sol, whatever you say."

"You better not be looking at my butt."

There is a small pause. "I wasn't until you mentioned it."

"What?"

He snickers. "I'm kidding. Let me go first if you're self-conscious about it."

"Whatever, it's not like I care."

"You're the one who mentioned it, but it's not bad at all."

"*Anyway.*" I check the handle of the door for the bell tower and it gives easily. "Once we're done with all of this you're going to owe me so much. I'm legit so close to bolting."

"I'm with you all the way."

We enter a small room that leads directly to a spiraling staircase. Slivers of light come from the barred windows placed along the steps. Unlike the previous building, here in the tower the floors are made of wood instead of stone. Every step we take causes the tower to echo, creaking all the way down.

"Do security guards check this building often?" Ethan's voice is a lot closer than I thought he was, which at this point has stopped surprising me.

"I wouldn't know." My knees hurt from crouching so I straighten up and move my legs. "It's off limits so I would assume they don't check it *as* often."

The staircase does not have a banister, and that's dangerous for someone like me, who falls down even with their shoes tied right.

"Either way, the bell ringing will alert anyone that something is going on." I place a hand firmly against the stone wall and climb. "Let's hope that the lights are still out by the time we come back."

Ethan follows me up slowly, and we have climbed up about ten steps or so when I notice he is being extra quiet.

"Everything okay?" I look over my shoulder.

"I . . . yeah, fine." His eyes flicker to the edge then back to me again, throat working.

"You afraid of heights?"

His Adam's apple moves as he swallows. "I, um, I know it's stupid, but—"

"Come." I reach out to him with my right hand. It's a bit

awkward but I want to make sure I have the left one pressed firmly against the wall. "We'll get up there together, can't have you falling behind."

He nods, grasping my palm as we climb faster than we did before. I look back at him every now and then to make sure he's all right.

At the end of the stairs there's a door too small for him to walk through without hunching his back, which leads to an even steeper set of stairs up to an alcove where the bell resides. It's larger than I thought it would be. The tower gives us a view of the city. Cool air brushes against my face as I march up the last few wooden steps.

Ethan hangs back.

"It looks amazing up here." The archive is close to downtown Westray, and while it is nothing compared to a large city, it's beautiful nonetheless. Houses and cars are still lit up this time of the night, and the bell tower is tall enough to make the twinkling lights appear like a Christmas celebration.

Ethan stands still, one hand firmly planted against the wall. "I'm sure it does."

"Ethan."

"Yeah?"

"We kind of have to do this now."

"I know." He keeps his eyes on me as he comes up the stairs. It takes him a couple of seconds but then he's standing next to me, hands balled at his sides. "A couple of rings, you shoot the video, and we're out of here, and if this ruins my life—"

"I'm going down with you."

He seems as surprised as I am to hear that.

"I was going to say I'd ruin the whole club," he says.

"The club going down would mean me going down too."

"You deserve better than that, Sol, you—actually, no time to talk, just film me."

I move back, pull out my phone, and open my camera app. Time seems to slow as he grabs the rope hanging beside the bell, the heavy bronze reflecting his figure as he pulls with what I can only guess is all his strength.

Then comes the bong. A physical shock to my body, I have to concentrate on both keeping a good grip on my phone and not letting out a yelp when the sound waves vibrate through my entire skeleton. Ethan nearly falls to his knees and covers his ears, but manages to grab the rope once more and pull it another two times. He is clearly in as much pain as I am.

We don't have time to recover from the auditory attack. I swiftly end the video, rush to his side, and pull on his arm. The bell is still swinging, though not as strongly and as terrifyingly as it had during the first rings.

"We gotta go now!" I yell, even though I can't hear my own voice, and push him to the small door and down the spiraling stairs. Anna said there would be an exit at the back of the building open for us to slip through, but didn't give us the exact location. I hope she meant the one at the back of the church or else we're screwed.

My brain doesn't catch up to the fact Ethan is scared of heights until we're halfway down the stairs. When I slow down he keeps going, which I take as a sign that he will be okay. By the time we're both on the bottom floor with sure, nonwooden ground under our feet, I sense a headache behind my right eye beginning to form.

There are two exits at the back of the church. I'm betting

on the one closer to the area where delivery trucks unload for events. Stained-glass windows line the wall to our left, the different colors painting the halls in an oddly beautiful and haunting way.

"Time?" I whisper, struggling not to pant.

"I'm guessing, like, five minutes, don't want to look at my phone." Ethan rests his hands on my shoulders as we pace as slowly as we can to the end of the hall.

We take a left turn, walking along the back area close to the confessional booth that was turned into a storage closet. The left side of the church is a merging between the modern and times past, the archive blending into the holy building and helping it stand. We take a right to the back of the building and enter the darkened halls modeled after the newer building, which will make the flashlight beam so easy to see.

A hand covers my mouth before I can even think of gasping. Ethan presses his body and mine against a wall, his forehead flush with mine. I can feel his breath against my cheek, and I clutch his arms, my pulse racing. If it wasn't for the sudden adrenaline spike, I might even blush at the sensation of him against me, and it feels like minutes go by instead of seconds as we are frozen in terror.

To our right footsteps grow fainter.

As soon as we can't hear the steps anymore, I gently push Ethan away and reach down.

"Shoes off," I whisper.

He doesn't question me. Once we're both in socks, I grab his free hand and make a run for it. We reach the door and push it.

It opens.

Relief makes me go weak in the knees but Ethan presses a

hand to my back, hurrying me along to Scott's van, which is parked along the sidewalk outside the archive's back entrance. We're not even a yard away from the archive when the lights turn on outside and adrenaline makes us sprint to the vehicle and jump into the door that opens from the back.

I get in first, Ethan following by launching himself in and slamming the door behind him. Scott hits the gas harder than I anticipate. When he turns the corner, I fall over Ethan's side and his arm quickly goes around me for support.

"Scott!" I manage. Ethan rests his hand on my shoulder when I sit back up. I drop my shoes on the floor of the car so I can wrestle my feet into them.

"Sorry, kiddos, gotta get out in case things get ugly," Scott shoots back.

Anna leans over the armrest, blue hair shining every time we pass under a street lamp.

"How was it? You guys had fun?" She's beaming.

If it wasn't for Ethan suddenly tightening his grip on my shoulder, I would scream at her. Why am I doing this to myself? To Ethan?

But Anna is still smiling, and Ethan is still holding me close, and we did just storm the archive—and somehow I'm alive.

"Fun," I exhale, resting a hand on Ethan's leg. "It was fun."

Ethan laughs and bops my bun once. I shoot him a look.

"Yeah," he says. "It was."

CHAPTER TWELVE

"Can we agree yesterday didn't happen?" I ask, sitting down in a booth of the café, the conversations around us low enough to hear the low jazzy music playing overhead. Taking a bite out of my blueberry muffin like it's the last meal I'll have in my life, I sit back and stifle a moan at how good it tastes.

"If there was a way I could erase it from my memory that would be nice." Ethan is drinking tea, something aromatic and calming, like chamomile with lavender. I would poke fun at him for it, but the boy knows how to rock his aesthetic, with a moss-green shirt, gray beanie, and denim jacket. "Why are you glaring at me like that?"

Because I wish I had your goddamn fashion sense.

"You've got a bit of glaze on your cheek," I lie, pointing at my own. He takes a napkin and wipes, and I nod. "You got it."

As he takes another bite of his cinnamon roll, I drink my

coffee. I stumbled home about one thirty last night. We dropped Ethan off first at his grandparents' house.

As he was walking away, Anna had snickered, "Oh right, I should have put two and two together about his grandparents."

"You should've warned me," I told her, not able to hide the annoyance in my voice.

"I'm sorry, Sol, I'm not allowed to disclose details."

"For something that breaks the law a lot, the club has a lot of restrictions."

"They call it organized crime for a reason. Every organization has their own set guidelines. Even the devil follows the rules of his contracts."

"Sol?" His voice interrupts my memory from last night. The café is a nice distraction from everything that is going on everywhere else, and somehow the buzzing around of the students makes this feel normal—Ethan and me grabbing a bite before class is surely something I wouldn't mind repeating more often now that we're on good terms.

"Sorry, I'm spacing out. What's up?"

"Nothing, you seem to be spacing out a lot today."

"I'm fine. I just haven't fully woken up."

"And you look nice today."

I stop drinking coffee midsip. Aside from my regular clothes, I braided my hair, which took nearly half an hour to get right. Also, I put on makeup because Ethan offered me a ride to school. While there hadn't been a lot of thought put into arranging my look, there might have been an extra bit of effort put into it when I knew I was going to see him.

"Um . . . thanks, man, that jacket is nice."

He smiles and turns his head. "Well, thanks, girl. You going to the library?"

"Yep." Checking my phone, I see I have ten minutes to clock in, and it takes about six to walk there from the café, so it's a good call from him to remind me. "I love my job, but I don't particularly enjoy working Sundays."

"I don't either. I hate working retail, but—" He shrugs.

"You gotta make that check, I get it. Thanks for the ride this morning. I would've probably been late if you hadn't messaged." I wasn't even sure if he had any reason to be at school on a day like today—most students tried to keep an ample distance between themselves and the educational system on Sundays, but he had been the one to offer a ride when I mentioned I had to work.

"We did stay up pretty late.'"

"No, I'm usually late. It's funny you think I go to bed at a reasonable time." I grab my bag and walk a few steps to quickly give him a side hug before taking my cup of coffee off the table and trying not to walk too awkwardly out of the door and into the February morning after saying an awkward good-bye.

The library is mostly empty on Sundays. It usually does not become hectic until it is time for midterms or finals. Karim and I do a round of rock paper scissors for who gets to pull the books for the hold list and he ends up losing. I spend most of my shift helping students with questions or fixing their printing-credit problems.

Miranda comes over once or twice to check on my work. By

check I mean she tells me about her day and what she is planning on having for dinner: candied-bacon cauliflower mac and cheese.

"The cauliflower cancels out the unhealthiness of the bacon," she assures me, and really there's no arguing with that mindset, and even I start to believe it by the end of the conversation.

While the library closes at five on Sundays, my shift ends at one o'clock. The doors of the elevator open to the main lobby area, and I can taste freedom in the air. As I quickly wave at Lucy in circulation, I see Carlos strutting into the area like he secretly owns the place. Dark hair slicked back, bright-green eyes under bushy eyebrows, he smiles at me.

"Ready to go?"

I give him a side-eye. "Where are we going?"

Carlos takes my backpack from my hand and puts it over his shoulder so that he can drape his right arm around my neck.

"Diane messaged me. Something about you meeting her girlfriend and needing a date or else you'll feel like the third wheel—again."

Wincing, I close my eyes. I had completely forgotten I agreed to do that, like, a week ago. It's not the first time—there is a reason Diane and Carlos have each other's numbers. Whenever I go MIA or do not show up in class one or the other usually knows where I've gone sulking to.

"Oh right." I look through my phone and sure enough there is a missed call from Diane. "Friend of the year, aren't I?'

"You're all right. I'm sure she doesn't mind." He lets his sunglasses fall over his nose as we step out into the sunny day.

"As long as she doesn't tell Natalie you're my boyfriend." I laugh.

"She wouldn't. Maybe friend with benefits."

"Oh God, no."

He snickers and tugs on the back of my braid. I push him away then pretend to take a swing at him as he flips me off. Carlos reaches over and grabs my arm, directing us to the sidewalk.

"Come on, Solecito, we're going to be late."

After Tyler broke up with me in late February last year, I had no prom date. There were no hard feelings about it, but I had already gotten the tickets, so Carlos and I decided to go together. It worked fantastically since I didn't want to be approached by anyone else, being fresh out of a relationship, and Carlos got to be eye candy for anyone who decided to look for him.

"Nothing gets someone going like someone you can't have," he'd said, grabbing a small plate of appetizers being passed around.

"That's kind of dumb, but sure if you say so," I'd replied. It was my first big thing after the accident; my arm was still in a sling and would be until I graduated, but my dress was sleeveless, and that helped me out.

After the party we went over to one of his friend's houses and amid the teenaged cheering, we kissed briefly. Something along the lines of us being friends for so long not making sense if we weren't attracted to each other, but I didn't feel anything. I was surprised, a lot of rom-com movies told me that that shouldn't have happened, that I should have realized I was secretly in love with my best friend, but I wasn't.

Turns out he felt the exact same way.

"It's different," he'd said, a couple of days later. "It's not like I feel like we should date, it's not like I see you *as* more or less of a friend because of it."

When I kissed Tyler it was nice—I felt cared for and there were feelings involved. Kissing my best friend was different. There were no butterflies or adrenaline. It was only a kiss, and we shared cheek kisses quite often as greetings. It was as if we had gone for a simple hello and missed, only to laugh about it later.

We were hanging out on the balcony of his place, our feet dangling three floors away from the ground. "No offense, I could not imagine dating you, but I know I want you there in the future," I'd said.

"Exactly."

"So, we're fine?"

"Yeah, Sol, we'll always be fine."

And we have been ever since. Whenever we need a date for events like family weddings, we're there for each other. Diane says we're technically friends with benefits.

"Nonsexual benefits, mind you," she assured me as soon as I protested. "You guys do what normal friends do, but he's also there at three a.m. bringing you ice cream because you watched *The Lion King* again and are crying. You would do the same for him. That's true friendship with benefits."

We meet Diane and Natalie at Liam's Dinner, a new, in-with-the-kids-but-with-an-older-kick restaurant that opened up a couple of months ago, and which I'd been eyeing since word got around that the shakes and fries were good. The floors are black tiles, and the booths and chairs a cherry red to contrast with the white countertops and teal-blue walls. "Put Your Head on My Shoulder" by Paul Anka plays overhead as Carlos and I walk into the restaurant.

"You guys made it." Diane gets up, her girlfriend following. Natalie is shorter than me by about a head, and has the type of pixie haircut I could never maintain without looking like a crazy person. She also seems to be the opposite of Diane, from their character to their looks. It's cute, how they steal glances, giggle, and touch whenever they can.

After everything that's been happening with Ethan, I've begun to wonder if I can go through something like that again. With what happened with my mom, there are things that are way more important than a relationship right now, but I still think about it from time to time.

"Diane says you're a history major," Natalie says, dipping one of her fries into her milk shake.

I nod.

"That's supercool. What's your favorite time period?"

"That's a tricky question. I don't think I can say I have a favorite time period per se. Things have always been hard for women and people of color. I'm not sure there is an ideal era that I would like to live in. When I study history, I ask myself, 'What did we do wrong in the past? Why are we still making the same mistakes today? How can we make it better in the future?'"

Natalie's eyes widen as she turns to Diane. "Wow."

"Told you she goes off." Diane raises her milk shake to me.

"Well, I'm glad I got to meet the friend Diane speaks about so much." Natalie smiles, and I can see she means it. It makes me glad that my friend talks a lot about me when I feel like there's not a lot to say about myself.

"She's spoken a lot about you too," I reply as Carlos gets back to our table with two drinks. He hands me one and I give him a quick thanks as he sits down next to me.

Diane looks away but I can tell she's a bit embarrassed by the previous comment.

"That's good." Natalie moves a hand through her hair. "Has she told you about all the movies she wants me to watch?"

"Don't even get me started."

"You both are simply not educated in the art of cinema, right, Carlos?" Diane says, pointing at him.

"That's right," he agrees, holding up his plastic cup so that Diane can clink it with her milk-shake glass.

"They're jealous because we're good students who don't have the time to watch movies all the time, don't listen to them." I turn to Natalie, who laughs.

"I mean, I'm not sure I'm a good student, I mostly spend a lot of time on my phone and napping," she replies. Her statement resonates in my soul.

"We all do, don't worry, girl, we all secretly do." Diane drapes her arm around Natalie's neck.

"Not so secretly." She rests her head on Diane's shoulder.

The nice thing about meeting your friend's significant other is that at the very least you can complain about them while they are sitting right in front of you. While that sounds like a mean thing to do, it does bring out the human aspects of a starting relationship—if they can get along with your friends and your people really like the person you're talking to, then it all should be smooth sailing from there. Most of the time.

"She seems nice," Carlos says as he drives me back to my place. I have reclined my seat so I'm nearly lying down, lo-fi music playing in the background as I watch the streetlights pass by outside the window.

Carlos's car is an old Mustang he and his dad put back together. It's a Marlboro red, and that's the last thing I remember because I don't pay much attention to cars unless there's a specific word or feature that stands out on its own.

"She does. I think they work nicely together."

"Like you and Ethan?"

"Oh shut up."

"I heard you guys had fun last night." With a quick pull of the lever, I am sitting back up and glaring at him, ready to give him a piece of my mind.

"Fuck that, I was scared for my life. We nearly got caught."

"In the act?"

I slap his shoulder. We're close to the college campus, and the various fast food restaurants splatter neon lights across his windshield.

"Ouch, Sol! I'm driving."

"Well, you said something stupid." Looking away from him, I watch the sidewalks snaking across the different apartment complexes dedicated to the students who want to live nearby. "I mean, I like him, and I guess you could say he likes me. I don't know what we have now."

"Have you thought of telling him?"

"What? No. You think I'm crazy?"

"I don't think you're crazy for liking him. I think you've been spending a lot of time with this guy and that you've gotten attached." He puts his blinker on to merge onto Thirteenth Street, which feeds into the larger neighborhoods in town, including mine and the Winstons'.

"I don't have time for a relationship. You know what I have

time for? School, work, the club, my cat, and my family. I don't need a relationship."

"I know you're a strong independent woman, but I saw you by the pool. Maybe you could make something out of it. Not something serious, but something." Without taking his eyes off the road, he reaches over with his left hand and pats the top of my head, which is nice until he digs his fingers down and messes it up, the way Dad often likes to do.

"You're so *fastidioso*!"

He laughs, and while he is as annoying as he can be, I wouldn't exchange this idiot for anyone else in the world.

CHAPTER THIRTEEN

The first rule of the history club should be: do not trust the club.

It's six in the morning on a Tuesday, the blinds in my room are closed, and Michi is sleeping peacefully by my feet. My slumber would have been undisrupted had it not been for the constant vibration of my phone next to my pillow. With a yawn, I take my phone in my hand and cringe at the amount of light it expels once the screen has been awoken. Reading the message makes me squint in disbelief at the normalcy of it.

Anna: Morning members :D I want to remind all of you that this upcoming weekend there'll be an opportunity to join the WCC festival of the arts! We'll be selling some goodies and spreading the word about the club. If you'd like to get a couple of community hours make sure to message me so I can add you to the roster (:

My first instinct is to message her "Bruh wtf" because she never mentioned us being a part of the festival, but my exhaustion wins and I go back to sleep.

The next time I wake up it's because my cat is on top of my chest, pawing at my face.

"Michi, I'm trying to sleep." I push her off but this only makes her meow harder. "I'm not feeding you, go away."

That doesn't appease her.

"Fine, fine." The fact that I'm talking to my cat doesn't make me question my sanity, but getting up at eight in the morning surely does. I pick her up before marching out of my room and into the kitchen, where Dad is stirring a cup of coffee.

"*¿Te caiste de la cama?*"

"No, I didn't fall from my bed, this one wouldn't shut up." I set Michi down in front of her bowl and grab a can of food from one of the lower cabinets. To be completely honest, I don't know what kind of cat Michi is. She was a birthday gift nearly four years ago from my parents. Now she's a bit round and lazy, but I love her, and she is like my child. When I was growing up in the old house, I would ask for an indoor cat but Dad would refuse because he didn't want animals inside the house. Even when they gave her to me he sternly told me she was only allowed to be at home because she was a kitten.

Michi has never stepped a paw outside unless it's for a vet visit, begrudgingly going on a harness walk, or moving into the new apartment.

"You should put her on a diet." Dad still thinks the outdoors is a perfect place for a cat to roam and be free, but Michi has grown on him. Besides, I really wanted an indoor cat, one to cuddle and buy a cat tree for—all those things that give me an idea of what my life will be like when I'm eighty and my only companions are my thirty-eight cats.

"Pa, don't say that! She's perfect." Michi purrs slightly when I pat her back, or maybe it's more of a growl because she's trying to eat. I smile and lean against the counter, trying to undo the knot my braid became during the night. "You didn't go to work today?"

"New job site. They're doing some paperwork and asked the workers to come around nine." He takes a sip from his coffee, bushy eyebrows shooting up. "Your ma says you haven't called her in a couple of days, is everything okay?"

If there is anyone on this planet who would sense something is wrong with me it would be her, even though she lives thousands of miles away. Some moms are faster than Russian hackers.

"Everything is all right, school has just been extra tiring recently, and I've been busy with club . . . activities." I try not to look guilty. "I'll call her later today once I come back from class."

"Don't stress out too much, corazón, it's not worth risking your health. You know no matter how hard school gets or how busy life seems, we're always here to talk."

Oh crap, there it is, the line parents use to make you feel like crying and like you are a disappointment.

I nod as he walks by and pats my head.

"You work too hard." He yawns.

"I learned it from you and Mom."

Dad laughs. "I know we always asked you for the best grades and for you to be well behaved when you were little. Though sometimes I feel like we might have asked you too much and not given you enough . . . I wish your mom was still here, and I know a father is not the same thing as a mother—"

"Dad, you try, and she's only a phone call away. I'm grateful for all you do. Aside from having Mom here with us, I would change nothing about our family."

I know that he partially blames himself for meeting her in the first place, because if she had married a citizen, she would already have papers. If he had started his citizenship application sooner, he would be a citizen and wouldn't have to wait for me to be over twenty-one to fix her citizenship. If only she had worked in a program that allowed her to apply for a green card, or if only she had been a Dreamer.

If only.

My grandmother used to hate my dad's guts because he was undocumented, which meant her daughter wouldn't be able to fix her papers until her children were old enough to petition for her or she left the country. That meant she was always at risk. Then he got his residency and it was my mom alone, in danger.

But if they hadn't met, I wouldn't be here.

Only a couple of days into February things around school have simmered down a lot compared to the last couple of weeks. Students have more of a grip on what's going on in their classes, so more people have started to skip said classes, unless attendance is mandatory. Being that I work for the school and spend the majority of my time on campus, I manage to be both forced to go to every one of my classes and still manage to be running late to all of them.

"Are we doing it?" Ethan says.

"Excuse you?" I stop in my tracks in the middle of the student path toward the square. I had been pushing my bike next to me to avoid hitting any students who were walking, and had no idea anyone was following me. He was clearly not here a moment ago, and yet his tall butt has appeared out of nowhere.

He pauses and gets really close to me, way closer than he usually does. He's wearing his denim jacket with a marine hoodie underneath. The fabric is cold against the inner skin of my arm when he hooks his elbow with mine.

"Are we going to do it?" he whispers.

"Oh! You mean the fund-raiser." I elbow his side, putting some distance between the two of us while appreciating the mildly pained face he makes. It's funny that he thought he could make me blush. "I'm not against doing it, but I'm pretty well set up with the community hours I get from the archive."

"Are you sure you want to go there after what we did that night?"

I pause. He's hiding his hands in his hoodie's pockets, and has a slight grin on his face.

"Are you sexualizing us breaking into the archive and ringing the bell? Because that's some weird-ass kink you got there." I continue walking, only catching his laugh as he follows close behind. Then, pausing for a moment, I add, "Who knows, maybe some people fetishize breaking the law or breaking into weird places to do it. Wouldn't be the weirdest thing I've heard."

"You realize you took my little comments and shot them off into the stratosphere, right?" We keep a calm pace, avoiding bumping into people as we round the fountain in the middle of the square. "But, I mean, there's a fetish for everyone."

"Oh really, Winston?"

"Soledad, we're not having a weird fetish conversation in the middle of the day at school."

"Hey, you started it."

"Did not."

"Did too."

"Did not."

"What you're trying to say is that you have a bunch of weird fetishes you're now too embarrassed to bring up." I wink. "All right, I see you."

Ethan clears his throat. I'll take that as a win on my side for who was trying to embarrass the other one in public. He is surely more playful today, which is nice to see.

"Anyway, maybe you'll want to stay clear of the archive for a week or so, in case they have some of the footage laying around or are still investigating what happened with the lights."

He's not wrong, as usual.

"Besides, I figured you and Carlos would be the first ones to volunteer for community hours."

"No, I think he's going to be with an engineering association. He's in a bunch of groups. He was surprised that we were going to attend the festival in the first place." When I called him before I got to school, he had yet to read Anna's text.

I turn my bike and cross the grass to where one of the overly used bike racks is placed in front of the Liberal Arts Building. There's a bright-red bike laying on the ground, no chain. Someone must have been running late to class, like I am. "If you're asking whether I still plan on attending without Carlos, the answer is maybe. But if you want to volunteer with me, I'm down."

The way Ethan looks at me when he smiles makes me want to punch a wall. He has no right to make me feel this way. Crushes in the twenty-first century: you either make out on the first day you meet or don't say a word about your attraction until both of you are dead and buried.

"Awesome, then I'll see you later, Sol." He gives a quick wave and walks away from my spot on the lush grass. I can't take my eyes away from him until enough people have walked between us that it's like he disappears.

As I stand there, under the February California sun, I come to the conclusion that I like Ethan Winston.

Throwing my shirt across the room, I put my hair into a ponytail and stare at my reflection in my mirror. It's a mess, my room and my life. In the corner of the mirror is a picture of Mom and Dad with me when I was about six. Next to it is a picture of me and Diane, and one of me and Carlos. I look happy in all of them.

Sighing, I turn away and grab a pajama shirt, unlock my phone, and find my WhatsApp icon. My aunts and uncles on my dad's side swear by this app, and once Mom moved to Mexico, it seemed like the best option for long distance communication. When my parents were young, they decided to move to California after my father's friend told him about the construction business here. My maternal grandmother was not happy about it, and the family drama that ensued ended with my mother cutting ties with her parents and seldom talking to her brother. Dad has two sisters in Texas still, and while he gets along with his family, they don't really see the need to see each other very often.

A couple of years ago one of my aunts friended me on social media, which provoked an avalanche of friend requests from cousins and relatives I hadn't heard of in ages. I was added to many a group chat, and yet I muted most of them.

I missed my call with Mom this morning to go to class, but I promised her that I would call her tonight to make up for it.

"Halo." Spanglish is my third language and I am very fluent at it.

"Hola, corazón." Mom is in her living room, the window behind her showcasing the city landscape, her hair is up in a bun, and thick-rimmed glasses are on, which means she was most likely grading papers. "You hadn't called me, I was getting worried."

Parents are always worried. We talk for about two hours, catching up. She tells me about the kids she's tutoring, how some of them remind her of me when I was little and trying to handle two different languages at the same time.

"They are so smart, but at the same time their papers are so bad." She laughs. "That's terrible to say, and they're great, they really are, but it hurts a little when I read their homework."

"Can you tell when their parents write their homework?"

"Of course! Sometimes it's worse than when the kids do it."

It's strange talking to my mother like she's a friend who lives far away. We make jokes and think up various vacation places we could all go to from different spots in the world. One day when we all have money we'll go to Europe, or another day, when it's calmer in Mexico, we'll go on a road trip down to Guadalajara. The long distance has made us into something closer to sisters than mother and daughter. I can't recall the last time we were in a fight like we used to get into when I was younger and wouldn't pick up my room. She's gotten more comfortable in Monterrey, and Dad and I are almost like roommates here in Westray.

There are times I look around my home and wonder if she ever lived with us. When we moved from our old house into a smaller apartment, we sold some of the stuff that wasn't going to fit. It's a strange feeling, knowing she was here a year ago, and now isn't. Like I'm forgetting pieces of who she was.

"I wish I could fix your papers already, not at twenty-one . . . or twenty-seven."

"That's the way things are, corazón." She seems sad too.

"I know, and it's stupid." I fall back against my bed.

Maybe I'm being selfish. There are thousands of people in the process right now. I know some families have it far worse than I do, but I can't help how I feel.

Ten years, ten long years I will be waiting.

It won't be cheap either. A consultation to speak with the immigration lawyer cost us $150, with the lawyer who spoke to us informing us that it would take about $4,000 to get the case rolling. Could be more or less, depending on the entirety of the case.

Part of me wonders where I would be if she was still here. Whether I would have joined the club and met Ethan.

"You're spacing out," Mom says, and I snap back. "What were you thinking about?"

"Homework," I lie, trying not to smile. "Same as usual."

CHAPTER FOURTEEN

When Ethan picks me up at seven thirty in the morning for the festival, I have the feeling we're getting set up for some sort of trick. The Westray Community College Festival for the Arts is a yearly event. There are food stands, dances, musical events, gallery shows, even theater plays and slam poetry readings. It's a week-long event that climaxes on Friday when all groups, no matter the background, can set up stands along the student path and promote their clubs—extra points if you give out food.

"What's wrong?" Ethan asks, turning left at the end of my street.

"Nothing. I just feel uneasy." Two cups of coffee from a local gas station are resting in the cup holder. "Wow, I didn't take you as a caffeine freak, Ethan."

"One of them is for you. French vanilla, right? It's the one in front."

"Aww! You remembered my favorite flavor?"

"We've gotten coffee a couple of times. It'd be rude if I didn't." At the café I usually get an iced vanilla latte, but I admire the hustle for getting gas station coffee, since it really does tastes different. Like early Saturday trips to the lake, or midnight gas station runs with Carlos after a college party he managed to sneak us into.

"I don't know your favorite type of coffee."

"I don't really have one. I'm more of a tea guy."

"Right. London Fog, then?" The cup is still warm as I take a sip.

"Yes. See, you know me too." We stop at a red light, morning traffic making the drive to school longer than usual.

"Do I? I'm sure there's a ton of stuff I don't know about you."

"What do you want to know?"

I hesitate. "You said that the night I broke into your house, you were already kind of upset and that I was the cherry on the top that made things worse."

"Yeah, no one sees an intruder and thinks, I wonder if she'd like to hear about my parents wanting to get back together?"

He brings the car to a stop at a light, although processing his sentence takes me so long that by the time I manage to figure out my follow-up question we've begun to move again.

"Back together?" He did mention his family dynamics being complicated at the archive, and that his dad wasn't in the picture while he lived with his mom in middle school.

"They've been split for a while. They've been an on-and-off thing for as long as I can remember."

"But—and I'm sorry if this is too personal—isn't it a good thing that they're getting back together?"

Ethan makes a face. "Sometimes you think you find your soul mate because you can't be apart, but *sometimes* that person brings out the worst in you. Even if you love them, you fall apart, and as soon as you're away you crave them. That's not a good relationship, that kind of love is an addiction. Addictions aren't good.

"I'm not saying I don't like my parents—I think they're both good people on their own—but it's difficult when they're together."

"I'm sorry." My voice is low.

"No, you're fine. I've lived with my grandparents since I was in eighth grade. I keep in contact with both of my parents and visit them when I can. Mom is always traveling, and I was actually just back from my dad's place in Sacramento when I caught you. My grandparents were on vacation, so I went to spend the weekend there, and turns out he wants to try it again with Mom." He puts the car in park and it takes me a moment to realize we're already at school. "But I think they'd be better off not getting back together. They're holding each other back from finding someone who truly makes them happy."

"You're probably right, I didn't mean to assume—"

Ethan laughs. "Sol, you're fine. No family is perfect, is it?"

I think of my broken family. "You're right."

"Cheer up, I can't stand seeing you all gloomy like that." He taps my cheek, and I want to kiss him. Right here right now, I want to grab his face with both of my hands and kiss his lips. And his hair, his curly hair, I want to feel it with my fingers, and feel his fingers hold my neck softly, then more firmly. I want to rest my forehead against his and breathe out after a kiss, open my eyes to see his, dark brown like mine, before he moves closer and we kiss again.

I want it and at the same time I'm too chicken to do it.

"Fine, I'll try to cheer up for you."

"For me?" He undoes his seat belt. "No, Sol, you need to be happy for you, but if I'm involved in the process of making you look less serious, I'll be glad to help along the way."

It's a pretty windy day, and we have a hard time setting up the table. In total there are five members: Scott, Ethan, Xiuying, Angela, and me.

Scott is a bit like Carlos, a sort of unofficial vice president who was never elected. He always seems to be involved with the club, but not terribly involved. In fact, he's always the driver who takes us to the challenges. An intriguing character, he's always cheery and uncaring, yet on top of things. I strive to be that nonchalant and cool.

Once we've managed to set everything up, with some rocks weighing down the papers on top of the table, we arrange chairs in a semicircle around the booth. Scott excuses himself to fetch some treats from his van.

Some of the clubs are actually cooking food in order to raise money, but that requires a food handler's permit, which takes about two weeks to get, and we did not have time to figure everything out. Instead, we have pamphlets about the club that boast about our members and their bright futures.

"What made you want to join?" I ask Angela and Xiu, who told us to call her that. They're both freshmen, like me.

"I only wanted to join some clubs, and this one went well with my academic track." Angela is dressed from head to toe in workout clothes, which makes me wonder if she's coming or going to the gym. "It keeps me busy."

Xiu, on the other hand, looks supercozy in a fuzzy sweater and a beanie. "Me too. It goes well with my schedule, I didn't think it'd be so—"

"Weird to get in." Angela laughs. "Yeah, what they made me do was weird as hell."

"I didn't really want to do it." Xiu looks around. "But I did it in the end, and here I am."

"Here we all are," I mumble. "How did you guys hear about the organization, by the way? Neither of you are history related, right?"

"I heard it from Alan, he's in one of my classes and I mentioned it to Xiu." Angela nods at Ethan. "You and I also have a class together, I had no idea you were joining until I saw you at the club."

"Oh right, chemistry lab!" he replies, and while he sounds surprised, I can see he's a bit tense.

"You're always quiet in class, I was surprised when I saw you pushed through the process." Angela leans forward. "Especially with the things they made us all do—"

"Gotten to know all of your dirty secrets already?" Scott arrives with a large box. He sets it down on the table and smiles. "Anna gave me this. It's full of club merch. There's some shirts in here if you guys want any, but I don't know your sizes, so you'll have to look for yourselves."

In the box are key chains and pencils I had never seen before, as well as a couple of well-made water bottles. I feel kind of offended they never gave us any of these fancy things.

Navy-blue shirts feature the club's logo on the front, and on the back say "Become a Part of History." Both of the girls and I take one but Ethan passes.

"Are you sure, man?" Scott asks. "I'm sure I could find one that fits you."

"Nah, I'm fine."

"Wouldn't go with his style," I say before I can stop myself.

"My what?" Ethan's forehead creases.

I pause. "You've got great fashion sense. I don't think I've ever seen you wear a T-shirt unless it goes with your outfit, and I don't see how this would work." *Oh my God, Soledad, stop talking, stop talking right now.*

He smiles.

"Hey, can I get pamphlet?" a guy asks across from the booth.

"Yeah. Here, you can get a pen, too, in case you want to write some stuff down." Scott pulls a pen from the box and hands it to the guy. "Like my number."

Ethan turns to me, eyebrows high. My mouth hangs open. Angela and Xiu look at each other similarly.

God I wish I was that smooth.

"Maybe I'll come 'round and get it later." The other guy walks away but not before throwing a quick look over his shoulder, a grin dancing on his lips.

"How?!" I ask Scott.

"What?"

"How did you offer your number like that? That was so smooth I could slip on it. I can't do that shit, man, I'd look like an idiot." Flirting is not an area where I am extremely adept. The banter with Ethan was as close as I've ever been, and even that was terrible. Carlos could woo a fern at a party if he so wished, and which he has tried to do when drunk.

Scott shrugs. "I thought he was cute, and it was worth a shot. The worst that could happen is him calling me some slur and stomping off."

"I wish I had that confidence," Xiu says.

"You can, you simply have to be able to pick and choose your battles. I wouldn't have done it if he looked like he'd punch me or something. Flirting is easy when you realize you don't have anything to lose aside from being rejected. If you are rejected, move on. But if your ego is bigger than your dick . . . err, boobs . . . then you have to do some soul searching about whether you're ready to be with someone else. No one deserves to be with a shitty person who thinks you owe them attention and affection. They gotta try too."

A silence follows.

"That's deep, man," Ethan says.

"That's not as deep as I can go . . . if you catch my drift." He winks and Ethan chuckles.

"Son of a bitch, you got me," he says.

"Nah." Scott pats my hair as he walks by me. "We all know you are Sol's man, wouldn't dare go near ya."

"Wait, he's not my man." My face is burning.

"My bad. You're each other's. Thanks for correcting me, Sol."

Angela gets up to help a student. Xiu smiles at me. I can't look at Ethan, so when a student walks by our table, I immediately get up to try to persuade them to talk about my shady club and its even shadier members. We hand out merch like it's candy and try to entice susceptible students with the opportunities to get community hours.

I mention to some students how the club is like a big family. What I fail to add is that it is like a family at a Christmas dinner, and you're the controversial cousin who never got married and disagrees with your relatives' political views, which causes tension to run high at all times.

But at least there's food at most of the meetings.

Time goes by with me ignoring Ethan, glaring at Scott, and making conversation with the girls. About halfway through the day, Scott lets us go to buy food. I'm starving after only drinking that coffee in the morning.

"Where do you want to go?" Ethan asks once I put some of the flyers down in a neat stack.

"We could split and find something on our own if you want."

"Nah, let's walk around and see what we find." He tilts his head to the side. "Come on."

I look at the booth, wondering if I should invite the other members, but I'm really happy he wants to walk with me. There is nothing rational about my emotions—I don't want him to notice the attraction I feel toward him but at the same time I'm hoping he does. The fear of damaging this blossoming friendship between us matches my need to tell him that I like his face, and I'm having a hard time handling that.

"What's wrong?" Ethan asks as we thread through the crowd.

"Wrong? Nothing's wrong." I nearly lose him among bumping shoulders and heads. "I'm thinking."

"About?"

"The Spanish Inquisition? I don't know. I'm thinking in general. Is there a problem with that?"

"Sorry, I was just wondering."

I stop and immediately someone runs into me.

"Sorry, I didn't mean to snap at you."

"It's fine," he says, but he seems distant.

"Hey." I slap his shoulder playfully. He finally looks at me. "Things get to me easy and the way Scott was talking about us rubbed me the wrong way."

Ours steps slow as we hold each other's gaze, and I would linger on how romantic this might seem to anyone who might spot us in the crowd, but the next instant someone walks right into me and doesn't even offer an apology.

"Hey, watch it, man!" Ethan says. "I don't think this is the best setting to talk about stuff like this."

"I would have to agree with you there."

"Here." He takes my hand, fingers intertwining easily. "So we don't get separated."

"We wouldn't want that."

"And have my comedy source taken away? No, I'd rather die."

"So I'm your comedy source? Might as well call me a clown. I won't take that, bye."

His hand tightens around mine when I move away, and with a light pull he moves me back closer to him.

"You know I'm kidding, sunshine."

Sunshine. *Sunshine. SUNSHINE.* I think I'm about to pass out.

"I know, but I still like to give you a hard time." The air smells like deep-fried food, and my stomach growls. "I'm like an annoying rock in your shoe."

"I like that rock, so I won't be taking my shoe off anytime soon."

"What?"

"Let's go, I smell fries. We could get some burgers from that tent and fried Oreos from the one next to it."

He moves faster, weaving easily through the crowd and pulling me along by the hand. Somewhere along the tents someone is playing pop music, and while the festivities seem to be starting for today, their enthusiasm is lost on me.

Ethan kind of said he likes me.

Holy shit.

CHAPTER FIFTEEN

"I'm dead."

"You're not dead."

"Yes, I am." I look away from my food and glare at Diane. "You don't seem to be concerned about my death."

It's been a day since the festival and when I messaged her as soon as I could about what Ethan had said, she agreed to a consoling session in exchange for food. Her dark eyes are judgmental underneath perfectly shaped, raised brows. "Girl, homeboy said he liked you. He didn't propose marriage. You don't need to die over that."

When it comes to Mexican families, everyone thinks they know the best Mexican place because of the vibes it gives off. A menu written in Spanish is a good sign, as well as some quality music; it's always a plus if there is no elaborate fresco on the wall of some sort of event or ancestral place the owners want you to connect to, but that's not necessarily a deterrent. My general rule of thumb is to try at least two things on the menu before shooting down a restaurant.

We're at my favorite Mexican restaurant, forty-five minutes away from town, but it's worth the drive. Casuelas can be described as a hole in the wall, but it has a lot of things I like when it comes to Mexican cuisine. Instead of focusing on a specific gastronomical inspiration, the menu rotates with the day of the week, and the owners take you through an experience that goes deeper than the free chips and salsa you get at most taquerias.

It's not my *mamá*'s cooking, but I'll settle for something that's better than my crafty concoctions. *Banda* music is playing through the loudspeaker and Diane moves her shoulders to the beat, even though all of the Spanish she knows can be boiled down to three phrases: *me llamo Diane, tengo hambre,* and *chinga tu madre.*

Translation: My name is Diane. I'm hungry. And, last but not least, fuck your mom.

I sigh, scooping some of the refried beans from my plate and into my mouth. My platter consists of a tamale, a tostada, and a chile relleno, which comes with rice and beans. While that is a lot of food, I've never been one to curb my eating habits. When my mom told me that at my age she weighed thirty pounds less than what I currently weigh, I nearly had a heart attack, but I bike a lot and sometimes *sometimes* go to the gym with Carlos. Besides, I haven't hated my body since sophomore year of high school.

Average-sized bodies are still being introduced in regular media, and it took me a while to realize that I'm built like my father. Where he is stocky and full of muscle, my mother is lankier, and seeing her high school pictures compared to mine used to get to me. Tyler was around my same size when we started dating, so we never had any problems with body image. As time went on, I began to understand there was nothing wrong with how I looked, somewhat, anyway—everyone has their bad days.

Ethan is pretty fit—not that I want him to be able to scoop me up, just press me against the wall while we make out.

"What are you thinking about?" Diane asks as she takes a bite from her tostada platter, minus chicken or meat or cream, or *queso fresco*, so it's basically a salad on top of a tostada, because veganism.

"Oh nothing. I like the guy a lot, but sometimes I overreact, and I'm scared I'll mess it up and he'll stop liking me."

"If he did then he wouldn't be worth it."

I'm about to tell her that she's probably right, but my phone vibrates. It's Dad. My dad is more of a call person. He was the last person in our family of three to get a smartphone, and even though he does text me every now and then, he generally sounds superserious because of his rare use of emojis.

"Papa bear, got to take this." I get up, clicking the Answer key. It's slightly rude to talk in front of other people in a language they don't know, or discuss topics they're not too comfortable with. "*Bueno?*"

"*Oye mija*, do you think you could pass by the store when you come home?

I can hear the roaring AC from his old truck in the background. He's probably heading home from the job site and is too tired to go shop.

"Sure, Dad, what do you need?"

"I was thinking of grilling some *agujas* or rib eye. If you want some T-bones, that's okay too. I'll pay you back once you get home. Oh and . . . that's right, you can't buy beer yet." He laughs. It's good to know he's in a good mood. "Just bring some sodas and stuff to make *pico de gallo* and salsa."

"Okay, Pa. After I finish eating I'll pass by the store but it'll be, like, an hour before I come home."

"It's okay, I'll drive by a gas station and get some beer, and we'll make a *carnita asada* later."

"Okay, then I'll see you later, papi. Bye."

"*Ándale,* bye."

I pocket my phone and am walking back to Diane when an older lady waves at me.

"Hi, I don't know if you're on break but can we have some refills?"

It takes me a moment to process what is going on. I'm wearing dark jeans and a military-green shirt, and my hair is not in a bun. Does she think I work here because I was talking Spanish?

"I don't work here."

The woman squints and laughs.

"I'm sorry, you looked like our waitress for a second. You Mexicans look so much alike sometimes."

My chest feels tight. I walk briskly away.

"What the hell?" Diane says after I tell her.

"Yeah."

"That's messed up. Who was it?"

"Some lady, it's fine."

"No, that's like her stopping me at a fried chicken place because I 'look like all the other staff.'" She leans back, crossing her arms. "Just because she didn't think it was racist doesn't mean it's not. It's insensitive and you shouldn't be afraid to call her out on it."

"I completely get where you're coming from but she's older. Older people tend to say more insensitive things than younger people. I'm not going to let it bother me too much."

"Well, it bothers me."

That's Diane. If something happens to her it's not a big deal, but if it's her friends, she's ready to throw some rounds.

"I'm sorry for telling you about it."

"Sol, don't start with me."

"I'm not starting with you."

"Then take it back. If some old ho told you some shit I want to know, okay?"

I stick out my tongue at her. "Okay, mom."

She throws a piece of lettuce at me. "Don't be rude!"

Leaning back against my seat, I look in the direction where the couple is sitting. Diane is right, being older doesn't make it okay to say that type of thing. I know I don't go through the same hardships that Diane and Ethan go through being black, but that little encounter feels like a slap across the face. Even if this will fade and we'll all continue our day like nothing happened, the sting is still there.

Diane drops me off at the store a couple of blocks away from my apartment. She wanted to give me a ride all the way back home, but I declined, assuring her I'd be okay and not get hit by a car while biking back. After getting my bike from the back of her car (where she had put the seats down so it could fit), and promising to send her a text once I was home, she leaned out the window of the driver side and said, "I know it's been a while since your ex, but don't let that make you anxious about making a move. If Ethan is good, good things will happen. And if he isn't, call me and I'll help you fuck him over."

I grin. "We're not fucking him over."

Diane winks. "No matter what happens, the offer stands."

When I enter the store, my eyes immediately go to the cashiers, but none are Ethan.

The meat section is pretty small at the market, but I find a pack of T-bone steaks and throw it in my cart before heading for the spices and rubs. Once I get those, I head to the produce section to get stuff for pico and salsa, as well as corn. Grilled corn tastes so good when an unhealthy amount of butter is slapped over it, or I can make some *elotes* later in the week.

I'm turning the corner of the soda aisle when I see him. Ethan is putting some boxes on the bottom shelf, nearly sitting on the floor next to a cart full of Dr Pepper, which is my favorite flavor.

As he reaches for another pack to put on the rack, he turns and my creepy cover is blown.

With one hand he removes his headphones, smiling. "Hey, sunshine."

I'm screaming inside.

"What's up?" I push my cart into the aisle as he gets up.

"Nothing much, finishing up here." He looks good in the company shirt and jeans, a red lanyard hanging from his neck. "Trying to hide for the last moments."

"I usually shelf books at the end of my shift to not deal with people."

"Yes, exactly." His eyes trail down to my cart. "Grocery shopping?"

"Getting some stuff for dinner."

"Did you come with someone?"

"No. Why?"

"I was wondering if you had a ride home."

"I brought my bike, it's not that far away."

I have an itch to do something with my hair to distract my hands, though instead of doing this, I simply grip the shopping cart harder to stop myself from doing anything weird.

"I get off in five minutes. I'll give you a ride home."

"I'm fine, but thanks. I mean, I don't want to be a bother."

"Sol, you live, like, three blocks away from my house. It's not a bother."

I want to cover my face and scream, because he makes me feel the urgent need to yell into the void.

"Really?"

"Really."

Maybe because the talk with Diane is still in my head I say, "Do you want to come over for dinner? My dad is cooking, but he's chill, it's not like he'll chase you with a machete. He'd appreciate the company because I'm fairly sure he thinks I'm a loner."

If there was an anatomically sound way to slap myself without appearing to be a crazy person, I would do so.

"I'd love to, but I promised my grandparents I'd make dinner tonight. What about another day? If that's okay?"

"Totally okay. It's great, actually, so I won't give my dad a heart attack, not that you'd scare him, I really don't bring boys home often, aside from Carlos, but he doesn't count. "

He smiles at my blabber, then looks at his watch. "I should be getting out right about now. Do you want to wait for me at the front of the store? I'll meet you there in a minute."

"Yup. I still have to pay, so take your time."

I move my cart past him, trying to get away from the awkwardness.

"Sol, aren't you getting soda?"

"Right."

Ethan walks out, jean jacket hooked under his elbow. The sun has gone down quite a bit, not too dark for biking, but it'd be a dumb move to cancel on his offer.

"God, my boss is annoying," he groans.

"What happened?"

"Scheduling issues." Ethan shrugs. "I'll get out of that dump someday, but in the meantime, I'd like to keep paying for classes and gas."

"I think I got lucky."

After we get in his car, he starts the engine and then reverses. Ethan says, "Got lucky?"

Ever since I stopped driving I've learned a lot by being the passenger. You can tell a lot about a person by watching them drive. Diane is the chillest driver I know, Carlos has road rage, and Ethan, well, he's pretty great.

"I like working for the library. My boss is okay and I get along with everyone. Besides, I don't have to pay for gas because I bike to school or carpool with friends like you."

"Oh, I'm a friend now?" He stops in front of my apartment building.

"Yeah, you're my friend."

He stays silent for a second. "Just a friend?"

Cue a record scratch as Ethan looks at me and I am filled with confusion and anxiety. All I can think of doing is opening the door and running out of his car like he has the plague, but he's clearly giving me an opening to flirt back, and I want to take it.

"I, I mean, maybe," I say.

"Maybe?"

"Maybe."

He inches closer. "Maybe more?"

I laugh and bop him lightly on the nose.

"Maybe more."

He smiles. "That's good to know."

"Really? Why?"

"Because you're more than a friend to me."

And because I'm *done* beating around the bush, I place both of my hands on his cheeks and kiss him. We were already pretty close to begin with, it was only a push that was needed to close that gap—I'll blame the universe later—but in that moment, I decide to take the matter into my own hands and do it. It's nothing romantic, in fact, I think it's over quicker than the time it took me to think of doing it.

His eyes are closed when I pull back, the light from the console casts a blue glow over his skin.

"That's good to know," I whisper, my hands still on his face. "Now, I'm about to run out of your car and into my house. It doesn't mean I don't like you, I'm about to have a panic attack."

Ethan grabs my wrists before I can pull away. "Why?"

I swallow hard. "Because I kissed you, and told you I like you, and I don't really do that." It takes me a moment to breathe. "And I don't have a plan after that."

Ethan lets my wrists go, carefully places his fingers along my neck, leans in and places his lips to mine. This kiss is slower, sweeter, allowing me to wrap my arms around him and feel his hair, the touch of him exploring the back of my neck, and his breath against me. He pauses, his forehead against mine.

"We'll figure it out, sunshine."

Nodding, I take hold of the door handle, and flash him a smile as I get out of his car. Only to remember once I'm on the sidewalk that I, too, own a method of transportation.

"Wait, the bike!"

CHAPTER SIXTEEN

Dad and I have dinner later that night mostly in silence while watching television in the living room. He doesn't ask any questions as I hastily wash the dishes and make a beeline for my room shortly after, with Michi following close behind. I thank him internally for this because all that happened not even an hour before is still haunting me.

On the one hand I did kiss Ethan Winston and he returned my feelings, but on the other one, I did make a split-second decision that I'm not too sure was a good idea.

While I don't want it to be a recurring theme in my life that I profess my feelings to people I like by kissing them out of nowhere, like I did with Tyler, it is an exhilarating feeling to have. Taking control of the situation is like a drop on a roller coaster. It's not as much of a power move as it is me being truthful to myself—opening myself up to rejection and being unafraid of it, like Scott mentioned at the festival.

I sit down on the edge of my bed, my cat following suit and pushing her head against my arm. The sudden rush of adrenaline simmers down in my body as it slowly converts into an anxious pool at the pit of my stomach.

This could be a terrible idea.

I'm not sure if I really like Ethan for who he is or because of the time we've been spending together, and that's scary to think; however, is it bad to try out a relationship with someone you've only known a couple of weeks if you think you like them because of that? After the friction at the beginning, he's been nice to me, and we've figured out a couple of things about our lives, from cat names to favorite colors. He even knows how I like my coffee. That knocks out most of the questions you ask your date when you match on any mainstream dating site.

Tyler and I started dating sophomore year of high school. The first time his parents had me over for dinner, his mom made enchilada casserole to make me feel included. I didn't like it, but it was a nice gesture. That lady was the sweetest—she drove us around and took me shopping after Mom was deported to make me feel better, even though Tyler and I had already broken up. I still send her texts on Thanksgiving and Christmas; it'd feel wrong not to.

Tyler broke up with me because I was "complicated." Mom got deported and I fell hard into depression, plus I was anxious that more bad things would keep happening to me. I relied heavily on Carlos, and Tyler didn't like that. Aside from his being funny, I can't remember what I liked about Tyler. He was the first boy I slept with, too, but a year out of that relationship I can't pinpoint why I liked him so much.

After Tyler, I went on a few dates the summer before college—those months were a blur. I met Taylor, a girl, at a party like that. The first thing I told her after she introduced herself was that she was named almost like my ex. She had laughed, said she hoped to leave a better impression. Taylor wore a floral perfume I liked a lot and had bright-green eyes. She was the first and only girl I've kissed. We fell apart about a week after that.

I don't think I ever needed a boyfriend, or girlfriend for that matter. I didn't feel compelled to go out and meet people because I felt the need to be with someone else. I suppose I did it partially to distract myself and because I thought that was what a normal person would do, go out and have fun, you know?

At parties I was the awkward girl with a glass of water in the corner, and I hated it. That wasn't my scene. I was trying to reassure myself that I wasn't *really* depressed, because I was going to parties, kissing strangers, and laughing a couple of pitches too high. That I wasn't someone who cried herself to sleep every other night. I was fine and was going to figure life out on my own.

Even today I'm not completely fine, but I'm way better than I was at the start of that semester. I met Diane, got the job at the library, concentrated on my classes, and Carlos stopped bringing me to his parties. He said it was because they weren't helping me, but he was still there for me. Carlos would drive to my house in the middle of the night and take me to IHOP when I felt like the walls in my room were closing in. I never told my parents I felt like that; I didn't want to break their hearts.

I sigh, turning to look at my alarm clock. It's 2:17 a.m. and

I can't fall asleep. Michi is purring away on the side of my bed, my perfect little angel.

Getting up, I take my phone from the nightstand and look through my contacts.

Me: U up?

Not more than two seconds pass.

Carlos: maybe . . . why?

Me: Can you take me to IHOP?

Carlos: Be there in five

After we're given our menus and order coffee, our waitress, a girl not too much older than us, leaves us to ourselves. We hadn't exchanged many words on the drive over to the restaurant. As usual, Carlos had pulled up to my apartment with the lights of his car off.

"*So, ¿qué pasó?*" He pushes his menu to the side; we order the same thing every time.

"I kissed Ethan."

Carlos laughs. "Wait, you're serious?"

"You think I'd pull this if I wasn't?"

"Maybe you were hungry." He messes with his hair. "Okay, fine, I believe you. What happened?"

I bring him up to speed up on what happened before I sent him a message, including all my mulling over the past summer.

He listens carefully, only interrupting every now and then to ask why I hadn't invited him over for carne asada and asking if our friendship meant nothing to me anymore.

"Are you guys ready to order?" asks the waitress, appearing from what seems like thin air.

"Can we have the appetizer sampler, the New York cheese-cake pancakes for me, and some chocolate chip for her?"

"Of course. I'll be right back with your iced coffees, my bad." She walks off, giving Carlos a quick once-over.

"She's into you." I kick him under the table.

"A lot of people are into me." He leans back against his seat and kicks my shin. I hit back again. "I'm good looking, I can't help it."

"Whatever."

The waitress returns with two vanilla iced coffees before disappearing again. I take the paper off the straw and dip it in so I can stir the thick syrup pooled at the bottom. "I promised myself I was going to focus on school and not let anything derail me."

"I don't think its Ethan that derailed you. It was the club."

"But you got me in the club, and I met Ethan because of the club."

"I didn't say it was a bad thing. In a way, it's kept you distracted from other things."

"But what if I mess it up?"

"How could you?"

"I don't know."

"Then why are you worried?"

"Because being with someone means accepting that you're going to be vulnerable. It means that at one point you'll have to open up. What if he just wants a fling? Maybe it'd be better for the both of us if it was a temporary thing."

"Here is your food." The waitress arrives with a large tray and a small table to place it on. She places our pancakes and the rest of our food down, asks if we need anything, and disappears with a quick "Enjoy!"

Carlos reaches for one of the chicken tenders and I for a mozzarella stick. We eat in silence for a few seconds.

"Look, dating someone isn't going to change the fact they deported your mom and your dad works all day to take his mind off things. In fact, it might give you more stress, because relationships work like that. But you like the guy and the guy likes you, and you've never been one to only have a fling." A small tip of his cup toward me. "You lose nothing by going on a date, you might actually lose more by doing nothing."

"Life," I mumble through a mouthful of cheese.

"As long as you keep living it it'll go forward. You know why I invited you to all those parties, even though it wasn't your thing?"

"Because I was holed up in my room."

"Even if you do nothing the world will keep moving around you, Sol. I know you don't need me to tell you that." He sighs. His hair is messy and wavy. It's always odd to see him without gel and his sunglasses—Carlos is always ready to impress, and whenever we're alone at IHOP, it feels nice to see him with his walls down.

"Are you good, Carlos?"

"I'm good, I always am." He rakes his fingers through his hair. "The thing is that I feel like whenever I try to bring you out of your comfort zone I end up doing more harm than good."

"Don't say that—"

"I mean it."

"I know, but it's not your job to try to bring me out of it. You have helped me out so much throughout these months, and the people at the club are really nice." I look down at the food in front of me. "I can't change what happened, you're right, and I should take the lead for myself. It's hard sometimes to face the truth."

"Hey, if you found someone because of the club, I'm happy for you, even if it meant breaking into his house." He takes another drink from his cup, finishing it up as our waitress is passing by. She smiles and quietly takes the glass from him.

"Thank you," Carlos says to her, then turns to me. "You've talked with lawyers, you've got years ahead of you, and your dad is safe. Live your life, Soledad. I'm sure Ethan's last worry is his key at this point."

"And what would be his main worry then?"

"To get you to date him."

The '60s playlist IHOP forces upon its customers fills the air. Outside, the dark night looks to be brewing up a storm. It's nice to see it from inside. We hadn't done a witching-hour breakfast run in a while. After all my tumultuous emotions have been laid out on the table and carefully examined, Carlos gives me an idea of what to do next.

It's nearly five in the morning when I get back home. I'm going to skip morning class because there is no way in hell I'm going to be awake enough to be functional, so I set my alarm for noon before opening my messages app.

> Me: Good morning, do you want to go to a park or
> maybe get some coffee . . .

I feel a bit giddy as I press the Send button. To my surprise, my phone vibrates and I nearly scream.

> Ethan: Morning and yeah that works sushi
> Ethan: Sunshine* half asleep

What a dork.

> Me: That's okay, sorry for waking you up
> Ethan: No you're fine, I'm glad you didn't ghost me
> Me: I wouldn't
> Ethan: Really?
> Me: Yup, I like you

There is a solid minute of me wondering whether he fell asleep or if I jumped the gun by telling him I like him this early in the morning.

> Ethan: I like you too Soledad, I've liked you for a while

I can't contain the giddiness inside me, and turn to my side to scoop Michi up in my arms. She does not appreciate me interrupting her sleeping only so I can lay her down on my chest and pet her head, but she quickly comes to prefer this over the other. There is no way to predict how tomorrow might go, but here's hoping it doesn't go as disastrously as the first time we met.

CHAPTER SEVENTEEN

Ten minutes prior to the time settled for a date is the ideal time to show up. If he comes in earlier than you and you make him wait, you're a bitch. If he shows up early and you're already waiting, you're desperate. In the possible case he shows up late and you have already been waiting, he's right on time. Ten minutes is enough of a sweet spot that shows you care but not too much.

No, the world will not give women a break, thank you very much.

The coffee shop we always come to is quiet for a Monday morning. At this point, I've begun to learn the baristas' names and which one of them makes my drink with the most love and care.

I take a sip of my coffee, allowing the caffeine to wash over my sleep deprived body.

"Hey, sunshine."

Because of the tall barstool-like chairs cafés like to keep, when Ethan wraps his arms around me we're nearly the same height. The warmth of his body contrasts with the rough material of his jacket, and when his cheek touches mine I can feel he has recently shaved, and carries the scent of aftershave on his skin.

Holy crap, he smells so good.

I have to clear my throat when he moves away. "You look really good."

He's wearing his jean jacket over a mustard-colored button up even though it's seventy-three degrees outside in February.

"Did you bike here?"

"Yes, I was here at seven for . . . work." A lie. I called Miranda and asked if I could take the whole day off. Karim covered my shift. Aside from my encounter with Ethan at the library a couple of weeks ago, I don't think I've given Miranda or anyone else at the library a hard time, so they didn't ask many questions when I called.

It takes him a minute to order his drink and come sit with me. "So we're both early," he says.

"We're a pair of nerds."

"You're a nerd?"

"I'll have you know I passed all my classes last semester with As."

"Were they all beginner courses?" Ethan ducks when I toss a rolled up piece of napkin at him. "I didn't say they were *easy*."

"You were preparing to be rude."

"I was, but to be fair, you're cute when you're a bit angry."

"Just a bit?" Placing my chin on the back of my hands feels a tiny bit goofy, but it's hard not to get lost in his features. The sharpness of his jaw, the way his eyes shine behind his glasses, the curve on his lips as he takes me in as well, fingers intertwined in front of himself.

"Just a bit, otherwise you're deadly."

"Ethan!" the barista calls, and that little pocket of infinite universe closes shut.

"What are our plans for today?" he asks when he gets back to the table.

"Aside from coffee I hadn't thought that far ahead."

"Same. Do you have anything else planned?"

"No."

Ethan taps his fingers on the table. "How do you feel about mini golf?"

"That's an idea . . . or we could watch a movie."

"Or go to a museum."

"I'd like to keep my distance from museums, bro."

He laughs. "What if we take these to go and think on the way?"

"Sure, that works too."

The passenger seat in his car is perfectly set to how I like it. As we pull out of the café parking lot, I lower the window to let some of the cool air inside. I straightened my hair this morning because my bird's nest was not cooperating, and I decided that damaging it with a hot flatiron was the best idea.

"You look really pretty." Ethan lowers the volume on the radio, which was connected to his phone and playing "Best Part" by Daniel Caesar.

"Thanks. Oh hey, we're matching." I was wearing this mustardy color, off-shoulder shirt with a pair of mom jeans that were literally from my mom's closet.

"Now people will know we dating."

"Are we?"

"I mean, we are on a date." Ethan stops at a light and gives me a quick glance.

"I mean, yeah."

"And we kind of match." Outside, Westray blurs in a mixture of greens and yellows, the buildings around the school shining in the late-winter sun that is warming up the town.

"True."

"I'm not saying we're in a relationship. Dating and being in a relationship aren't the same thing."

I slap his arm. There's no real meaning behind going out on dates aside from the fact that we like each other, and in a way I like that, but there's no denying that knowing whether or not we'll get into a relationship would be an added bonus.

"Woah, what?" he laughs, jokingly rubbing his arm where I hit it.

"Smartass."

"I'm the smartass?"

"Yes, very much so." I rest my head against the half rolled–down window, feeling excited about this new opening. For the first time in a long time I don't feel stressed about what happened in the past, and I don't find the future frightening—the focus is on the present and what's happening today. There'll be enough time to worry about what I'm going to do, and what I've done before, but now the present is brimming with opportunity, and it feels good.

"Well, I learned from the best."

I flip him off. "That means I'm a good teacher."

Suddenly he jerks the car to the right and enters the parking lot for a grocery store, and I hit my head against the glass.

"Ethan, what the hell?"

"Sorry, I got an idea."

"What kind?"

For some reason he seems eager. "A picnic."

Shopping with Ethan is somewhat of an exhilarating ordeal. As we grab sandwiches, cake, and the like, he makes random jokes, we dance to the background music in the middle of the coffee aisle, and we laugh too loud and get disapproving glares from other customers.

I have never seen him this relaxed.

We end up at a lake on the outskirts of town. From the shore you can see the mountains, and they have little benches for picnics and BBQs. I've been here many times when I was younger, with my parents on the weekends. Dad would make carne asada and Mom and I would play volleyball. In the summer you can rent little paddleboats from a shop nearby, and sometimes Dad would take me out on the weekends Mom was working on schoolwork and we'd try to fish the afternoon away. We never came back after Mom was deported.

"You chose a good spot," Ethan says, after taking a bite out of one of the sandwiches we bought.

"I know what I'm about, son." The moment he suggested a picnic I knew exactly where I wanted to go. There was a probability that coming here would make me sad, but as soon as we drove through the entrance to the park, the one with the large wood carving of a bear by the gate, I nearly felt right at home. It was comforting. "I haven't been here in too long."

"Why?"

"Life."

We sit in silence for a moment, listening to the waves crash against the rocks. A few ducks quack over the sound of water and the wind picks up around our table, rustling the bags we brought with us, which are weighted down by our food.

"You look, upset," Ethan says.

"I'm not, why do you say that?"

He shrugs, picking a piece of red pepper from his sandwich and tossing it to the side. "I don't know, the way you said 'life,' and turned away, it felt sad. It's a beautiful place here—I've lived in Westray the majority of my life and I don't think I've ever been here."

"I used to come here with my parents, before my mom . . . moved to Mexico."

"Work related?" I wonder if he knows what I'm alluding to or if he genuinely believes Mom moved because of work. I'm not ready to tell him the truth.

"Something like that." I pause. "It's weird how things happen in life and you are in a completely different place from where you pictured yourself years ago."

"Life hasn't been fair to you has it, Sol?"

I hold in a laugh. "Ethan, life isn't always fair to everyone is it?"

Ethan sips from his bottle of iced tea, which he bought to make up for the coffee he drank in the morning. "I think some people are given a better hand when they're born. Then life takes over and that's when you really realize whether those first cards matter or not."

"What does that even mean?"

He straightens up.

"Now I'm not saying I'm the most privileged guy, but both of my parents are lawyers—they met in law school. Despite the divorce, my childhood was pretty damn good, being the only child and all. You've seen my grandparents' house, we're not in a bad position. My parents are paying for the majority of my college fees, so I could've gone anywhere, but I decided to stay here." He reaches over and takes a grape out of the bag before chucking it on the ground. A duck quickly waddles over to our table. "Moneywise, life has been fair to me."

"But that doesn't mean it's been *fair*," I say. "I'm sure your parents' divorce and the constant fighting has affected you."

"It has—"

"And I don't mean to *assume*, but I don't think your parents have a house in the Bahamas and a private jet, do they?"

"No."

"Simply because you live comfortably doesn't mean you live in luxury. I mean, there's people out there who have everything in the world who still think life is not worth living. If you're trying to tell me I have somehow had a less fair experience because my mom isn't with me, you're wrong.

"Is it shitty? Yes. But guess what? There's people who have it way worse. People who don't have both of their parents, or have terrible parents, and don't have any money to get by. But that shouldn't erase your struggles or make you feel like yours don't matter. I know you have more struggles than money—you said it yourself that you can't put it into a way that I can easily understand, what it's like to grow up as a black boy, and that's okay. You shouldn't feel guilty simply because of money."

Dad and I have a savings account to save up for future lawyer fees for Mom's citizenship process. It does not have much money in it, but it's something to look forward to. In terms of money, we're not in the worst of spots, and in fact, aside from missing my old house and the things we used to have, I think we can figure out a sort of happiness one day.

A few ducks have gathered around our table, waiting for a meal, so I grab the entire bag and start giving out grapes as I continue talking.

"I had a very happy childhood, I really did, even if I grew up with no siblings or cousins to play with. I was happy with what I was given, and even now I wish I had cherished it even more than I did. Just because I never had the money to splurge doesn't mean I'm jealous that you might have. And whether you were the governor's son or dirt poor, I honestly wouldn't give a shit as long as you're a decent person—which you are.

"Does money make a difference? Yes, yes, it does—sometimes it makes a great big difference when it comes to food, education, and shelter. There should be a way we as a country can make a difference in other people's lives, but it doesn't make *you* a different person. Life is never fair, Ethan. It's a gamble, and what you choose to do with your first coins is up to you. I don't want pity for what has or hasn't happened to me. I want to look forward to what I can change in the future."

Ethan blinks. "Did you take my comment and make a whole speech out of it?"

"I didn't make a speech out of it."

"Even if you didn't, that was kind of hot."

I hit his leg with my foot and he smiles, returning the light kick.

"I like that you're . . . you." He reaches across the table and places a hand on top of mine, the warmth of his skin sending a giddy sensation throughout my system.

"A person who takes your argument and runs wild with it so they can compliment you on your background even though you were trying to say you're more privileged than they are?" I ask, squeezing his hand, which gets a laugh out of him.

It's always nice to hear him do that; I never get tired of it.

"No, I like that you're genuine—I can read every emotion on your face, I can tell when you're angry or sad, and I could clearly see when you felt guilty for what happened. I might be an idiot for saying this, but that day you offered to help at the playground, I could feel you meant every word, Soledad." His fingers interlace with mine. "I knew it didn't make sense for me to trust you, but I did. I still do."

It is hard to hear him say this because throughout all of that time I was sure he hated me, that there was no way in fresh hell that I could gain his trust. Even now, when he is sitting right across from me, I'm having a tough time believing he had any trust in me back then, and yet here we are, joining hands a few feet away from the shores of the lake that meant so much to me growing up. Maybe this is a step toward something better. Right now it doesn't feel like a fling, and the way his eyes lock with mine tell me all I need to know about what he said. Maybe this can work out if we do make it a thing.

We haven't said a single word since we got back inside the car. Westray is calm as we drive onto Main Street; today the businesses close a little bit early, and the twilight is settling over the mountains. On the radio indie music plays softly, the drifting sentiments left open in the park floating between us until the questions I have are too much to hold inside anymore.

"So."

"So," he echoes, attention still on the road.

"Are we dating?" I had made my hair into a somewhat decent side braid and play with the end of it to distract myself.

"Didn't we go over this earlier?"

I glance out the window. There are some small shops and not a lot of traffic.

"Ethan, pull over."

"What? Why?"

"Just do it."

And he does, I'll give him that. In a maneuver reminiscent of what he did earlier today to get us to the grocery store, he weaves into the right lane and enters the first parking lot available. Once he's stopped the car, he looks at me.

"Are we dating?"

"Yeah." He laughs. "Sol, we—"

"Are we in a relationship? Because I like you and what you said earlier rubbed me the wrong way. To me dating has always meant more than a date. I have to ask because if I don't I will torment myself about it until three in the morning, and I'll wake up late for my class, and will fail my tests, and become a failure in life."

Ethan unbuckles his seat belt. "Come here." He hugs me over his cup holder thingy.

"What?"

"Breathe."

"I am breathing."

"And you're speaking a hundred words a second." He pulls back to rest his forehead to mine. "Why are you so anxious about it?"

"I'm not anxious, I'm . . . wary."

"Why?"

"Because I don't like not having definite answers, and I like you."

"I like you, too, and I don't want to move too fast. I'm sorry if I wasn't being clear earlier. I also don't want you to overthink me asking you out on our first date. What if you think I'm trying to use you?"

I smile. "That sounds like something I would overthink. I also don't want you to think I'm trying to jump in the first instance I got. I know I sort of spewed all that out but I really do want to take it slow too."

"But if you're okay with it . . ."

I lean forward and press my lips against his. Slowly at first, then as he kisses me back, picking up the pace, feeling the soft press of his fingers on the back of my neck.

"I'm okay with it," I say. "But maybe we should stop kissing in your car or it'll become a habit."

"That's a habit I wouldn't mind keeping."

He drives me home as soft music plays in the car. Our fingers are interlaced over the armrest as he drives, and we don't say a single word the whole way. Even when he parks in front of my apartment, we simply sit in the darkness of his car. He undoes his seat belt, and as I step out onto the pavement, he rounds his vehicle and with one of the most delicate moves I've seen him make, puts his arms around my shoulders and rests his chin on top of my head.

"We're good, Sol," he whispers against my hair as we sway slightly from time to time, and in that instance, as we hold each other in the early night, I believe him.

CHAPTER EIGHTEEN

Diane's room is what I hope I can achieve one day when I no longer live with my father. Her apartment is a four bedroom that she splits with three other people I seldom meet. Her room has tapestries all over the walls, plants decorating every single corner, and fairy lights that dangle from the ceiling at such a perfect angle that I'm surprised an Instagram model hasn't recruited her as an interior designer. It doesn't even matter how small the square footage of her place is because of how great she uses it.

"So the answer was yes," says Natalie.

"Pretty much," I say.

Diane gives me a suspicious look. Natalie is sitting next to her, across from me, chin resting on her palms as she listens intently. I've given them a complete summary of my love life, gruesome details about my ex, my party kissing sprees, and friend with real benefits included.

"But he never said it," Diane says.

"No, but the intent was there." I could tell from the way his arms felt around me that he meant every single thing he said.

"The boy is clearly into you, so I guess there's no questioning it."

"You asked me out." Natalie pokes Diane in the side.

"But that's the way I am." She combs one hand through Natalie's hair.

"My God, you guys, get a room." I grab my backpack from the floor. Diane's place is close to campus and it's nice to come here between classes sometimes. I'm somewhat surprised how little it's changed since she started dating Natalie. It's always nice to see when couples don't try to change their living ways for one another, it means the connection is right.

"Sol, have you studied for the history exam?" Diane asks.

"Kinda." The first history exam is an essay written in class. The professor will give us five questions and we have to choose three out of those to answer in essay form. They all have to do with the eras we'd covered so far, from the Civil War to the Gilded Age, as well as the reading materials we had been given. However, because of club activities and work (and laziness) I hadn't gotten around to studying for it.

"You haven't studied a single term have you? Have you even bought an exam booklet yet?"

"No." I stand up and throw my backpack over my shoulder. "I am going to go buy one and study right now and won't get distracted. When is the test again?"

"Friday, in class."

"You see? It's Monday, I've got plenty of time to prepare for a one—"

"Three."

"Three essay questions no problem." I blow a kiss when she gives me a disbelieving glare. "Bye, Nat, bye, Di, you guys have fun. Ima go be a good student!"

"You do that, girl, and text me later!" Diane yells as I head out.

In fact, I do go to the library and force myself to read over everything from the most recent topics to the very first ones that we went over. There's something about the Gilded Age that feels slightly close to what we're going through right now, what with the superrich and seemingly expanding wealth gap, the high levels of materialism in influencer culture and the massive following that lifestyle has, not to mention the cultural tension and immigration problems that were present back in those days.

Even the darkest times in America can be tinted golden.

I look down at my notes.

I've gone over one page.

My phone buzzes.

> Anna: Surprise meeting! I need all of you guys to swing by the club at four ;)

It's 3:27 p.m. Not even a minute after I read the message I get a call, which isn't the greatest when you're at the library.

"Give me a moment, I'm at the library and need to pack my things," I hiss.

"I'm close to the library, I'll pick you up," Carlos replies.

He's waiting by a small area with couches and a coffee table.

"You know what this is about?" I ask once we're out and walking.

"Nope, it's a surprise to me as well."

"You're such a liar." I hit his shoulder with mine.

"I'm not lying. She didn't say anything to me. You okay with Winston?"

"Yep, we're a thing now."

"Wow, graduated from the singles class. I'll have to find someone else to use as my scapegoat for declining people's advances." Carlos and I use each other's photo as our phone background to keep unwanted people from flirting with us. It works great.

"You can still keep my photo and call me."

"Is that so?"

"Of course, you're still my favorite annoying person."

"I take pride in that." He tugs on the end of my ponytail. "Can't afford to lose my IHOP buddy."

"You're never losing *that*."

We drape our arms over each other's shoulder like we're exiting some '90s movie. I can't think of ever being without Carlos by my side. Now that Ethan and I are a thing, I can only hope my friendship with Carlos isn't something to be scared for. It was a big deal in the past with Tyler, but Ethan has seen me and Carlos hang out before, and he's never seemed the type of guy to be intimidated by a friend. No matter what happens, it'll still be something we can always talk about. And Diane and Natalie appear to be completely okay with me hanging out.

Friendships don't end simply because you start dating someone.

"Thank you for coming on such short notice." Anna is sitting on top of the front desk in the classroom. After her blue hair washed out, she dyed it a bright mint green. It went well with the sharp bob, and the length of her hair only sharpens the appearance of her face.

Aside from Carlos and me, the other members in attendance are Ophelia, Scott, Alan, and Xiu.

"As you all know, we have midterms next week, which sucks, but I do have something for you guys to look forward to: spring break." She jumps off the desk, pacing like a general talking to her soldiers. "We're going on a trip."

"Where?" Carlos asks.

Anna pivots, pointing at him. "Thank you for asking. Of course, I'm aware not everyone will be able to make it since it's so sudden, but let's say I have *acquired* a lake house in the mountains for the last weekend of spring break. It will be private, and as long as everyone pitches in for groceries, most dinners will be provided for you. It's not mandatory but think of it as a gift to you for being members of this lovely family."

That doesn't sound shady at all.

"Sounds good. Do you need drivers?" Scott asks.

"Depends on how many of you guys decide to go, but we'll cover your gas. We'd go Friday morning come back on Sunday. There's a grill and a boat. It'll be fun, I promise."

A weekend to relax and not think about the crushing responsibilities of college. I suppose that's why students go to the beach and live in a drunken stupor. To forget they have tests, essays, and the ever-looming possibility of being their family's disappointment.

"Sounds good, I'm down." It's a bit surprising that I'm the

first to say that, because I usually am *not* the first one to do so.

"That's two of us." Carlos puts a hand on the top of my head.

"Everyone who's coming, please sign this form." Anna pulls out a white sheet of paper with some hand-drawn lines from a folder on top of the desk and hands it to Ophelia. "I'll text everyone to make sure the list is up to date. Don't forget your regular community hours, we've got to make sure everyone keeps on top of that! Other than that, the meeting is done."

The rest of the members get up and form a line to sign the form.

Scott bumps Alan out of the line, who then turns around with fists raised, ready to start a pretend fight, which they do, though it is more cute than funny. I step around them and make my way to the front of the line where Anna is standing on the other side of the desk, hands pressed over the top, her gradient nails matching the minty shade of her hair.

"I heard the good news about you and Mr. Winston."

"From who?" I haven't told anyone aside from my close friends, and I know neither would've said anything.

"A little bird told me." She beams. "I was rooting for you guys all along, as I'm sure the other club members were."

The ink is still drying on the sheet of paper as I move it back over to her. The ease with which she learns things has always unnerved me, but when it comes to matters about Ethan, I am more than ready to argue for him.

"What about his things?"

"Oh, he didn't tell you? I gave the key to him the same night you guys finished his initiation." She takes the paper from me and holds it over my shoulder, allowing one of the guys behind me to take it from her. "Not that it matters anymore, right?"

"No, it doesn't matter anymore." I pass her the pen I used to sign my name. "I'm glad he got them back, though."

I don't wait for a response; instead I take my backpack from the chair it had been resting on and march out the door. Outside the club room, Carlos and Ophelia are in deep conversation that is sufficiently killed once I've shown my face.

"You all right, Sol?" Ophelia asks.

"I'm okay." I push my hair out of my face. "Anna told me something I didn't know."

She nods. "Anna can come off as a bit intimidating when you first meet her, but she's superchill once you get to know her. She looks out for us all here. Even when it seems like she learned something out of nowhere, there's always a source of information."

What Ophelia is saying makes sense, though it's not Anna knowing about my relationship that hurt my pride but rather that Ethan didn't mention having the key back.

Carlos drives me home and I ask him to come in and stay for dinner. After I place the frozen pizza in the oven, because I'm way too lazy to actually cook, we lie down on my bed together. Michi jumps into the middle. Sometimes I wonder if Carlos misses my old house like I do. Dad used to joke around that he'd have to make the guest room a Carlos room because of how often he used to visit when we were in public school. We used to study for classes that we didn't even have together simply to hang out and spend time in my backyard.

Carlos would joke about how he preferred my place to his

because he preferred my parents to his own. While I used to tell him not to say that, I began to understand the older we got. His father was always away on work-related trips and his mom was too busy working during the day and taking classes at night to pay attention to him. They'd often fight, too, because of cultural clash, and Carlos felt stuck in the middle of a great divide.

He found some attention through parties and meeting other people, he says, like little pieces of love scattered throughout the bodies of the people he met.

"Your family feels like a home, though. The moment you see you guys together it's like a little portrait over a fireplace," he once said, sometime in high school. "It fits so nice and you guys get along. Not a lot of people get that, Sol."

"What's wrong?" he asks now, scooping up Michi in his arms.

"Nothing's wrong."

"Liar, you think I don't know you like the back of my hand?"

I reach over and pet Michi's head, feeling her purr against my hand.

"Do you want to watch *The Devil Wears Prada* and *Legally Blonde,* eat pizza, drink unhealthy amounts of soda, and ignore all of our responsibilities?"

Carlos picks up his head. "Don't we do that last bit all the time already?"

"I'm adding the first bit, though."

He pretends to think about it for a second before saying, "It sounds like a good plan. We can even invite Diane over, she'd like that."

"Sounds good, but you know what's going to happen first?"

"What?"

I take a pillow from underneath my head and try to hit him

but he rolls off the bed, laughing and grabbing another pillow. Launching my body off the bed, I throw the first feathered object I find within hand distance, and immediately duck his swing at my head.

Michi runs off in the middle of our pillow fight.

Laughing and screaming, we chase each other into the living room as my dad enters through the main door.

"Hola, papi." I push my hair back, kiss his cheek, and try to catch my breath. "Carlos is hanging out for the rest of the day and Diane might come over. We have pizza in the oven and leftover wings from yesterday. Do you want anything else?"

"I'm not hungry right now, *mija*. Thank you, though."

He turns to Carlos who is still standing with a pillow by his side. "Hey, Carlos." Dad shakes Carlos's hand, a smile on his face. "Nice to see you, it's been a while."

"*Gracias*, Mr. Gutierrez. I'm always glad when Sol invites me to come here, feels like my home."

"You know this is your home too." He turns to me. "I'm going to call your mom and have a beer on the balcony. Don't make too much noise, though, or the neighbors will get mad."

Mom and Dad can be on the phone for hours. Sometimes when he gets home from work he has already been on the phone with her during the car ride. I like to think that's true love. He walks off to the kitchen, then opens the fridge to grab a beer. Carlos and I look at each other.

"Fight until the oven tells us to stop and we settle down to watch a movie?" he says.

"Sounds good." I swat him with my pillow before he can even get in a fighting position.

Diane ends up being busy for the night but promises to have

us over the next time we want to watch something. Carlos and I are halfway through watching *The Devil Wears Prada* and nearly done with our pizza when I put the movie on pause and turn to him.

"Did you tell Anna about me and Ethan?"

"No."

"Someone told her." I take a bite out of my slice. "It doesn't bother me, I just find it weird."

"Well, she does know everything."

"Isn't that strange?"

"A little bit, but who knows? Maybe it was Ethan who told her. Anna doesn't have superpowers, information always comes from a specific source. You heard what Ophelia said earlier."

I grab my phone. "I'll be right back."

Michi meows as she follows me into the bathroom, as all cats are legally bound to do, and I wait for her to get inside before closing the door. I put the toilet lid down and sit as I dial Ethan's number. It rings two times before he picks up.

"Hey, sunshine, what's up?" His voice sounds deeper over the phone, and this is new information that I did not know I would find so attractive.

"Quick question. Did you tell Anna about us?"

"Actually, funny story. She came into the store earlier today with her boyfriend and mentioned you while they were checking out. Did you go to the meeting? A lake house, it sounds . . . interesting."

"Yeah, I think it'll be fun. Another thing. She said she gave you the key which is great, I only found it odd that you didn't tell me." Michi puts her front paws on my leg, demanding pets.

"Oh fuck, I'm sorry. I completely forgot about that." He

sounds genuinely surprised. "That night when they dropped me off at my place Anna gave me the key. It just dawned on me right now that I never told you about it."

"Don't be sorry, it's not something bad."

"It's kind of important, though."

"Is it? I'm guessing you can't get out of the club since you're in it already."

He laughs. "That's true."

"I'm not mad. It's strange how the club works things out. Not just Anna, she's another member like us and had to go through the process too. I sometimes wonder if she's as frustrated as we are and simply can't say anything . . . I don't know."

The way Anna appears to be confident about how things will work out makes me wonder what her process was. She must have had to make some hard decisions herself, and worked hard for her position.

Ethan stays silent for a moment. "Sol, are you happy in the club?"

"I'm not *not* happy. I like the people, it's . . . messy. I wish things weren't the way they are."

It still doesn't sit well with me, the things that we did. Even if they aren't outlandishly illegal, they still made me feel guilty. I haven't lied to my parents about the club, but I've kept things from them, and I've done things now that could possibly jeopardize my relationship with them. "But there's no going back, is there? If I had known then what I know now, maybe we'd both be in better spots."

"What if . . . no, forget it."

"What?"

Ethan sighs. "Nothing. Sometimes I wish things had gone

differently, too, but I know you because of all of this madness, and I wouldn't have it otherwise."

"Me too. I don't want to sound like I was freaking out because you didn't tell me about the key, I really value communication." It was the way Anna had commented that she was surprised he hadn't told me that made me feel insecure. It's not her fault either—after all, she did say she was rooting for us.

"You're okay. I should've told you, that was my mistake. You want to grab some burgers tomorrow to make up for it? My treat."

"You're learning the way to my heart is through food. That's dangerous."

"Hey, the same can be said for me. We're okay?"

"We're okay, we always were." I get up. "Now I should get back, I was watching movies and eating pizza with Carlos."

"Awesome, you guys have fun. I just got off work—I need a shower and then I'm crashing, but I'll see you tomorrow, right? I can pick you up."

"That works perfectly for me."

It's good to get that off my chest, even though I knew nothing was probably wrong. The fact that Ethan was so open and honest with me is a fresh breath of air when it comes to history club shenanigans. With that out of my mind, I am able to put my phone back in my pocket, pick up my cat like she is a baby, and saunter back into the living room, ready to bask in early 2000s nostalgia.

CHAPTER NINETEEN

On Thursday morning I finally tell Mom about me and Ethan. Yes, I skimmed over a lot of important details like how we met, but that didn't matter anymore because she was very interested in my love life at the moment, and I hadn't been able to give her love drama like any other teenager would.

"He's nice?" Mom says.

I smile, pouring milk over my cereal. "He is. We had a picnic the other day."

I haven't spoken to her regularly in a while, and that was gnawing at me. It's like the club is taking over my life little by little when I should be concentrating on the important things in life, like school and my family.

"How come I haven't heard about him before?"

I pause. "We met at school but I didn't want to talk about it because it would sound like it might take away from my education."

"Sol, you're eighteen nearing nineteen and you've had boy-friends before. I know you're a good student, I know the daughter I raised." She gives me this meaningful look that makes my stomach knot. "I'm happy for you. Maybe one day I'll get to meet Ethan."

"You might have already. He's the Winstons' grandson."

"Oh right, the ones in the old house. They were really nice."

"It's one of the oldest houses in town, they even got an award for it. I think it was built in the late nineteenth century." Most of the information I know was provided by Anna, but I can be well assured that if I liked a boy he'd tell me these sorts of things on his own, and Mom wouldn't be the wiser.

"Wow, where did you learn all that?"

"Ethan." I am so getting coal for Christmas.

"I think I do remember him. I'm pretty sure I invited his grandparents for one of your birthday parties and they brought him over. His parents were getting divorced or something."

I wonder if we ever met each other before, then. If by any chance Ethan hit my piñata, or we ever hung out with some of the neighborhood kids. He is older than me, so I know we wouldn't have met in school, but now that Mom has mentioned him, I've noticed I can't place him in my memory. Only his grandparents stand out when I think of my childhood.

"Yeah, he doesn't have the greatest relationship with his parents. Like I said, he lives with his grandparents now."

"A family doesn't always have to be a mom, dad, and a son, sometimes it's a single parent and a child, or grandparents and a grandchild, or even a couple with no kids. Sometimes it's better when the parents are apart."

"Not us. We were better together."

"That's true, but we'll work through it. How are your classes? You're taking midterms, right?"

"I have one later today, which I should be studying for, and another one tomorrow. Then I'll be done. Oh, I'm going to a lake house at the end of spring break with the history club."

"That sounds like a lot of fun." She glances at a point above her camera, the sign that she has to leave soon.

"It won't keep me from making good grades." When I was younger we would have a family meeting when I got a grade lower than an A to talk about why my grades had dropped and what we could do as a family to raise them.

"You'll be fine. Don't strain yourself too much, okay?" She straightens up, messing with her hair like I oftentimes do, to try to make it look presentable for class. Her hair is as dark as mine, but unlike me, Mom got blessed with straight, sleek hair that doesn't fight her when she decides to do anything with it.

"I won't if you don't."

She points at me. "Don't talk to me like that. I'm your mother."

It's a joke, because everyone in our family is a workaholic.

"I love you, Mom." I wave good-bye.

"Love you too, corazón, good luck on your test." She reaches over and the next second the frame freezes before showing her information. It's a bit strange but I'm beginning to get used to this form of communication with her. The morning calls, the messages, Skype calls at dinner time with her and Dad—they all feel somewhat normal now, and I don't entirely like that.

I get that math is important and we wouldn't have gotten to do many things as a human race without nerdy kids throwing numbers around. However, if someone announced we've done all the math we need to do as a society, I'd drink to that.

The student sitting two seats away from me lets his head fall on the paper with a loud thud.

I feel that.

Thirty minutes later I force myself to get up from my seat and turn the test in. My professor looks like he feels terribly sorry for the pain he's causing us. Stepping out of the room is like a breath of fresh air.

I take my phone out of my backpack and turn it back on to check on what I missed while I was taking the exam.

> Ethan: Hey beautiful, do you want to come over to my house for dinner later?

My heart beats slower.

> Me: For sure I would love that
> Me: I don't have to dress up fancy or anything do I? lol

Feeling a bit like an idiot after sending the second message, I shove my phone in my back pocket. I exit the mathematics and physics building.

"Hey, Sol!"

I don't recognize Angela until she's right in front of me; in fact, her cute military-green backpack covered in pins catches my attention before I realize who she is.

"What's up?" We walk together since staying still on a busy college path is a great idea only if you want to get shoved out of the way.

"Nothing much, walking to my next midterm."

"Oh no, you have more than one today?"

She grimaces. "Yep, and they are my least favorite classes."

"That sucks."

"Are you going to the club getaway?"

"Yes, it'll be fun after all this bull. Are you?"

"Yeah. The club is kind of crazy, but I'm sure the lake trip will be like the initiation party." Her light-brown hair falls a bit past her shoulders in pretty, beachy waves. The fact that we are in the middle of midterm season shows true commitment on the part of those actually styling their hair in the morning. I have nothing but respect for her now.

"For sure. I didn't think I'd end up in a club like that, but it's changed my life," I say, a tad surprised at how truthful that is. The club is a part of my daily life, no matter what. Whether I'm spending time with Ethan or hanging out with Carlos, if I'm having a conversation with Diane, or if I'm home working on homework, the club always looms in the back of my mind.

Angela nods. "I kind of feel the same." Then, a bit lower. "I sometimes feel though that things would be better if it wasn't a thing, though."

"How so?"

She makes a face. "You didn't hear this from me, but I pretty much desecrated a grave. It scared the crap out of me. There's a high possibility if any of this blew up, I wouldn't go to jail but I could be fined and put on probation."

We round the corner outside the building, following the path to the main square. The sky is clear and birds are singing; it'd be a nice day to have a picnic if it wasn't for the ever-present stress of the college students around us running to the next midterm that could make or break their semester.

"I mean, I get it. I feel like I went against myself doing what I did," I reply. At least she understands the consequences; I feel like I followed everything blindly until it was too late.

"Exactly! It's like I betrayed myself doing what I did." She sighs. "I don't even feel like it's worth it."

"Tell me about it, I tell myself the same thing every day." I doubt there's a single day since my dare that I have not questioned my place in the club.

"Right? I wish it was all gone sometimes, but hey, at the very least they're giving us a place to stay during spring break. Well, I gotta turn here, but I'll see you next weekend." Angela gives me a smile, holding on to the straps of her backpack as she walks away with a tilt of her head.

"All right. Good luck on your test!" I call.

As I look around to figure out exactly where on campus I am, I remember I left my bike chained up outside the math building.

"Crap."

Ethan is trying not to smile while driving. The AC in his car is on full blast as I sit back and try not to sweat my butt off. Turns out wearing a long-sleeved sweater on a day that goes up to eighty degrees is no fun, to the surprise of no one. I didn't expect it to get so hot in the first place, but I should have known my cute outfit would eventually backstab me when I'm trying to meet my new partner's family.

"You forgot your bike and had to walk all the way back." Ethan laughs.

"It wasn't the first time nor will it be the last time I do that." It was worse when I first started biking to school. I would get out of class and walk to the parking lot all the way across campus and then remember I didn't have a car anymore. That's truly how my leg muscles started developing.

"What am I going to do with you?"

"Appreciate me for who I am." We come to a halt in the driveway of his house.

"I do that already." Ethan runs the back of his fingers against my cheek. "I appreciate the hell out of how weird you are."

"First of all, that's an insult. Second, it's not that weird to forget things." Or perhaps it's a thing only me and Dad do, without Mom to remind us of things we always misplace or when we forget the simplest things. His lunch, for example, or the keys inside the house, or reminding me that I have homework and only realize that three hours before it's due.

"Fine, quirky."

I scrunch up my nose. "Nah, I don't have enough Instagram followers to be quirky."

He laughs. "Okay, then we're back to you being weird."

"Fine. Your grandparents are having dinner with us, right?" I get out of the car and grab the bag of pastries I got on the way back home.

"Yes. Are you nervous?"

"No! I feel weird because the last time I was here I . . ." Slowly,

I rotate my hands toward him, aware that he knows what I'm getting at.

"Broke into their house? I didn't tell them anything about that."

"Really?"

"I told them I was changing the locks because it is a good idea to change them every couple of years." That's a relief. Doesn't make me feel much better, but he takes my hand as we walk to the main door nonetheless, and the warmth of his fingers against mine brings me some comfort.

Life is good.

As soon as we enter, the smell of comfort food is nearly overwhelming. Maybe it's because I've gotten used to eating out or cooking myself, but I haven't had a good homemade meal in a while.

"Mima, I'm home." Ethan takes off his jean jacket and drapes it over the armchair where their cat, Muffin, is sleeping. Of course, I instantly go over and pet it. The cat purrs, pressing its head against my arm. I don't even know anything aside from its name, but I would die for it.

"Hey, baby." Mrs. Winston comes out of the small dining room, wiping her hands with a rag she's carrying. She is about a head shorter than me, which makes the difference in height compared to Ethan as she walks next to him adorable. Her glasses are thick and the wrinkles on her face make her smile warm my heart as she moves toward me. "Is that who I think it is?"

I step toward her and offer my hand.

"Hi, Mrs. Winston, it's been a while."

"Stop that. Come here, baby girl." She wraps her arms around me, squeezing me as hard as I think she possibly can. Her limbs are shaky and she appears frail, but I can feel the pure happiness she carries. "I haven't seen you in so long! How have you been?"

She turns away from me and looks toward the stairs. "Samuel!"

"I've been good, life has been . . . interesting, but here I am."

"I heard about your mom, I'm so sorry. Here, take a seat." She takes my arm and leads me to their small dining-room table, where I can drop the bag of pastries and sit down. It's so strange, being here again.

"What was that?" Mr. Winston rounds the corner of the dining room as Mrs. Winston sits next to me. He is a bit closer to Ethan's height compared to his wife, but he walks with a bit of a hunch, though is not slow as he walks toward us. There is a hearing aid in his left ear, which he turns toward Mrs. Winston.

"It's Soledad, remember? Margarita and Emanuel's daughter."

Mr. Winston squints, then takes his glasses out of his breast pocket and puts them on. He has been doing that since I was little.

"No, I don't remember her."

My smile falters.

"I'm joking. Of course I remember you, kiddo."

That makes my night. He, too, gives me a hug. When I offer to help Mrs. Winston, she shushes me and tells me not to worry about it.

She made meat loaf with this drizzle sauce that is still steaming hot when she puts the plate in front of me, as well as mac and cheese, steamed veggies, and fluffy golden mashed potatoes. In the center of the table, there is a pitcher of gravy, as well as biscuits covered in melted butter. I almost feel like crying.

"How are you, honey? How's your dad?" Mrs. Winston asks.

"He's good, working hard as usual."

She nods. Mr. Winston laughs and sounds so much like Ethan it's almost scary.

"Your dad worked sixty hours a week and acted like it was nothing." He drizzles more gravy on his food.

"Yup, that's Dad."

"How's your mom?"

"She's good, still teaching English." I gather a bit of mashed potatoes with a piece of meat loaf. "She misses us and we miss her, but there's nothing we can do at the moment."

"It is such a shame," Mrs. Winston mumbles. "Must be so hard on you too."

"With the system right now nothing can get done," grumbles her husband.

"Not until I'm twenty-one." I take a sip of my water. "Well, a real case can't get started until I'm twenty-one, and then I have to wait six more years since she is in a ten-year ban. All the lawyers my dad and I have spoken to have told us to wait."

"But she had no criminal record, she's the sweetest lady—" Mrs. Winston says.

Mr. Winston interrupts her. "All immigrants are criminals to the government right now."

I couldn't agree more, but if I speak my voice might break.

I can feel the weight of Ethan's gaze on me. He's never asked why Mom works in Mexico, or about my living situation. It didn't occur to me that he might not put two and two together, or maybe he was waiting for me to tell him.

"Hey."

"Yeah?"

"Are you okay?"

We're sitting on the ledge of his window, the same one I jumped from. The slant on the roof seems a bit more dangerous now than it did then. After dinner and dessert, the elder Winstons settled down to watch TV while Ethan and I went upstairs to his room.

The walls are painted gray and the accents around his room are white. He keeps things neat and tidy, more so even than I do. A small fish bowl rests on his desk, where a little betta fish swims around. His desk is scattered with papers and his laptop is placed in the center. A large, dark map of the world hangs over top of his bed, and a couple of pictures are scattered across his nightstand.

"I'm fine, lost in thought."

"That's a scary thing."

I scoff. "Why?"

"Because you're usually a chatterbox and it's honestly terrifying when you're silent."

"You should feel very terrified, yes." I hope he can hear the sarcasm in my voice, though it is hard after being lost in my own thoughts for a while.

"You're admitting you didn't feel okay and then lied to me saying you were fine."

"You know what? This conversation is over."

He laughs. "You said that that night too."

I look at the tree, partially disbelieving I fell from that height. "I was so high on adrenaline, I can't believe I did it."

"You can say that again." He sighs. "I didn't know about your mom. I mean, I had a hunch, but I didn't want to pry."

"I should have told you." My fingers hurt because of how many times I've twisted them into knots tonight. "It's never a good time to bring up that your mom got deported."

"You didn't have to tell me. Now I feel like a dick for the comment I made about your mom probably not making a lot of money."

I rest my hands on his knees. "You didn't know. She's a teacher, and a struggling one at that, but she's getting by. We all do that, don't we?"

"Get by? We do." Fingers lightly tap my arms. "Do you want to talk about it?"

There is the sound of a car driving nearby, the rustling of the leaves of the oak tree branches as they sway in the breeze and wait for spring to come around to show off its full range of color. In the grand scheme of things, I do want to talk about it, I just don't know where to start, or even how to do that to begin with.

"So I was learning how to drive last year, right." It was a beautiful day, almost too beautiful. Mom woke me up and told me to get the keys because Dad was sending us for groceries so we could make a meal later on at the park. "I was excited since it was the last week of winter break and she had promised to give me driving lessons more often. Anyway, um, we decided to go to the Walmart on Washington Street since it was farther away, and I could practice getting on and off the highway. But as I was driving down the late closest to the entrance, someone, let's call her Beatriz, decided it was a great day to speed down the highway and not check her mirrors."

Ethan's shoulders tense up. "Jesus."

"She took out the entire back side of my car, and the impact was so strong and so fast it sent me and Mom skidding across two lanes of traffic and onto the grass. I lost consciousness after that and woke up with my dad giving me the news that while Mom was talking to me, screaming for someone for help, when the police showed up not only did I not have my instruction permit with me, but my mom had an AB 60 license, and while the police couldn't do anything to her, he or someone in the truck that hit us, called ICE while I was being checked in an ambulance. Dad goes: 'Your mom is getting deported and you have a broken arm and bruised ribs.' It was a great end to my break."

"Sol, you don't have to continue . . ."

"And it's—shit fell apart from there, Ethan, I don't know what to tell you. The past year of my life has been such a haze it might as well have been a blackout. Up until I stumbled into you."

He leans into me, a warm palm resting against my cheek.

"I'm sorry you had to go through that."

"I want her back and all the signs point to that not happening until I am ten years older, and even then it seems like a complicated uphill legal battle."

"My parents aren't immigration lawyers, but maybe they know someone who could help," he offers.

"It's okay. Thank you, though. We've talked with a couple and they say we're better to wait for now. Depending where we are in a couple of years, I might take you up on the offer." I inhale. "Sorry I spewed out a lot of tragic backstory to you. I promise I don't do that very often unless I really like someone."

"That's okay, though I want to know you better." He brushes his hand through my hair, the sensation sending tingles through my skin. "You can tell me about your tragic superhero backstory at any moment, Soledad."

I smile. "They say you never truly know a person."

"Yeah?" He's so close to me he barely breathes.

We're kissing, slowly, sweetly. Then I push back against him, biting his lip as I twine my arms around his neck. He moves his face away from mine and kisses my neck, the light scruff on his chin bringing different sensations. I move him away, grab the front of his shirt, and bring him to me again so I can kiss his lips, this time more needy.

The thing is, we're still sitting on his window ledge. Me being the klutz I am, I try to lean back and forget that there is no support, and for one moment all I see is the starry night over the roof of his house. My stomach drops and I feel the shame of all my ancestors.

This time I would have died for sure if it hadn't been for Ethan grabbing me.

"Holy shit, Sol."

"Oh my God, I nearly died," I manage to get out between laughs.

"You know who would have had to deal with that? Me." Ethan presses his hands to his forehead. "Are you okay?"

"Yep, the universe is a cockblocker." I get up, adjusting my shirt. "I should go home, I'm not here to disrespect your grandparents."

"I wasn't planning that with them downstairs." He tousles his hair before pulling me into a hug. "You scared the crap out of me."

"I think it's an omen that I should go."

"Roger that. I'll take you home." Ethan touches his forehead to mine. "I'm really glad you came today, and that you met my grandparents even though you technically had already met."

"I'm glad you invited me over. I'm sorry for nearly falling out of your window . . . again."

"Let's make tonight the last time."

I give him a light peck in the lips. "Sounds good to me."

Ethan holds out his hand and I take it immediately. As we walk to the door of his room, I look over my shoulder once more, at the window I jumped out of that first day—at the exit and the entrance to this strange part of my life I hadn't known would exist.

CHAPTER TWENTY

The light filters through the blinds over the kitchen window. Sunlight makes patterns over the mug of coffee I've placed on top of the table but have refused to touch since preparing. It's the type of quiet morning that I love, where the world seems to be dragging slowly through time, and the little details of life seem to be basked in the golden sun, but I would appreciate it more if I wasn't so tired.

"You're awake already?" Dad yawns as he enters the kitchen.

I glare at the microwave clock, marking six thirty in the morning.

"Yes, they told us to be ready by now." In all honesty, Anna had never told us what time we were leaving for the cabin, or where exactly the lake was.

I spent all of spring break being lazy and refusing to go out. I stayed home, redecorated my room, helped Dad move stuff around the apartment, and marathoned about five shows online. It was the first time in a long time that I had pure free time for myself and I made sure I used every last second of it to enjoy my solitude. Of course, that meant I stayed up until ungodly hours talking to Ethan on the phone last night.

So when Anna had called me, and the rest of the members I'm assuming, some time around four in the morning with the news that I had to get ready because Scott was coming to get us around five or six in the morning, I was not prepared.

Dad snorts. "You didn't even brush your hair?"

"Um, no." I look like I rolled out of bed, and the simple explanation to that is that I did. "I'll throw it in a bun later."

"When do you come back?"

Big props to my dad for being up this early, all dressed for work, and still having enough energy to worry about his daughter's school trips.

"Sunday afternoon."

He takes a sip of his coffee, nodding. "Well, be very careful. You got the pepper spray I bought you?"

"Yep, always carry it with me."

"That's my girl."

He walks past me to grab the pot of coffee. I managed to make some food last night to use as his lunch today. I made some rice with corn and green peppers, as well as *milanesas empanizadas*. It's simple, but it'll be filling enough for him. I didn't use to cook as much when Mom was here, and it is a steep learning curve, but Dad has never complained about my food.

My phone dings as I'm taking a drink out of my cup.

Carlos: *Yo, we're parked outside your house, come out*

"Bueno, papi, I need to go." I put down my cup before jumping off the kitchen counter and giving him a kiss on the cheek.

"Okay, corazón, be careful. Don't drown in the lake and tell Carlos if anything happens, I'm coming for him."

Grabbing my duffel bag, I stop by the chair where Michi is sleeping to plant a kiss on top of her head, which I'm sure she does not appreciate.

The sky is a hazy purple, and dew is still scattered on top of vehicles and plants. Scott's soccer-mom van is parked right outside our apartment complex, and I can nearly distinguish the loud '70s music playing inside of it.

Sure enough, when Xiu opens the sliding door, "Dancing Queen" is booming inside.

"Holy shit, Scott, isn't it a bit early for this?" I pass my bag to Alan, who is hanging out in the back of the van with the rest of the luggage. Xiu and Angela are in the middle seat with a spot left for me, and Carlos is riding shotgun.

"Sol, it's never too early for ABBA!" Scott shouts back. "Now, get inside. We've got a four-hour drive ahead of us."

Thankfully, he lowers the music once I'm buckled in and we're on the road.

"What about the other members?"

"Anna is picking them up," Carlos says. Like me, he looks like he could use four more espresso shots to be at Scott's level of enthusiasm this early in the morning.

While I wish we were in the same vehicle, we're all going to the same place, so I'm not too worried. Still, I grab my phone to see how he's doing after being up all night on the phone.

Me: Morning, our car is full so you're going
to be spending some quality time with
the other club members

He answers almost immediately.

Ethan: *We're on our way already. Can't wait to see you*

That brings a smile to my face. Scott is singing along to his songs, and next to me Xiu and Angela are swaying with the sound track as well. I feel like we've been transferred to many years in the past where a band of friends could get together and road trip. So I close my eyes and let the sound of the music create cheesy music videos in my mind as we get on our way to the lake house.

Nature is mind boggling. The way the roads bend into hills, and the hills into mountains. When they're farther away they're blue and gray but as you get closer the colors change and so do you. Mountains have always reminded me how small we are.

They also remind me how scary it is to be in a car with five other people while the driver vibes along to Andy Gibb's "I Just Want to Be Your Everything," taking sharp curves up the steep path. I have to give it to Anna. Once we step out of the van and walk through the trees to the main entrance, the size of this place settles in. There are three spots in the garage, with a walkway that is lined by lush green bushes.

The two-floor house is made of dark wood and has a deep-gray shingled roof. It has double doors made out of the same material the walls are, but with frosted glass and golden details. Four windows along the front wall are also adorned with twisted iron.

Scott whistles. "This sure as hell costs more than my tuition."

"You're trying to tell me this is someone's second home?" Angela mumbles as we open the door.

From the foyer you can see a balcony on the second floor. We quickly stumble upon a living area where one of the walls is completely made out of glass that reveals the deck and lake.

The living area is furnished with sofas that curve around a circular table and a plasma TV with a Nintendo Switch plugged into it. Underneath the TV, there is a fireplace, and different potted plants decorate the space.

"Great, you guys are here." Anna is wearing a white T-shirt and jean shorts covered by the type of robe you'd wear when you murder your rich husband. Her hair is up in a ponytail, with a few loose strands framing her face.

"Where is here?" Alan asks, and Scott extends his arms to him.

"One of our nice members lent us their lake house. Amazing, isn't it? We stopped at the last McDonald's nearby, so you guys are just in time for breakfast, come on."

We follow her into a massive kitchen, complete with an island that can accommodate six people. The kitchen also overlooks the lake, as well as a grilling section made out of stone that contains a fire pit and patio furniture straight out of a garden-decor magazine.

Around the kitchen island are the other club members, eating McDonald's biscuit sandwiches out of a large bag placed in the middle.

Ethan perks up as soon as he sees me, and I can't help but smile goofily when he gets up to hug me.

"Hey, stranger. Holy crap this place is so nice," I say.

He only needs to widen his eyes while squeezing my hand to let me know he agrees.

Once everyone finishes breakfast, Anna takes off her murder robe and walks to the center of the kitchen, stopping right in front of the island.

"As you can tell, our sponsor was very generous by letting us stay here. Please be respectful. There are four rooms and there are ten of us, so on the west side we'll have the girls. Xiu, Melina, and Angela will be in one room, while Ophelia, Soledad, and I will be in the other. The boys will be in the east wing, Ethan and Carlos in one room and Scott and Alan in the other. Each room has its own TV set, but try to spend time with your fellow members. Also, there are two full bathrooms, but since there are so many of us either figure out a shower schedule or take very quick showers.

"Fridge is fully stocked thanks to your twenty-dollar donations. As you saw, we're kind of removed from society, so as far as I know no one delivers all the way up here. We have a boat and three Jet Skis for anyone who knows how to use them. Please don't injure yourselves, I don't want to call a helicopter for anyone. You can go hiking, swimming, or play video games all day long, it's up to you. Have fun.

"Go wild, my children." She raises her hand. "But not too wild."

The first thing I do is take my duffel bag to my room. It takes me a hot minute to find the stairs, which are past another living area. It doesn't have a TV—instead, the focus of the room is an ornate fireplace, above which hangs a meticulously detailed painting of the lake.

I take my best guess at which side is west and journey down the hall until I find a door with a small dry-erase board that says "Ophelia, Sol, Anna."

Scott was wrong. This place is probably more expensive than all of our tuition costs added together.

There are two queen-sized beds neatly made, and so comfy looking I have to fight the urge to take a twelve-hour nap.

A large TV is mounted on the wall above a vanity. There are a few toiletries, like makeup wipes, with a small note that reads: These are new, feel free to use them (:

"I feel like a sugar baby," says Ophelia as she enters the room.

"Right now, we're all weird, sugar cousins," I say placing the note back down. If this entire lake house belongs to one of the former members of the club, I'm beginning to wonder how much power they might have out there in the world.

"I've been with the club for two years now and they've never done something like this." She lets her bag fall on the bed closer to the window. "Then again, it's the first time Anna is the president."

"She seems to stay strict to code." Leaving my duffel bag next to hers, I look through my clothes until I find my bathing suit. There's no way I'm coming to a lake house and not taking a dip in the water.

"You'd be surprised, the last president was extremely strict about hours and who could join. Anna tries to keep things fun." She stretches, yawning. "She works hard."

Ophelia is not completely wrong. The pool party and now this are certainly things I didn't expect to come out of the history club of all things. While I'm still not happy about some of the things done to get into the club, it has truly been an entertaining (and thoroughly stressful) ride.

Once we make our way back to the first floor, we find Alan and Xiu playing Super Smash Bros. while other members are hanging out on the covered part of the deck. I'd changed into a one-piece swimsuit and shorts and Ophelia had changed into a moss-green two-piece and was wearing a sheer robe à la Anna, as well as a wide-brimmed hat and some round shades. She looks right out of a summertime photo shoot, and I wish I could hold that power.

On the deck, I lean over the railing. Scott and Carlos are ripping over the water on Jet Skis, chasing each other.

"That looks like fun," Ophelia says, taking her copy of *The Handmaid's Tale* with her to the shore of the lake, where there are reclining chairs and Anna is currently reading a book as well.

"I feel like I'm in a movie," Ethan says, encircling my waist with his arm. I feel the warmth of his skin against mine before I realize he's in his swim trunks.

Jesus Christ, how are you so fine?

It doesn't feel like a movie. It feels like a dream.

"I'm going to take a dip," I say, pulling on his hand. "You coming?"

"Right now?"

I'm already halfway to the pier, undoing the buttons of my shorts. "Right now."

I take off my shorts and leave my sandals with them on the chair next to Anna's. Running down the pier, I pick up speed and exhilaration courses through my veins as I reach the end and jump.

I'm only airborne for a second or two, but it feels longer.

If I could take a snapshot of my life the past couple of months, I'd make it this. Right here, where everything seems so easy and simple. Where the members of this strange, cult-like family are talking and laughing among each other. Because right now I don't have to worry about school, or my family, or anything else.

Right now I'm just a girl, jumping into a lake with her friends.

The rest of the day is a blur. We swim in the lake. Carlos gives me a ride on the Jet Ski. I take a shower, and we all play Mario Kart.

Around seven o'clock we decide to make dinner. Alan offers to grill burgers. Carlos suggests we make s'mores over the fire pit, and we cheer. We raid the fridge and cabinets for food then make our way to the deck.

The sun is setting over the lake, giving it a bright-orange glow. I sit next to Ethan on a small love seat close to the fire pit.

Scott comes out with a portable speaker. Tame Impala plays soothingly around us.

"Did you think you'd be here two months ago?" I rest my head against Ethan's shoulder.

"Jesus, has it only been two months?"

"Like, two months or less." That does sound like a very short amount of time to have known him. Before that time, I didn't even remember he existed; I didn't even know the rest of the members existed for that matter. Yet here we all are.

Scott sits down across from us, grabbing a few of the s'mores ingredients on the table. "Where are you bitches going after Westray?"

"What do you mean?" Xiu asks.

He pushes a stick through his marshmallow. "What are your plans? I will probably be homeless for a while and backpack around. See the world, leave my shitty family behind."

"Why am I not surprised?" Alan laughs, closing the top of the grill, where he had just flipped the patties he had shaped himself. He and Scott share a long look before he responds to the question himself. "I want to go to grad school, but there's no money for that, so I'll find a job."

"I want to go to grad school too." Angela gathers her hair up with a scrunchie before taking a bite of her s'more. "Hopefully get a job doing research, bank some money, and go traveling when I'm not stuck in the lab."

"I want to be a get a PhD and teach classes," Xiu says. "Not here, but somewhere."

"I want to build things, make things better." Carlos looks at me. "See people around me happy."

"Carlos, my man, you make people happy by showing your gorgeous face." Scott manages to put an entire s'more in his mouth. Between mouthfuls, he points at me. "What about you, Sol? Ethan? You guys? The golden couple."

"I want to switch my major and minor, to study computer science and hopefully get into IT," Ethan says, but I feel disconnected.

What *do* I want to do?

I don't know if I've ever known. When I was in high school all I wanted to do was get into college and figure out if anthropology was for me. My parents wanted something more viable than that, but all I wanted to do was figure out past events and human patterns. When Mom got deported, I figured I'd understand the world more with a political science minor, and since WCC doesn't have an anthropology degree, I decided to zero down on history. It didn't feel like a path, though; it felt like I was merely finding something to write down on a piece of paper.

"What about you, Soledad?" Alan asks.

"I don't know. I'm still trying to figure it out."

"Yo, I'll drink to that." Scott lifts up his Arizona iced tea. "Our generation says we want to do all these things, but honestly, no one knows."

There are a few nods of approval, as the smell of sizzling food fills the air. The music plays softly in the background as more questions about life roll around, but my mind is elsewhere—in the imminent future that will come to sweep us all away no matter what.

Stars glitter in the sky, clouds muddling their shimmer every now and then as the darkened leaves of trees make them look like cosmic puzzle pieces. As I get lost in the sea of starlight, I realize no one asked Anna what she was planning on doing with her life, but when I look around, I don't see her.

CHAPTER TWENTY-ONE

It takes me a minute to remember where I am when I wake up. The ceiling is high and slanted, and the light entering the large windows to the right is scattered because of the trees surrounding us.

I turn on my side. Ophelia is fast asleep, but I hear the tapping of keys, so I sit up. Anna is on her bed, legs crossed, with her sleeping mask up on her messy hair. Her fingers are tapping swiftly; she doesn't seem to notice me.

"Morning," I say. "We missed you last night."

"Something came up." Her eyes stay locked on her phone.

"Is everything okay?"

"It's personal." She gets up with a small smile. "Thanks for asking, though."

Anna leaves the room, taking her mystery with her.

The bathroom of the girl's wing is busy, so I can't take a

shower. I drop my bag back inside the room and make my way downstairs to the laundry room, where we were able to dry our swimsuits, and change into mine there.

Out on the deck, the boys, except Ethan, and two of the girls are using the grill. Carlos is lounging on one of the chairs with dark sunglasses on and a light-teal button up open to expose his pale chest, which is exactly where I slap him.

"Ah, Sol!"

"Sorry." I snicker. "You were so vulnerable. I couldn't help it."

"That's exactly what a serial killer would tell her victim."

"You big baby."

He shoves my hand away when I try to grab his cheeks.

"I will throw you in the lake, woman."

"No, you won't."

"You think I won't?"

"I think you're a chicken."

A sinister smile creeps up his face.

Oh fuck.

The next moment he's wrestling with me as I try to make my body heavy.

Let me tell you, I'm not the thinnest girl. I will hands down eat the last taco left standing, but Carlos is a fitness addict. When he snakes one of his arms around one of my legs while the other grabs me from underneath my torso, I am beyond impressed and horrified.

"Carlos, stop, we're gonna fall and die!"

He laughs, walking us down the pier. "Look at it this way, you're already wearing a swimsuit."

"I swear I'll bring you down with me." I'm falling, screaming bloody murder before my body crashes through the water.

Boy, it is cold as fuck.

I swim to the top, ignoring the numbness in my arms and legs. Carlos is laughing hard at the edge of the pier, like some sort of evil villain in a children's movie.

"I fucking hate you!" I yell.

He blows a kiss my way. "I love you, too, gorgeous. Go for a swim, I'll call you when breakfast is done."

With a quick flip off, I turn and swim around in the lake. Once I'm moving, it's not as cold, and with the morning sun my skin starts warming up.

I let myself drift a little, making sure I'm not too far from the shore, but far enough so I can't hear the mutter of everyone's conversation. Scott's groovy music is the only sound aside from nature itself. Fluffy white clouds obstruct the sunlight every few moments. I close my eyes, think of what I have accomplished so far this year. I met Ethan. My grades have not dropped, despite the amount of time and stress I dedicate to the club. I have a good relationship with my parents, even though I feel guilty about not talking with my mom as often as I used to.

I wonder how things might be different if Mom hadn't been deported. Before she was taken, I had applied to different schools in Southern California, far from where we live now. I was more than ready to move away, become my own person, and leave my little town behind.

Would that have been better? I don't think I will be able to know now. I'm not even sure I know the girl I used to be before the crash. The little girl who'd run around her house and drag her parents to parks, the teenager who'd argue with her mother about future tattoos and piercing ideas, the young adult who wasn't scared of the future.

Me.

And Ethan. If Mom were here I wouldn't have met him. There is a selfish side of me that says I would be okay with that as long as I could have my mom back. But I do really like him, and I am happy he is in my life.

If I had known who he was before I broke into his grandparents' house, I think I'd do it all over again.

"Sol!" Carlos calls.

I open my eyes, the light of the sun nearly blinding me.

"Food is ready! Swim back!"

Rolling in the water, I prepare to swim back to the shore. I feel the weight of the current over my shoulders and the reality of my life settles in. There is no way I could have anticipated the things that happened, and the choices I've made ever since, whether they were made willingly or taken in the spur of the moment, have shaped the course of my life.

We have a feast for breakfast. Red potatoes, seasoned and seared to perfection, accompanied by sausage and fluffy eggs jazzed up with spices. In the middle of the table there is a bowl of diced mangoes, bananas, and green apples, drizzled with honey and sprinkled with roasted almonds. Next to it is a bowl of guacamole for the toasted bread that is slathered with butter.

Ethan and the others are already eating when I get to the deck. I lay down a towel and sit next to them. Scott passes me a glass of orange juice.

"This is the life, isn't it?" Alan asks, grabbing a bit of the guacamole to spread on his bread.

Scott laughs. "None of us is living here any time soon. Unless your families are well off, because mine sure as hell isn't." He pauses. "But if any of you guys *is* well off, you have my number."

"We're all going to Westray Community College, come on." Melina laughs. "I'm sure none of us have the type of money to bribe our way into an Ivy League."

"Doesn't stop a boy from doing his hustle. If I don't end up marrying Alan I gotta get someone who'll take me traveling all over the world." Scott tips his glass of orange juice at her before taking a drink.

"You mean someone who can stand you all over the world," Alan retorts.

"Look at it this way." Carlos sits up. "If this house was provided to us by one of the former members, they've got money. Even though none of us has this kind of money now, it shouldn't stop us from dreaming. The system is fucked up, but we have to fix it. This generation, I mean."

"Holy shit." Alan laughs. "Run for president already."

"I'm not doing that shit, man. I just want a good life." We continue to eat, glasses and silverware clinking over our plates. It reminds me of Ethan's mention of how the other half lives, fairness being given to a chosen few throughout life, but then again, I'm here sitting next to him, enjoying breakfast by the lake.

"Has anyone seen Anna?" I say.

"She was gone by the time I woke up," Ophelia says.

"She went out to get some food," Carlos says, turning to me with a quick tilt of his face. "Said something personal had come up."

"Well," I say, cutting up a piece of my sausage, "I hope she's okay."

Everyone helps put stuff away and wash the dishes. It is nice seeing us all work together, really, like a kids' show singing about teamwork. Afterward, some of the members settle down to play games while others go back to their rooms to watch TV.

I decide to take a shower and wash the lake water off me. Like the rest of the house, the bathroom is fancy. While the floor is made out of the same polished concrete as the rest of the house, the tub is pure white marble, as is the sink and the accent handles on the drawers. The mirror is made out of a material that doesn't get foggy, so I don't have to wipe the steam away when I brush my hair.

I'm changing into a pair of shorts when someone knocks on the door.

"It's busy!"

Ethan's voice comes faintly through the wooden door. "It's me."

I open the door, my hair still a bit too damp for my liking. "What's up?"

He's wearing a T-shirt and joggers; the first time that he hasn't been dressed like a fashion icon.

"I was wondering if you wanted to go for a hike."

"Sounds like fun." I look down at my outfit. "Let me find something to wear and I'll meet you on the deck."

He smiles and kisses my forehead. I melt inside like the corny fool I am.

"Okay, I'll see you there."

Once I'm in the only pair of leggings I brought and my beat-up running shoes, I meet him on the deck. The sun has already peaked today and it's on its way down. There is a little trail off the deck that leads to the woods. We walk around the edge of the lake. Since there are no people on Jet Skis disturbing nature, a few ducks have settled to float on the water.

"It's so nice and calm here," I say, hands deep in my hoodie pockets. The breeze is cool thanks to the water. Even in early March, Westray can get fairly hot, but temperatures tend to be cooler in the mountains.

"Right? I woke up this morning and forgot I had come here yesterday."

"How was your drive with Anna, by the way?" We bump arms for a second.

He snorts. "She was mostly talking with Ophelia about all the things she planned to do here. She asked me about you, but I didn't answer because privacy."

"Thanks."

He holds his hand out to me and I grin, taking it and letting our fingers interlace. "I know you're a private person too."

"I am. I don't like surprises, they unsettle me." He moves over a root, pulling me toward him so I don't fall over it.

"Oh, I *unsettle* you." I get really close. "That's nice to know."

"Sunshine, you scared the hell out of me. Crashing into my life out of nowhere. And there you were, at the library. Suddenly you were everywhere, even my grandparents knew you. At the beginning I was upset, but the more I got to know you, the better I understood why you did certain things. When I learned about your mom, it's like everything clicked."

We stop walking, and I can't see the lake house anymore, it blends so well with its surroundings. Ethan and I are standing in a little clearing with grass beginning to grow into wilderness; a few birds sing overhead.

"It doesn't make how we first met right." When I look up at him, I grab a hold of his other hand, taking in the expression on his face.

Ethan tilts his head to the side. "No, it doesn't, but it feels like we were meant to meet. You make me happy, Soledad."

I wrap my arms around his neck, having to tiptoe a little, and hug him as tight as I can.

"You do, too, even if I want to fight you sometimes."

"Just sometimes?"

"A lot of times, but don't you ruin this moment." I can feel him let out a breath before kissing the top of my head.

We continue walking up the trail, stopping every now and then to steal a kiss. The path becomes steeper, and sometimes he has to help me climb. Finally, we get to a high point that overlooks the lake, which shines triumphantly blue like the sky, shimmering reflections of the sun. The trees around it follow its contours perfectly. We are in the valley between two mountains, and they rise around us like gentle giants, stark shades of green trees and gray to blue rock reaching for the sky.

I wish I could take a picture all of this, take my old camera out and capture this moment. When Mom left the country, I found it near impossible to go through my old pictures. They were little memories frozen in time that I refused to look at. They reminded me of an era that had been closed off to me. A hobby that brought me joy at one point no longer felt appealing when I became unhappy with my place in life. I couldn't pick up my camera after that.

However, as I walk through the vivid scenery, I feel oddly at peace with the thought of framing this moment up if I could.

Maybe I can start again.

"Holy shit, this is gorgeous." Ethan is standing with a hand against the side of the mountain, not going anywhere near the edge, which is where I am currently standing. I almost forgot he was scared of heights until he tensed up at the sight. "Crazy how we'll only get to see this once."

"Who knows?" I walk next to him; he wraps his right arm around me and pulls me close, and I rest my cheek against his collarbone. "Maybe the club will bring us back again next year."

"Maybe." He kisses me, his lips soft against mine. It never occurred to me before how different people show affection, but every time Ethan kisses me, I feel nothing but warmth in my chest. It's always so careful and caring. "I'm glad I'm here right now, with you."

"Me too." I look up at him. "I really liked meeting your grandparents last week. You were right, they didn't deserve what I did."

His lips pout as he breathes out. "My grandparents have always been involved with Westray. They raised me when things got complicated in my family without demonizing either of my parents, they've donated to the school and other charities, and they're literally the coolest pair of eighty-year-olds out there."

"I know I'm a bad person for still doing it."

"I don't think that's the way to look at it. It was a dumb choice and I was so pissed when it happened, but look at where we are now. You've apologized many times, I think it's time I accept your apology."

"You hadn't accepted it yet?"

"Acceptance comes in stages, sunshine." He rests his head back on top of mine. "We're good now, though."

"Good."

We stay on top of that lookout point for a while, seeing the sun high up in the sky as it marks the afternoon, and the clouds moving like slow boats in a sea of blue, the landscape becoming reminiscent of an expressionist painting, with different spurts of color mixing in. It makes me so happy to be here with him—no matter how we met, or where we go from here, right now it feels good to be in this moment.

Going down is a lot harder than going up. More so because that's when you realize the strain your limbs made while hiking and the climb starts catching up to you.

Once we're back on the dock, we see people gathering in the kitchen thanks to the glass walls.

"You guys!" Scott says as we enter the kitchen. He's holding about five boxes of pizza. "Homegirl Anna came through with lunch."

Anna, sitting on the kitchen counter and smiling, shrugs. "What can I say? I'm pretty awesome. It was a long drive but I made it back in time for a late lunch."

"Truly, the queen we deserve." Ophelia laughs and opens one of the pizza boxes.

As everyone sits around the kitchen island, passing plastic plates and pizza boxes, I look at Anna. She's laughing along with the jokes, eating pizza, and acting like her normal self.

Something feels off, though.

Ethan looks at me with a smile on his face and squeezes my shoulder as he makes his way to the first pizza box, Scott already pulling out another bottle of iced tea from the fridge. Anna turns in my direction, hand holding a can of soda, and shoots me a wink.

Maybe I'm overthinking things again.

We have another Mario Kart contest later that night. Afterward, Alan tosses some hot dogs onto the grill and we all hang out and talk about our lives. The fire pit comes alive with our stories once more as the stars twinkle in the sky above our heads. The shadows of the woods around us appear less mysterious and more homely.

After Scott describes all the ways he's broken a large majority of his bones, we decide it's time to head back inside. Once in the living room of the house, we settle down with some ice cream and Alan browses through some movies before choosing the first horror movie he can find. Xiu and Angela mention they're not the biggest fans of the genre, so they head up to their room to watch TV on their own.

Ethan and I sit on the edge of the large, C-shaped sofa, and I tuck my legs close to my body, resting my head against his chest as the movie starts.

"This is nice," he whispers, setting his cheek against the top of my head. "I'm glad I'm here with you."

"Me too." The reality of this fact surprises me a little. Being in a room with people I used to think of as strangers, who have now become a bizarre group of friends, lying next to someone I can call my boyfriend is a simple but true form of happiness I wasn't aware I had available before.

I'm happy, and the moment I feel Ethan's arm around me bring me closer to him, I know he is too. It's as if the universe saw me running all this time and noticed the ache in my muscles, and for the first time has told me I can take a rest. It's comforting and gentle, a sort of calm I didn't know I needed and that, for a moment, allows me to breathe a little easier.

CHAPTER TWENTY-TWO

The light that cuts through the white curtains at the lake house wakes me up the following morning. The room is cold, and when I turn to my side, I notice Ophelia has stolen most of the blanket we were sharing. She is still fast asleep, and I wrestle with the idea of going back to bed for another hour or so, but decide against it and instead sit up to stretch my arms.

Anna's side of the room is empty.

I tiptoe out of the room, trying not to wake our still-slumbering roommate, and close the door behind me. Thankfully, the bathroom is empty.

I take a bath to soothe my sore muscles from the hike yesterday. Also, when you have a crazy nice marble tub, you *have* to take a bath. There is an assortment of bath bombs on the sink of the bathroom with a note that says we can use them. The pile seems smaller than it was yesterday, so I'm sure some of the other girls also took advantage.

While I'm soaking, I text my mom and dad that I'm okay and having fun. Then I watch some YouTube videos on my phone. Once the water turns lukewarm, I get out.

I get dressed, and since I didn't get my hair wet, I unbraid it and let the partially stiff waves down over my shoulders.

Because it's early in the morning, and I'm assuming everyone is asleep, the best option is to watch Netflix in the living room. As I turn to the main hall that leads to the stairway down, I nearly bump into Carlos, who looks like he just saw a ghost.

"Are you okay?"

He doesn't look at me.

"Carlos." I put a hand on his shoulder and he startles. "Are you okay?"

"Sorry." He runs a hand through his hair, slipping his phone into the pocket of his jeans. Clearly he's been up longer than I have, which is mildly surprising considering how many times I've had to continually call him to get him up and ready for class.

"What's wrong?"

"Nothing."

"It's not nothing. You think I don't know you like the back of my hand?"

He looks at me for a couple of seconds, then grabs my elbow and nearly sprints down the hall. I don't ask questions. I've never seen him like this. Our steps intensify throughout the house as we make our way to the first floor. I wouldn't be surprised if the other members wake up because of us.

We arrive at the laundry room and once inside, he closes the door and speaks in a hushed tone.

"Look, no one can know this yet because we're still getting information. Someone spoke."

"What do you mean?" I whisper.

"Someone talked about the club to the police. Names, phone numbers, everything." Carlos swallows. "Someone on the board messaged Anna yesterday. There is a full-on police investigation of the club and its members. Of us."

The realization of what he's saying falls over me like ice water or a punch to the stomach. Thoughts fly as my mind tries to find a way to properly make sentences.

"Carlos, are you . . . joking?"

"I wish I was." He moves back to the door. "We're told we need to go back to Westray as soon as possible, so after everyone has had breakfast she's going to break the news to them. Anna is going to drop by the police station to make a statement because we don't want them coming after every single member."

He keeps talking but I can't hear.

I can't breathe.

I put a hand against my chest as if that might help me make words. Carlos puts his hands on my shoulders; his mouth is moving but I don't understand anything he is saying. The world feels unstable around us, like the floor is about to give out at any moment and the only thing that is tethering me to the now are his hands on me.

When I was little, about six or seven, my family went out to the lake I took Ethan to, and while my dad and I were on a boat fishing, I slipped and fell into the water. I didn't know how to swim then, and panicked. Every time I'd try to push up into the surface it felt like I was only dragging myself down. I was drowning, there was no way up or down, only the everlasting embrace of the water, until my father pulled me out.

Right now, in the laundry room of the lake house, it feels almost like that. It's like waking up all over again in that hospital room. Bad news being delivered all over again.

I'm being investigated by the police.

"My parents are going to kill me," I choke out. "I'm going to get kicked out of school for this."

I don't know how we end up on the floor, Carlos holding me close.

"Sol, breathe, you're going to be okay."

"Carlos, I'm going to go to jail."

"No, you're not. We're all going to be okay."

"And if I go to jail, what if they don't accept my request to bring my mom back in the country. I'd have a record, I'd . . ." I trail off, the sudden terror of the thought of never seeing my mother again gripping me at the throat.

After a minute or two, I manage to pull myself together. Carlos is going through this, too, and I'm not going to fall apart in front of him again. He's seen enough of me falling apart over the last year, and I have to be there for him no matter what.

"It'll be okay," I say, though my heart is still beating terribly against my rib cage.

Maybe if I lie enough I will believe it.

We leave the laundry room. Scott, Alan, Xiu, and Melina are in the living area; some have bowls of cereal on their lap, and they're watching *Jeopardy!*.

Scott perks up when we walk in.

"These fools are getting the simplest questions wrong. You wanna join us?"

"Yep," Carlos says.

"Sol, are you okay?" Xiu asks.

The room still feels like it's spinning a little and I don't trust in myself to not say anything about what's happening, so instead I think up the first excuse I can to get out of this situation.

"I think the pizza didn't sit well with me. I'm going for a walk to get some fresh air." Carlos looks at me and I nod; he understands I don't want to be around when the news finally drops.

As soon as I am far enough from the house, I run. It's hard not to trip on the twisting roots of the trees.

I follow the same path Ethan and I used yesterday, but instead of climbing up, I continue along the lake. The water blurs until I have to stop and rest my hands on my knees.

The sound of my blood rushing in my ears is the only thing I can hear aside from my desperate struggle to breathe. My hair sticks to the sweat on my face, and my skin is as hot as the stones baking in the sun.

My legs feel weak, so I sit on one of the large roots by a tree overlooking the lake.

I did this to myself.

Everyone calls me Sol because I ask them to, because I always felt like my name is too sad. Soledad means loneliness in Spanish. It feels so fitting now.

My phone vibrates more than once but I don't bother to look at it. A black bird flies down and perches next to me. We gaze at the water, the currents carrying leaves and ducks by. The next moment, it flies away and I'm alone again.

"It seems like I scared your bird friend," Anna says, sitting in the bird's spot. "Ethan was losing his mind looking for you. I told him I'd find you."

"I don't understand," I mumble, tears brimming in my eyes. "Why the hell are you so calm through all of this? You're always on top of everything. You said nothing would happen and here we fucking are. I—"

She doesn't seem phased at all by my words, her eyes focused on the lake in front of us. I want to stand up and shake her, scream and demand that she do something with this stupid club she keeps praising.

"Everyone responded differently to the news." She extends her legs, her bright neon-blue shoes contrasting starkly with the ground. "Xiu and Angela shut down, Melina stormed to her room, Ethan got really angry, and then you have Scott, who said he was going to drop out anyway."

"Do you really not care?"

"I care a lot, Sol—don't think that because I've learned to handle my emotions better than most doesn't mean that I don't care what happens to me or other people. You have no idea what I've been through with this organization."

"Then why do you never say anything? Why the hiding information, why the stupid dares to get in?"

"Why do fraternities haze the freshmen? Why do other organizations ask you for ridiculous amounts of money? Why did you or anyone else accept to doing that dare, Soledad?" The sound of the water fills in the void her words leave. "You wanted to be a part of something, you wanted to belong because anywhere else you felt inadequate. You think I don't understand that? Do you know how hard it was for me to get here in the first place?

"It's tradition. The members have connections, we all benefit from knowing each other, there have been years of this, and no one's said anything until now. It's about who you know—how else do you think we're here? What do you think we're all doing except making connections that can help us get ahead later in life when it really matters? You want to be able to own a house like this one day? *You* made a sacrifice, *you* put your neck on the line.

"This isn't Princeton or Columbia, Sol, it's a small community college in a small town where nothing will change no matter how much time passes. To put your name out there you have to be brave enough to take risks."

"I *can't* afford to take risks, though!"

"You did! You did and so did I, and so did everyone. It's not a death sentence. In fact, it's hardly a jail sentence."

"I can't even afford that! My life is on the line, my mother is on the line!"

"Then why did you do it, Soledad?" she screams back, and for a moment I can't hear the lake or the trees anymore, only the pounding of my own heart. "Why did you do it?"

"I—" Different reasons come to mind. Carlos, my resumé, Mom encouraging me to join organizations, the flashy flyers, the fact it happened to be a club related to my major, but none ring true to me. Nothing but the void inside my rib cage feels true.

"Figures." She sighs.

I want to yell and tell her she's wrong, that somehow there's something different about what I did to get here, but every time I start chasing that thought, I end up in the same place.

"Are we all going to be expelled?" My voice sounds like sandpaper.

Anna sighs. "Honestly, Sol, I'm not sure what's going to happen. I'm going to call up the founder and see what's going to happen next, possibly a hearing with the school. Then depending on what happens there, they might start charging different things, especially the criminal cases." She turns to me, the mention alone knots my stomach over. "There's no deaths or drug intake, surely there's something that can be used as college kids doing stupid shit. Vandalism, breaking and entering, as well as some stealing is as far as we go. At the moment, the most we can do is head back to town."

"Do you know who it was?"

She rests her chin on top of her knees. "I have a good idea, but this isn't the time to point fingers. I don't want the risk of fights breaking out in a place that doesn't belong to us."

"I'm guessing you're not allowed to talk about it either."

"You would be guessing right."

I grab a small rock and toss it at the lake, the plop in the water followed by a slumbering silence. Ducks float peacefully along the water; the world is peaceful around this perimeter of chaos.

"What's going to happen?"

"I don't know."

"Tell me anything, Anna, goddamn it. At least tell me what the other members did so I can have an idea of what everyone is getting into. It's not fair that we're in the dark at all points."

"Melina went up to the bridge at the entrance of Westray and had to spray paint WCCHS on it, we go by the history club so history society is not necessarily a given. She did this while hanging some twenty feet above the river underneath it. Angela was given a series of tasks that ended up with her digging in the local graveyard under the oldest grave, from the gold rush era, to retrieve a medallion that was placed there for her. It's something creepy, especially at two in the morning.

"Xiu had to convince her boss in the biology department to lend her keys for the lab. After school she took some chemicals and used those to damage a photograph of the past chairman of the Liberal Arts department. No one found out, of course. And, well, you know what Ethan did. I vandalized school property, Carlos nearly damaged his self-image, and Ophelia had to go into the mines area, which is closed to the public, and find something placed for her there. Scott broke into the college president's office, and Alan stole an artifact from the archive." She pauses and turns to me, her bright hair falling over her cheek. "Feel any better?"

Pacing around, I chase for something else to demand from her, some sort of divine explanation that will make everything make sense again. Then again, nothing about this made sense from the very beginning. She might be right—the club might have the connections to get us out of this mess. After all, she did say other members had been found out before, but the way she's reacted doesn't appease any of my fears.

The biggest one being me staining my record and that jeopardizing any future petitions for my mother's citizenship. It was a thought so far away from me, the realization still makes my lungs compress. I risked too much for gilded coins, foolishly believing we were untouchable. I should have known better, I should have *done* better.

The possibility of a happy future is crumbling in front of me, like a boat sinking into the water. I've once more taken a decision in my life that has the power of breaking me in half, and just like last year, I can do nothing but watch in horror as it unravels.

"No." There's strain in my voice, words that could be used left unsaid. I straighten up, feeling the weight of my own body, the ache in my feet from running and hiking, the tiredness of my soul as I turn away from Anna and make my way back to the lake house.

CHAPTER TWENTY-THREE

Aside from the soft jazz music playing on the radio, Scott's van is deadly silent. We hit the road sometime after five in the afternoon. Our rooms, the bathrooms, and the kitchen had to be cleaned to a certain extent, but Anna assured us there was a professional cleaning crew coming.

I rest my head on Ethan's lap. We're in the back of the van, with all of our luggage. I watch the trees blend into each other out the window. Ethan is stroking my hair absently, headphones plugged in, eyes lost in the landscape too.

We get to Westray around nine thirty. We drop the girls off one by one. They don't say good-bye, everyone lost in their own world.

Alan gets dropped off next. He leans over and kisses Scott so quickly that I nearly wonder if I made that up.

Next is my apartment.

"You're going to be okay," Ethan says, giving me a hug as I reach for the handle of the door. I nod, shouldering my backpack before leaning in and brushing my lips against his.

Stepping onto the sidewalk, I watch Scott give me a military salute before he drives off.

There is a cool breeze rolling through town that I take a moment to appreciate. I let myself smell Westray. Like wet earth, when you don't know whether it will rain or not, the uncertainty of it making you pack an umbrella.

My keys jingle as I unlock the door. My cat is asleep on Dad's lap as he watches crime shows on our old TV.

"How was your trip?" he asks.

I drop my duffel bag on the floor and cry. Awful, ugly sobbing. Michi meows and the next moment Dad is kneeling in front of me, because I'd fallen to the floor.

He places a can of Coke in front of me. We are finally using the small kitchen table that we seldom sit at. The light in the kitchen is the only one on at the moment, making this feel a bit like an interrogation scene. My body shakes with hiccups every now and then, but I've stopped shedding tears. I feel like an empty shell.

Dad didn't speak at all while I blabbered everything to him. "So, are the police going to come look for you here, or what's going to happen?"

I shake my head. "I don't know, I don't think so." My lips feel dry. "They said the police are conducting an investigation, but no one knows what that really means. If they were looking for us, they would have already come to each of our houses."

"Well, I feel responsible for what's happening, corazón."

"What, why?"

"I thought we taught you better, that you'd recognize not to . . . to willingly join some sort of thing like this." He's looking down at his beer, forehead resting against one of his palms. "I don't want to say I'm disappointed, Soledad, but I feel like you pushed yourself too much and you put yourself in unnecessary risk."

"Papi, don't." I was wrong, I *can* cry more. "All I wanted was to make you and Mom proud of me, but there's nothing I can do and I—"

"Soledad, your mom and I are already proud of you. It wasn't necessary for you to get in a club or anything like that. Seeing you grow from a girl into a young woman is enough to make your mother and I happy. But right now, I feel like I don't recognize you."

"I'm sorry, papi."

He puts his hand on mine, finally looking at me. His face is weathered from the sun, wrinkles on his forehead are strained, and his eyes are tired. It's this that hurts me more than what he said to me. There's been stress added to his life that wasn't there before—trust was breached, and aside from his work and his wife, now he has his daughter to worry about.

I did that.

"I know you are, baby. Your mom and I are here for you, but whatever the consequences we taught you to know you must face them."

"I'm going to call your mom." He gets up. "You should get some rest."

Michi follows me closely to my room, meowing for attention. I can't even bring myself to be cheerful for her.

My room is as I left it, the bedsheets messily scattered because of how early I woke up on Friday. I place my bag on the floor by my desk. My laptop, still broken, serves as a paperweight for the exams I had been studying for.

In the mirror I see how truly horrible I look after having cried nonstop for about an hour.

As I sit in my rotating chair, I check my phone. Ethan called twice, Carlos texted, and strangely enough Angela both called and sent a string of three messages all with the same five words:

Angela: Please call me. It's important

While I want nothing more than to ignore everyone and go to sleep for the next couple of days, I dial her number.

"Sol?"

"Hey, I got your messages."

"Thank you so much. I know it's superlate, and with everything that has been going on I didn't expect you to reply, but I'm glad you did." She pauses. "You're a nice girl, Sol, and I know you and Ethan have this whole thing going on, which is great. He kind of got roped into all of this because of you, and what we did was different compared to other clubs, but everyone had their bag of stones with them, you feel me?"

"Angela, what are you getting at? I'm not following you at all." Angela and I aren't very close—I've had some encounters with her in the past, but nothing that indicates friendship.

"We all knew what we were doing was not good. Really it was more me and Xiu, but Ethan was involved at the beginning."

"What is it? Spit it out."

"I was the one who called the police. At the beginning it was me, Xiu, and Ethan. We had been planning it since we joined the club because it's not right what they make members do. That time at the festival, I mentioned knowing Ethan from a class to see if you knew that Ethan and I knew each other, but he pretended he didn't, so I figured he hadn't told you about it yet.

"Then afterward Ethan wanted out because of you, and then you guys started dating, so Xiu and I decided to keep going. The trip to the lake was the perfect time because no one would expect it."

I have no words.

"I'm sorry. You're not the only member I want to apologize to, but I don't regret it. Please don't be mad at Ethan. There are rumors about the history club everywhere, but no one thought it was true. When we found out about it and what happened to Ethan and possibly will happen to other people in the future, we didn't think should go on."

I press End Call faster than a lightning strike and get up. Strange energy flows through my limbs as I grab the keys to my bike lock and run out of my room.

Dad is still sitting on a chair outside on the balcony, so he doesn't see me as I sneak out the front door.

Westray is cool outside. The breeze carries the static of a storm nearing and a few droplets fall on me as I pedal. The wind sings in my ears and my breath becomes heavy with the strain of going as fast as I can along the middle of our little streets. This late at night there are not many cars, so I take the liberty of avoiding the speed bumps by riding between them.

By the time I get to Ethan's house my energy is so high I nearly jump off my bike, letting it fall on the sidewalk as I march to the front door and ring the doorbell. When there is no answer, I call him on my phone.

No answer.

I find the tree that I fell from, grab a pebble, and toss it. It misses. I try again, I miss again. This happens about five times before I finally land the window.

"Sol?" I finally see his face as he pushes open his window. Flashbacks of when we first met and he looked at me from the same spot make my stomach twist. "What are you doing, I was nap—"

"You idiot!" I scream, tears welling up again. "You helped them! I thought I'd gained your trust, I thought you liked me."

His eyebrows dip together and then his entire expression falters, understanding softening his features as he covers his eyes.

"Soledad, please listen to me."

"You never even mentioned it."

"I tried!"

"No, you didn't!"

"I did, but you seemed so happy, and I was scared of taking that away. I told the girls not to do it because of you!" Ethan moves away from the window, hands on his head, before returning just as fast. "I asked you multiple times if what you thought was going on was okay and you'd give me these mixed signals. I didn't want to hurt you, especially after you met my grandparents—I learned so much about you."

"It's not only me, Ethan! It's my family! It's the other members! I'm not the only member of the fucking club." I'm tired of screaming, tired of being angry and sad, and everything in between. "I'm going home. Don't call me."

"Wait, Sol!"

I ignore him and walk back to my bike. My limbs ache, as do my eyes; all my body wants to do now is shut down. As I'm about to get on, he opens the front door and sprints toward me.

His hand grabs mine, but I recoil, "Don't touch me."

Ethan backs away. "I'm sorry, Sol."

"It's over. My parents won't look at me the same way again, they won't trust me anymore. I might have ruined any way for my mom to come back . . . it's all my fault." The relationship with my parents was crafted through hardships, and while I know we'll be able to get through this together, it won't be the same as before. I willingly kept things from them, and that will leave an emotional scar I hope time will heal. "I really liked you, Ethan, I really did. But my life is hard enough without this bullshit."

"Sol, you've got to think about what you did for the club."

"What did I do for the club? You said we might have been meant to meet. You said you were okay with me feeling guilty about breaking into your place, but aside from that what did I *do*? I went to meetings, I volunteered for the archive, and I made friends. I helped *you* break the law. What did I do Ethan? I helped keep secrets? Guess what? So did you." I think of what Anna told me about the other members, the things even Xiu and Angela did to become a part of the organization. "We all played a part in this, and I know things will get resolved one way or the other, whatever that might look like, but you could have said something to me. I promised to get your things back to you, you could have at least told me what you were planning."

"Sol, please."

"You got what you wanted. You have your key back, the club is gone, and I'll probably end up in jail. Might be a miracle if I ever get to see my mom again." I get on my bike, readying my foot on the pedal. "Justice was served."

He calls my name once more but I can't hear him as the wind picks up around me. Rain begins pouring shortly after, soaking my clothes as I pedal back home.

CHAPTER TWENTY-FOUR

The police department in Westray is a sight to behold when you're wondering whether or not you'll be detained inside of it. It is made out of red bricks, and all of its windows are barred with thick black iron. Inside, the floors are a pale beige and the walls are painted a pasty blue, and, like a hospital, it carries that strange feeling with it, as if no one should be there and yet people end up in there no matter what.

Dad didn't speak a single word as he drove me here a couple of minutes ago. He has been tense since yesterday, and while Mom and I haven't spoken yet, I know she's likely as worried as he is.

I have to do this, though. No matter what happens, I have to try doing the right thing.

"Soledad Gutierrez?" An officer walks out of the office into the little lobby in which I've been waiting. The woman who took my information glances quickly at us before looking back down at her paperwork.

It would have been easier to call and give an anonymous tip; in fact, maybe that would have been the smarter thing to do, but I haven't been able to sleep since last night.

"Yes, sir, that's me." I get up, making sure to keep a safe distance from him. Dad says officers don't like to feel like you're trying to intimidate them. He gave me a lot of tips on how to act around the police and how to comply. I can only imagine it's from so many years of being afraid of being found out as illegal, and later on being scared of his wife being found out.

"Please follow me." He makes a motion with his hand and I walk silently behind him.

We make our way past the security door and enter a room where desks are laid out in an open area. A couple more officers are sitting and working on their computers; one of them is also on their phone. I half expected them to all turn to me with accusatory glares the moment I walked into the room, but none of them pay us any notice as we walk by. The officer takes me to an office on the right side of the building, separated from the open area by a glass wall and a wooden door.

"Please take a seat, Ms. Gutierrez." He moves past the chairs and into the back of his workstation. His desk is stacked high with papers and in a bit of a disarray, but the center is clear of any objects, and a small golden plaque tells me his last name is Salazar.

"What can I do for you today?" It's a simple question, something that shouldn't cause panic to rise up my throat and make me want to bolt out the door.

"I'd like to report some illicit activities going on at Westray

Community College." This wouldn't be the first time they're hearing about it if Angela and Xiu already reported what was happening. His face shows no sign of either surprise or knowledge of my comment, instead he nods and takes out a small notebook and a pen from his breast pocket.

"What would you like to report?" he asks.

"So, what you told them?" Dad asks when I open the passenger door of his truck. From the faint smell of tobacco in the air I can tell he's been waiting desperately for me to get out of that building.

"I didn't say any names, or which things I took part in, but I told them the truth." The engine comes alive with a loud whine at the beginning, the sun outside tinting the earth a yellowy brown. It's about to become spring but the heat of summer feels like an omnipresent god, the fear of fire season escalating every day. "We'll see how the system works now."

"You feel better?" You know things are serious when Dad tries to communicate with me in English. It shows he's giving his full attention to the matter. I'm not too sure when I began noticing this trend, but it's his thing.

"No. *Pero vamos a ver que pasa.*" We'll see how it goes.

He sighs, reaching over and cranking on his old radio. Los Tigres Del Norte's "La Jaula de Oro" plays as we drive back home. I move over and roll down the window, resting my head against the ledge and letting the warm air brush over my face.

Shelving books at the library is soothing. Once you get the hang of the alphabetical and numerical method, you pick a book from your cart and find its home. I have most of the floors in the library memorized by now—the halls filled with tomes might seem endless to some but their mazelike structure brings me a sense of serenity.

It has been three days since we returned from the lake house. Two days since I filed a report at the police station. Aside from Angela and Ethan, I've heard nothing from the other members, nor have I tried to reach out to them.

On Monday evening, we received a message via Anna through the group chat.

> Anna: So here's what's happening. We had a hearing with the Department of Student Involvement here at Westray Community College and are now being dismantled as an organization over the leaked material and the club and its members are now being investigated by the police
>
> Anna: The police are looking to classify our group as an extralegal organization and this could mean that they could come after any member of the group as a co-conspirator. What's important to know is that in these types of investigations the focus tends to be around the leadership or people that they can prove without doubt participated in illegal activity. Someone went through my bag and dorm and took some of the members' items. I have now found out who this person is, but I will not make it publicly known after their request

Anna: All information had to be turned in to the author-
ities and they will be cross-referencing for validity the
statements given by me and Carlos. Be calm at all
times and cooperate with law enforcement. The past
members as well as the founder of the club and I will
ensure all steps are followed so nothing falls on your
shoulders, however this might change based on the
scenario and charges pressed by other individuals

Anna: I'll keep you in the loop as things come up

Only Scott answered her messages with a link to Sarah
McLachlan's "Angel."

It felt strange reading those messages while brushing my teeth
before school that morning. It was a confirmation that this was
really happening, and even when she assured us we would be
okay, I couldn't help but feel like the earth was going to crumble
underneath my feet at any given time.

Of course, I called my mom. Our talk went a lot like my
talk with Dad, except with fewer tears. She never said she was
disappointed in me; in fact, she didn't say much aside from men-
tioning things would work themselves out.

Now we are all waiting, wondering what might happen next.
For the last couple of days all I've been waiting for is for someone
in a uniform to come to talk to me about everything.

"Hey, Sol."

Miranda peeks her head over the edge of the aisle. Slowly, a
police officer walks around her. "This gentleman would like to
speak with you."

It is bizarre how I was mentally preparing for this already, and
yet seeing him standing in front of me again is as nerve-racking
as the first time.

"Absolutely," I say as if I have never seen him in my life before, putting my book on the shelf and walking toward them, making sure to keep a safe and nonthreatening distance. "Soledad Gutierrez at your service, sir."

He's in his late twenties, and despite the circumstances I have to admit he's good looking. Light-brown skin, well shaved, and with a buzz cut that suits him very well.

"Ms. Gutierrez, I am Officer Salazar. My partner and I are here to ask you a few questions about an organization you were allegedly a part of." He's holding up a little notepad. I wonder how many members they've interrogated already. Or if he still has the notes from Monday. "Is all of this okay with you?"

"Yes, sir." Dad mentioned how police need warrants if they want to arrest you at home or work. He also went into what to expect in an interrogation. Sometimes the places he worked at got raided by ICE and he would get asked if he worked with any illegal immigrants, but aside from your identification the police can't ask you for answers you don't want to give.

"Just say, I don't wish to answer, *pero calmadamente*, and they legally can't make you say anything."

"You are not being arrested, Ms. Gutierrez, and you are free to leave at any time, and do not have to answer any questions. Do you still wish to talk with us?" He knows I do, after all he's the same person who took my statement at the station.

"Yes, sir."

"Please follow me, Ms. Gutierrez." The officer smiles and I wonder if it's supposed to bring me some sort of comfort. I've never truly trusted the police, considering how risky it was to have my mom around; after she got deported I felt the same. While I understand they are doing their job, I can't help but feel slightly uneasy as we walk between the shelves that usually are my sanctuary.

As we walk through the library, the other students stare at us. Would any of them figure out a way to take another video of me? Who knows? At this point, if the worst is that I lose my job, I'll consider myself lucky.

He takes me to a study room where another officer, a woman who looks like she could be a student here, and who has high cheekbones and piercing hazel eyes, is waiting.

The male officer says, "Please take a seat, this won't take long. We've gotten most of the information needed from you already."

I choose a chair against the wall so he won't think I'm trying to escape. He takes a seat as well, pulling his little notebook and a black ballpoint pen from one of his pockets once more. I thought this was going to be a good cop-bad cop scenario, but the female officer leaves and stands in front of the door.

I guess that kills any chance of escaping.

"My partner and I have been investigating a case regarding the history club here at WCC. As you mentioned before, you are a member and were part of some of said activities, however we still have further details to iron out."

"Yes, sir. I'll try to answer them as best as I can."

"Thank you." He clicks his pen once and flips over his notes. *How many people has he questioned already?* I imagine him at the Winstons' house, or maybe at Ethan's work. Even though I was the one who cut things off, I hope he's okay.

"We've been informed that you joined the organization earlier this winter, after one of your friends recruited you last December. Your 'trial' as they called it was to break into the oldest house in town and steal something from said property. Is that correct?"

I knot my fingers underneath the table. "Yes, sir, it is."

He writes something down on the notepad and I notice that one of his fingers is callused from what I assume is the way he holds the pen. "Ms. Gutierrez, were you fully aware you were committing a criminal activity while fulfilling your duty to this club, specifically a misdemeanor by breaking and entering private property?"

One . . . two . . . three . . . four . . . I could bolt

"Yes, sir."

"Ms. Gutierrez, were you at any point complicit with any other illegal activities performed by other members of this organization?"

I think of Ethan. Of the way he held me against the wall at the archive, keeping us from being caught. Why did he do that if he wanted all of this to be found out?

"Yes, sir." I clear my throat. "We stayed past closing time at the historical archive to ring the bell. It wasn't breaking and entering, though."

"Who was with you that night, Ms. Gutierrez?"

Ethan, who so delicately brushed his fingers against my cheek, saying how I made him happy. The press on top of my head as we watched the lake from the cliff. Him laughing when I made him pinkie promise. Checking on me at the pool party to make sure I was okay.

"I choose not to answer that question, sir."

He looks at me for a moment, and my stomach tenses. Then he nods, writes on the paper, and puts it inside the folder.

"Were you part of any of the following club initiation processes including, but not limited to: vandalism to WCC property, vandalism to City of Westray property, desecration of graves at the local cemetery, disorderly conduct, trespassing on private property, or unlawful break-ins at WCC?" He taps the pen at each of these mentions.

I glance at the glass door of the study room. The other cop is still guarding the door. How much have the other members told him? I told him all I could the first time I met him, so are most of these questions simply routine?

"Before you answer that question, I would like to mention that one of the chemicals used to deface the photograph of Chairman Warwick is also a precursor chemical in the manufacturing of explosives." He pauses, holding my gaze as his tapping stops. "If I wanted to, I could involve the Department of Homeland Security and have each and every one of you wrapped up as being a part of a terrorist organization."

My mouth parts. This escalated really quickly from being a mere precursor chemical to the *t* word being dropped. I can't imagine the thought of Xiu sitting down where I am today, going over the possibility of having my life ruined by a liquid in a bottle. Then again, she was one of the ones who turned us over, and maybe did that on purpose.

"Now, I don't want to do that. I would like to think that this was a prank that got wildly out of hand, but I need you to be candid with me and tell me what I need to know."

I shake my head. The prank was a completely different mess that I was not involved with, and I plan to keep it that way.

"No, sir, I was only involved in the first one you asked me about and the one I mentioned."

"Any involvement in the *planning* of such events?"

"No, sir."

He looks at me and makes sure I maintain eye contact.

Whether he sees another college student doing something dumb to impress their friends or a petty criminal who'll one day do something like this again and will amount to nothing in life, I can't tell. Maybe he sees a sister or a cousin, or perhaps he's thinking about lunch. No matter what, I try to keep my expression at ease.

"I think this wraps up our interview. We might have more questions in the future. Why don't you let us know if you plan on leaving the state." He closes his notebook and stands up.

I'm a bit shaken by that, and without being able to help myself, a question flies out of me.

"Wait, that's all?"

Officer Salazar turns to me, hand on his breast pocket as he puts his pen away once more, notebook still in his other hand.

"Is it? Is there anything you'd like to talk about?"

"I, no, I don't know how to react. What happens now?"

"No one filed a police report for your break-in, Ms. Gutierrez. The victims refuse to press charges. As for your club, someone came forward and assumed all responsibility for their members. We're making sure all the facts line up. Contact us if there are any more details you would like to share. And if you ever do anything like that again, you won't get off with just a warning. You broke the law—do you know how serious that is?"

"Yes, sir."

I get up and follow him out of the room. My limbs feel like lead but also shake a little as we leave the little study room behind. The world is swaying around me as I try to regain my composure.

This was good—this was really freaking good—and yet I felt like something didn't add up.

The female cop looks at her partner and they both nod.

"Thank you for your time, Ms. Gutierrez," she says and they both walk away.

Someone assumed all responsibility for the members.

"Anna," I whisper. The lawyers and her assurance that everything would be okay still linger in the back of my mind, but as I see the cops walk away I wonder if there's something else at play.

I forgot how hard it is to bike under the sun just past midday. Weeks of rides to and from school have spoiled me. The good thing is Carlos's apartment is not too far, so I've only broken into a light sweat by the time I arrive.

Carlos is lucky he doesn't live with his parents anymore. He had offered to room together after we graduated from high school, but I couldn't afford to move out of Dad's place.

I knock on his door, three strong knocks followed by two short ones. Because I have to be annoying, I also send him a text.

> Me: I'm outside your place, are you home?

> Carlos: Just missed me, I went to get some stuff but I'll be back soon. You can get my key from the usual spot if you want

> Me: I'm good, I'll hang out by the park until you get here

> Carlos: Cool, I'll be back in like fifteen mins

Me: Bring me something to make up for it

Me: Preferably sweet

Carlos: Oh you know I will ;)

Carlos's apartment building has a little playground for kids, as well as a dog park. Sometimes after a late-night IHOP run we go to the playground to stargaze or play on the monkey bars.

I sit on one of the empty swings. The metal chains creak with the weight of my body as I push my feet back and let momentum move me back and forth a little. The park is well covered by the canopies of the trees, which makes the heat of the sun more bearable.

Picking up my phone, I call my mom via WhatsApp. Her last morning class is at noon, and it's currently two thirty in the afternoon. Night classes don't start until six.

"Hola, *mi amor*."

I smile, not sure why I expected her to still be mad. Mom has never been a very strict parent, that was more so Dad's job in the family, but even then he gave me a lot of space to stretch my wings. Whenever I'd see angry representations of Latino parents in movies and social media it made me wonder if I grew up different because of how distanced I was from my other relatives, because my parents have been nothing but kind and understanding throughout all the phases of my life.

"Hola, mami." A bird that looks a lot like the one at the lake sweeps down and lands on top of the monkey bars. "The police came to talk to me. I'm not going to jail."

"Thank God." She sounds like she's released all the air in her body. "I was praying to the *virgencita* these last few days, I was so worried."

"I know I disappointed you and Dad. I know that while trying to be the best I could be I became the worst I could be." I kick at the pebbles underneath the swing set. "I know I've failed you."

"Sol, you didn't fail us. I never expected you to be a perfect daughter, I love that you're imperfect."

The pebbles under my feet blur together as I blink.

"You wore yourself thin trying to do all these things you thought would make me proud that you didn't see you were failing *yourself.* That's what hurts me the most, Soledad, the fact you never spoke about how you felt to me and your dad."

"I'm sorry, Mom."

"I know you are. It'll take a while to earn our trust back, but know we're not angry at you. We're just hurt."

"I know." I wipe my face with the back of my free hand. "I love you."

"I love you, too, darling."

"I wish you were here."

"I wish I was there with you, too, honey. No matter how far away I am, know I still adore you and so does your dad, okay? Don't be afraid to talk with us." She sighs. "I have to go, I'm going to grab some lunch with a few of the teachers."

"That's okay. I'm meeting Carlos to talk about all of this."

"*Y le dices que no se junten con mala gente.*" Don't hang out with bad people. I know I can't tell her the people I hung out with weren't bad people; in fact, they were great folks to be around.

"Okay." The black bird flies away, which is a bit sad again. "Talk to you soon?"

"Yes."

"Was that your mom?" Carlos leans on one of the poles of the swing set, three grocery bags hanging from each hand. He has a slight tan after the two days at the lake house, but it looks good on him.

"Yep." I jump off the swing. "Need a hand?"

"That'd be nice." I take a hold of one of his bags and we move through the park and walk back to his apartment.

"Can we have the appetizer sampler, the New York cheesecake pancakes for me, and some chocolate chip for her?"

The waitress writes down our order, having left two vanilla iced coffees on the table.

"What's going to happen?" I ask, swirling away at the sugary syrup in the glass.

Carlos shrugs. "Legal stuff—Anna still sounds positive that we'll be okay. I might be called in to testify in court but members who didn't hold a position are not required to. Unless you're a key component like Angela and Xiu, maybe even Ethan. I'm worried about Anna most of all."

"I feel like I made a mistake."

Ethan has kept his distance, as I asked, which I appreciate yet grieve.

"My mom said my not talking to her or Dad hurt more than my mistakes. I told Ethan I felt hurt because he hadn't confided in me about his plans to bring the club down." IHOP's vanilla iced coffee triples your blood sugar levels, but I can't help but drink a quarter of it in one sip. "I blame him for doing exactly what I did. Maybe I made a mistake by breaking up with him on the spot."

"You know I feel responsible for everything that happened, right?" Carlos flicks a piece of his napkin at me. "I was the one who recruited you. Your parents will hate me for the rest of their lives."

"No, they love you." I smack his foot with mine. "Besides, I've already forgiven you. In the end, it was my choice to join. The mistakes I made were mine from the very beginning."

Carlos holds up one finger, then reaches inside his jacket and extracts an envelope.

"Anna gave me this a day ago, said it was the only thing they didn't take as evidence and that you'd know what to do with it." He places the envelope in the middle of the table. "As far as I'm concerned, meeting Ethan was not a mistake. You seemed happier, more in the moment, even."

Slowly I trace the outline of the waxy paper of the envelope. "I really was."

As far as my friendship with Carlos is concerned, I wouldn't change anything about it. He's always tried to help, even if the choices weren't stellar per se. He's been through the hardest thing to hit me before, and I'll be there for him no matter what. "How have your parents taken it by the way?"

"Well, Mom is furious, says she'll give me some *chanclazos* whenever she sees me next. Dad laughed." I'm not too surprised. His dad is very lenient. Carlos says it's because he's an American and more laid back than his mother. "I know she's worried sick but . . ."

The waitress arrives at our table to deliver our meal. The chicken tenders and mozzarella sticks are steaming hot and still have a few dabs of oil clinging to them. We take a moment to delight in the food, dipping a bit into our orders of pancakes before he continues.

"But I know I fucked up too. I don't even think I want to pursue a history minor; I think mathematics would help way more with my major." Carlos rubs his cheek to get a dab of strawberry syrup off his face.

"That's great, I'm happy that you've figured out what you want to fix with your career." Just like me in the lake, I think we all need to make decisions about what we want to do with our lives, otherwise life will choose for us.

"We won't get to hang out as often, though."

"Carlos, I've known you for, like, seven years of my life. I think no matter whether we see each other once a week or once a month, we'll be okay. Besides, we live in a small town—there's only so much area you can cover without bumping into me." I steal the mozzarella stick he was about to grab and take a bite in triumph. "After all this legal stuff blows over we'll be okay."

"Shit." He sits back. "You're right."

With a wink, I let him know I am aware of this. So we continue to eat and make jokes about the unforeseen, but welcome, future. Knowing that no matter what happens we'll make it through to the other side.

CHAPTER TWENTY-FIVE

Chiles rellenos are possibly one of my favorite dishes. They're also a pain to make. You have to roast the peppers and put them in a bag, pull the skin off, beat the egg whites, prepare the stuffing, fill the peppers, coat them in flour, coat them in egg, and then finally hope the egg fluff stays stuck to the pepper as it sizzles in a pan full of oil.

Usually my mom would make stuff like this while she made me cook yellow rice and refried beans. She'd make two types of filling, cheese and this ground beef *guisado*, with pieces of carrot, potato, onions, and spices, that was so good I'd scoop it out by itself on my plate.

While Mom is a fantastic cook, I'm content with not setting the kitchen on fire.

"*Pues*, they look really good." Mom smiles, serving herself cooked rice across the table. She looks better on my new laptop. Diane was right, graphics sometimes do make a difference.

"You're saying that to make me feel better." I scrunch up my nose and pass my dad a plate.

"En serio." She pauses. "From here I can't even tell they're burnt."

"Because they aren't Mom."

Dad laughs. "I'm not sure about that."

"You guys are rude."

"How's school?" Dad cuts up a piece of his chiles rellenos and runs it across his beans.

"Good. I'm going to study at Diane's tomorrow, and they scheduled me for a shift at the library on Sunday. I didn't lose my job—Miranda knew all about the history club and she said that college kids should be free to make mistakes and be forgiven. I'm lucky. They're also opening up the classes for next semester next week, so I'll have to come up with a rough list for what I want to take. Seniors get first pick, so my turn won't be until Thursday."

"No breaking into houses?" Mom takes a sip of her water.

"Nah, that's for next week."

We laugh. While I can't change the past, my parents have moved on . . . a bit. Mexican parents never let you live down your mistakes. They'll tease you about it until the end of time. At least they're past the we're-very-serious-during-calls-because-you-need-to-think-about-what-you've-done phase.

I scoop some rice onto my spoon. "I'm switching my major next semester."

Dad waits until he's done chewing before responding. "Really? Why?"

"History is not for me. It's not too late to change it, I need to meet with my advisor, which I'm planning on doing before I choose my fall classes." After I talked with Carlos at IHOP what he said resonated with me. It's not that I don't like history; in fact, I love learning about what happened in the past to understand how we can shape the future for the better.

I want to understand the system more, be able to help families like mine, who have been held up by a system that punishes you for wanting to be close to your family. A legal net that catches hardworking people with the same indiscrimination that catches criminals. I don't want kids fearing that their parents will be ripped out of their arms at any moment.

"What would you change it to?" Mom asks.

"Political science." I look at her. Perhaps there's nothing I can do now, or in many years, but there's a lot that I can learn in those years I will be waiting. "Switching my minor and major won't affect me, and I want to see if I can make a change, maybe even get into law school."

Mom and Dad look at each other from across the glass screen, eyebrows raised. Dad never finished high school and Mom was only allowed to get her associate degree due to her status where she lived at the time. The thought of their daughter striving for a law degree must be more than a little surprising, but that's okay with me. For the past year I've debated what to do with my life over and over, and now I think I'm finally starting to see a path I can follow.

Me: Hey Anna, I'm not reaching out through the group chat because I wanted to pick up on the last conversation we had

Me: You were right, I joined the club and did my dare
of my own volition. I even helped Ethan with his. I
think I was looking for acceptance as you said. I don't
think you were a bad president, in fact with this legal
ordeal and you taking the fall it shows that you truly
do care for the members

Me: In a way the club getting disbanded has lifted the
weight off my shoulders, I wonder
if it's the same for you

Me: I hope things work out, and maybe one day in
the future (if everything is still okay between us) we
can go for coffee and talk about it. Carlos would
probably be down too

Me: Also, I have no idea when you'll be reading this
if at all, but thank you for the gift. I do know exactly
what to do with it

After exam season is over, fewer students gather at the coffee
shops on campus, aside from the hipsters and art kids typing
their novels. Calm saxophone and piano music drifting in the
background is a nice change from the quiet of the library, where
I had been for the past four hours.

One of the bells placed on top of the two entrances to the
café jingle, and I immediately meerkat to see who's come in.

I might have been doing that for the last fifteen minutes,
but this time Ethan stands at the threshold. We lock eyes for

a second. Thank God he responded positively to my message about meeting here.

"Hey," I say as he sits across from me. "You're not going to get anything?"

"I'm okay." Ethan carefully places his hands on top of mine. "How are you?"

"Better." He seems well. It's been over a week and a half since we've seen each other. I thought about reaching out to him multiple times, but as I was thinking up what to do with my classes next semester, and receiving updates via Carlos on how the club case was going, I didn't have the time to focus on fixing something I really should have.

"What about your parents?"

"They're still somewhat walking on eggshells, constantly asking me questions, but I think they're settling back to their usual selves." Last night we had had a normal Skype family dinner and no one said the *police* word even once. "How are your grandparents? You must have had cops visit you."

"They laughed it off and said that's what teenagers do. Said nothing of value was taken so they were fine." He rubs his thumbs over the back of my hands. "I assured the police I changed the locks and—"

"That you didn't want to press charges. I know."

"Sol, I can't begin to say how bad I feel for not having told you. I should have—"

"Ethan, you're fine. You did what you felt was right." I grab the envelope from my backpack. "This won't make things right, but you should have this."

His forehead wrinkles as he takes the envelope, carefully unfolds the top flap, and extracts a fork.

"Now you have everything back—the fork, the keys, and your life." With one hand I zip close my backpack.

"Do I get you back too?" he whispers.

I shake my head. "Look, what happened doesn't change how I feel about you, but give me some time to heal, to figure out my life." Pausing, I reach over and interlace my fingers with his. "I'm really sorry about the night after the lake house. I shouldn't have screamed at you, I should have listened."

"You're okay, I shou—"

"Don't apologize. Once everything blows over, when legal things have been set aside and we've both had some time to breathe, I'd like to see you again."

I want to make sure I like him not only because we were forced to spend time together because of the club. Emotionally, I want to get my feelings together and assure myself that I'm not using the people around me to make me feel like I belong to something. I want to take the lead in my own way.

"Take all the time you need, sunshine." He leans down to kiss the top of my hand, something that makes my stomach flutter. "I'll be waiting for you on the other side."

I get up and round the table to give him a hug, and the feel of his strong arms wrapping around my waist is comforting. When he pulls back his eyes linger on me before we pull away from each other and prepare to go our separate ways. The concrete floor of the café is sturdy under my feet as I walk away from him and into the hot March afternoon, ready to continue on my own way.

EPILOGUE

"You want to hear a fun fact about the history club?" I ask, lying down in the back of Diane's car, camera in hand, ready to take some random shots.

"Sure," Diane says, turning left. Natalie is riding shotgun.

"It was never a history club to begin with. When it was formed three decades ago, some guys decided to make up this prank society, but they got threatened with suspension so they covered it up by creating a different club. The main dude was some history major who took advantage of the fact that no one had made a history club for the school." I flip through the images I've taken of Diane and her girlfriend, as well as the ones they took of me at the ice-cream parlor we went to.

"That actually makes a bit of sense," Natalie says. "How come no one put two and two together?"

"The main guy was the son of the mayor. Then he became

disgustingly rich after graduating and getting into politics." I scrutinize a photo in which I like the pose I was doing while holding a double-scoop ice-cream cone. I'm smiling, too, and the ice cream is dripping down the sides of my fingers. "He pulled a lot of strings for his name not to be mentioned at the trial, and was the one who hired the lawyers to ensure everything went smoothly."

I'm still adjusting to my new shoulder-length haircut. Cutting it felt liberating. I liked who I saw in the mirror when the stylist turned my chair around. After doing a lot of research online, I figured how to get it to not poof and the style suited me.

"At least you don't have to worry about those things anymore." If there was anyone aside from my parents who had nothing to do with my crazy shenanigans and was with me through it all, it was Diane. She believes in complete freedom of choice when it comes to screwing up your own life, and I wouldn't change that about her.

Today is the first day of summer break. Not being in the club gave me the time to focus more on my studies and the other clubs I had joined at the beginning of my freshman year. The club was dismantled by the school. Anna was called into court, Carlos testified, as well as Scott, who had been the driver for each dare.

"You should have seen the judge, he seemed so done with all of it." Carlos told me as we were hanging out in his apartment the day after he appeared in court. "They all thought we were stupid kids. At least, that's what the defense ran with. The school wanted to expel Anna at the very least, but even she managed to get off without a scratch as long as all club activities and ties were cut. I'm sure she's had enough of a hard time herself, I'm just glad she's out as well."

"Do you think the founder had anything to do with it?" I had asked. After all, every time the club was involved in something it felt like there was something more to it than met the eye.

"What, like the founder had some things to do with the legal department or the school? He'd shrugged. I mean, maybe, Sol. Be happy that our lives will go back to normal now—the world is run by shady businesses every day."

After the trial, the club members became like long distance family members that you saw every now and then or got a message from time to time. From what Carlos had filled me in on, Scott and Alan were dating now. Occasionally, I'd see Ophelia and Melina at the library, and more than once I saw Angela and Xiu on my way to the science building. I don't hold them any ill will. Carlos was right, maybe we should just be happy that our normal lives have been given back to us.

Carlos and I see each other every other day or so. As we say, trash that becomes friends together stays trash forever.

Dad and I call Mom almost every single day for dinner, and I am finally feeling at ease with them again. I'll never be a perfect daughter, but they're okay with that as long as I am honest with them.

I put on my sunglasses and sit up and rest my elbows between Diane's and Natalie's seats.

Diane takes the next right turn onto the Magnolia Street I know too well, from having grown up in it. As we pass the Winstons' house, I see Mrs. Winston watering plants in her front garden.

"Can you drop me off here?" I say, unbuckling my seat belt in a single motion.

"We're still a couple of blocks from your place."

"Ethan lives here."

Diane seems surprised but still brings her car to a slow stop. "You be good, and text me when you get home."

"I will. Bye, Diane, bye, Nat." I push the door open and step onto the road.

The day is hot but the street is lined with trees, and the shade they give makes the area cooler. It's a gorgeous neighborhood, and memories of me driving my bike down the sidewalk on summer days like today are ever present as I make my way to the Winstons' house.

"Looks like a lovely day to garden," I say to Mrs. Winston, turning over my shoulder to wave at Diane as she drives away.

"It sure is, baby girl. How are you?" Mrs. Winston responds.

She extends her arms for a hug. I wonder how forthcoming Ethan has been with his grandparents as I wrap my arms around her. As she pulls away, I realize she has a necklace with a pendant on it, and for a fraction of a second I pause.

"Is Ethan home?"

"Yes, he went to get me a bag of fertilizer from the garage. My joints can't handle that weight anymore."

There's a loud thud, and we both turn to where Ethan is standing, arms extended, a bag of fertilizer on the ground.

"Sol."

"Hey." I smile. "I think you dropped something."

"Let me get you a glass of iced water, or would you prefer iced tea?" says Mrs. Winston, moving away from me and heading toward the porch. There's a voice telling me I must be hallucinating, but the charm on her necklace looks almost identical to the history club's logo.

"Water would be fine, thank you." It's almost like I can hear

Anna's voice in my head, telling me not to worry about it, and at this point, I won't. I finally have time to enjoy my life, and that's exactly what I am going to do.

She takes her time going up the stairs, but that's fine because Ethan and I slowly walk to each other as she closes the door.

"How've you been?" he asks.

"I've been good, great even. I'm glad finals are over."

"I feel the same way."

"I always loved your grandmother's garden." Marigolds and daffodils adorn her plot, along with some sunflowers that nearly reach my knee. "Especially the sunflowers."

"They're my favorite, because just like them, I'm always looking at the sun."

We laugh.

"Even you've got to admit that was a bit corny," I say, bumping his arm with mine.

"I don't regret saying it. I was struck the moment I saw you."

"Careful, Winston, you might make me fall in love."

He raises his hand and touches the side of my neck where my hair now stops.

"Good, because that would make two of us."

I take both sides of his face and bring him down to where I can kiss him. His fingers curl on the back of my neck as I move back a little.

"This is not exactly the slow start I was shooting for again, but I wanted to see if you'd be okay with trying again. From the beginning, middle, or end, I'd want to, you know . . ." I trail off, focusing on his eyes.

"Soledad, you don't even have to ask." He places a kiss on the top of my head. "Of course we can."

"You kids out here having fun?" Mrs. Winston carries a tray of water and a bowl of fruit. "Come to the porch, it's getting hot out there."

Ethan holds my hand as we walk up the steps of their little porch. There are three chairs surrounding a wrought-iron table where Mrs. Winston has placed the food and drinks. We sit next to each other and she scoops some fruit into a bowl before placing a fork on top of it and passing it to me.

A fork I know too well.

Ethan catches me staring and laughs.

While my life is far from perfect and there are many things I still have to figure out and do on my own, things are fine right now. I'll take it a day at a time and keep my eyes on the present. Right now, I'm exactly where I want to be. Where it all began: in the same place, with the same fork, and most importantly, next to the same boy.

ACKNOWLEDGMENTS

First and foremost I'd like to thank my Wattpad readers for making this happen. I was a young high schooler with the need to express myself, and Wattpad offered me a platform. I did not know at the time that it would completely change my life. Thank you for your support and your comments, they have helped me out through the difficult parts of life.

I'd like to thank my publishing director, editor, and overall awesome person Deanna McFadden for helping me along the way to publishing. Thank you for reading this book over and over and helping me polish it; I wouldn't have been able to do this without you. Marcela Landres, who had to read through the first draft and who was incredibly nice to point out ways I could improve this story. Rebecca Mills for her incredible work and eye to spot details I would have never found. Gwen Benaway for her insights and suggestions. Also an incredibly big thanks to Monica Pacheco, Samantha Pennington, Robyn Cole, and everyone at Wattpad Books and Wattpad HQ who has made this book possible. I cannot tell you all how much I danced in my living room, jumping around when I was told *Historically Inaccurate* was getting chosen to be published. It was truly a dream come true.

There is no way I'd be writing this without the help of my parents, whom I will be translating this for, but whom I love with all of my heart. They did what they could to raise three girls in Mexico, and when hardships struck they decided a life in the United States would be the best path to take. They inspire me every single day with their hard work and the love they have given me and my sisters, and I have nothing but respect for them. My sisters are two chemists, who are way smarter than I am, but who have both aided my journey as a writer. Jenny, when you lived in Mexico while our residency situation was being fixed, I sent you a letter with very badly written fan fiction about my favorite video game characters, and you sent back a response saying I'd become a great writer one day; that really touched my little thirteen-year-old heart. Naila, you were the first member in our family to read anything I uploaded to Wattpad, and you actually liked it. As embarrassing as the story might be to look back on, I'll always remember you asking me about my characters and for updates.

I must also thank my friend from across the world, Theodora Cristea, because we met through Wattpad, and now we've been friends for almost eight years (time flies)! Thank you for being honest about my writing and helping me out whenever I asked for constructive criticism. Thank you for the book recommendations and the late-night texting. I promise I'll finish writing that secret project one of these days, and you'll be able to hold it in your hands like this book. We also do need to do a road trip through the Romanian countryside; don't think I've forgotten.

I'd like to thank Louis, my partner, who jumped up and down shouting "Yeah!" when I told him that I was getting published, and who keeps my life filled with joy and entertainment. Whether it's bingeing an entire series on a streaming site all afternoon, napping the day away, or going out for a cup of coffee in the warm Texas sun, I wouldn't change you for anything. Thank you for helping me with American idioms, for giving me tips on my pronunciations, and for keeping me sane while I went through the editing process. Be it Texas, Iowa, or Tennessee, as long as I'm by your side I know I'll be happy.

Thank you also to my college professors: Elizabeth Garcia, Philip Zwerling, as well as Amy Cummins, for aiding me in my journey as a writer.

Finally, I want to give a quick round of thank yous to all my writer friends who have helped and inspired me along the way. Anna Sophia, Nessa Brown, Wendy Perez, Heather Provost, Ashley Lovie, Zulema Paredes, Dennis Kim, Kell, Patty, Donovan, and simply the entire Twitter group that started as a one-thousand-word-a-day challenge, my NaNoWriMo cabinmates and buddies, and all of my other writer colleagues at Wattpad. Thank you all for being an inspiration for young writers, and for following your dreams.

Lastly, I want to thank you, whether you bought this book or e-book, borrowed it from your local library, or found it at a random thrift store, thank you for reading *Historically Inaccurate*.

ABOUT THE AUTHOR

Shay Bravo is a Mexican-born author who has now lived half of her life in the United States. She began sharing her work online through Wattpad when she was fifteen years old and has connected with over 114,000 followers. *Historically Inaccurate* won the 2019 Watty Awards and is her first novel. Shay currently resides in Houston, Texas.

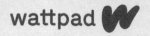

Where stories live.

Discover millions of stories created by diverse writers from around the globe.

Download the app or visit www.wattpad.com today.

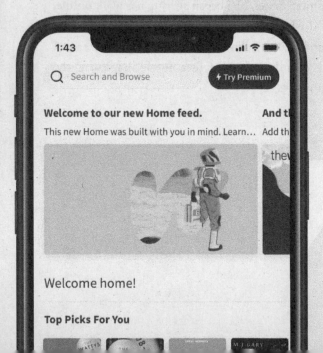

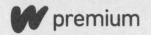 premium

Supercharge your Wattpad experience.

Go Premium and get more from the platform you already love. Enjoy uninterrupted ad-free reading, access to bonus Coins, and exclusive, customizable colors to personalize Wattpad your way.

Try Premium free today.

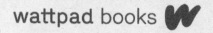

Want more? Why not try . . .

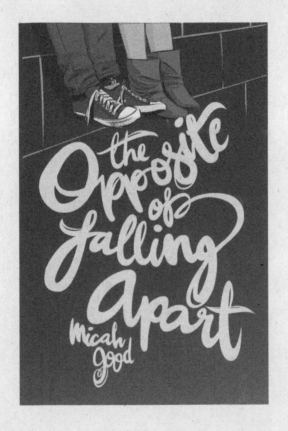

Can Jonas and Brennan help each other
to stop living in the past and start
dreaming about the future?

Want more? Why not try . . .

From the outside, Everest has it all, but
there's only one girl who can see
him for who he truly is.